DEATHLY SUSPENSE

When the police break into Joe Creeney's
Liverpool home, his dead wife is hanging
by a rope from the banisters, Joe is
walking away holding the ladder and there
is nobody else in the house. Yet Joe's sister,
Caroline Spackman, is convinced her
brother is innocent, so amateur PI Jack
Scott is called in by solicitor Stephanie
Grey. Now Scott, following a trail of
violence and lies from a murder for which
Creeney had been previously convicted,
must also examine links to a woman's
death in North Wales . . . and watch as
more bloody killings lead him to a
shocking denouement.

Books by John Paxton Sheriff
Published by The House of Ulverscroft:

A CONFUSION OF MURDERS
THE CLUTCHES OF DEATH

John Paxton Sheriff was born in Liverpool and spent much of his childhood in Wales. He served in the army for fifteen years, married his childhood sweetheart and had three children before moving to Australia. Returning to live in Wales, he realized his dream of becoming a full-time author and has written extensively for local newspapers.

JOHN PAXTON SHERIFF

DEATHLY
SUSPENSE

Complete and Unabridged

ULVERSCROFT
Leicester

First published in Great Britain in 2007 by
Robert Hale Limited
London

First Large Print Edition
published 2007
by arrangement with
Robert Hale Limited
London

British Library CIP Data

Sheriff, John Paxton, 1936 –
    Deathly suspense.—Large print ed.—
    Ulverscroft large print series: crime
    1. Scott, Jack (Fictitious character)—Fiction
    2. Private investigators—Great Britain—Fiction
    3. Detective and mystery stories 4. Large type books
    I. Title
    823.9'2 [F]   \ \ ⍵

    ISBN 978–1–84782–027–3

Published by
F. A. Thorpe (Publishing)
Anstey, Leicestershire

Set by Words & Graphics Ltd.
Anstey, Leicestershire
Printed and bound in Great Britain by
T. J. International Ltd., Padstow, Cornwall

PROLOGUE

Shockingly loud above the sound of rain beating against the windows, a door slammed. The woman sitting at the bottom of the stairs started violently. She turned her head, her eyes straining to see along the dark hall.

The tall man came through from the back of the house. He was wearing a brown fleecy jacket, jeans, Nike trainers. His face was wet. He was smiling. In hands covered by thin black-leather gloves he was carrying a stepladder and a coil of bright orange nylon rope. She turned to watch him, shock widening her blue eyes. In the faint light shining down the stairs from the open bedroom door her blonde hair was damp with sweat, strands plastered to her forehead.

When she saw the objects he was carrying, she began to tremble. She looked away. Conscious of her weakness, perhaps determined not to show fear, she pushed down on the filmy nightdress with her clenched fists and clamped her bound wrists between her knees. She made no sound. Above the crimson silk scarf tied across her mouth her

1

nostrils flared white as she struggled to breathe.

'Not long now,' he said softly. 'Be over soon. No more worries.'

He leaned the ladder against the side of the stairs. As he squeezed past her carrying the coil of rope he touched her hair with his fingers, lifting wet strands off her neck. She jerked her head away. He laughed deep in his throat. Then he climbed to the first-floor landing. He took one end of the rope and tied it tightly to the oak banisters. The rest of the rope he let fall into the stairwell. It uncoiled like a striking snake, hung swaying. The end, dangling five feet above the hall floor, was a heavy hangman's noose.

The man thumped down the stairs. He was impatient now. His knee hit her shoulder, hard. She whimpered. Her eyes closed and her throat moved as she swallowed. Tears slid down her cheeks to darken the upper edge of the crimson gag.

Now the man was in the hall. More banging. She knew he was erecting the stepladder, but she refused to turn, refused to watch. So far she had not seen the position of the rope, the ugly noose.

Then he came for her. One gloved hand reached for the wrists clamped between her knees, the other grasped her upper arm.

Unable to resist his strength as he pulled, she stood up, the soles of her bare feet squeaking faintly on the polished parquet flooring. He moved her away from the stairs and turned her to face the ladder.

Air hissed in her nostrils as she drew in a sharp breath. She reared backwards, suddenly squirming, fighting — moaning. Again he laughed, held her without effort. One arm was wrapped around her body, his hand holding her wrists. He lifted the other, clamped his gloved hand over her face and pinched her nostrils shut.

'Still. Will you keep still?'

For a few moments there was no sign that she had heard. Then, as the seconds passed, she nodded. His hand came away. Her breath whistled rapidly, painfully. She sagged in his arms.

'Just take it easy. This is not going to hurt.'

He took her to the big stepladder. When he pushed her against it and told her to climb, again she struggled.

'Get fuckin' well up there,' he snarled — and she shuddered and lifted a bare foot, stood on the first rung with toes curling, reached for the second.

Awkwardly he climbed with her, behind her, his body supporting her soft warm weight. There was a small platform at the top on which home decorators would stand — perhaps a foot square. He forced her all the way up, went most of the way with her. She took the last step up onto the tiny platform, swayed, whimpered as he held her waist.

'Turn around,' he said. 'No problem. Do it nice and easy, then stand up straight. Rest your back against the edge of the landing . . . while you wait.'

He held her until she was steady, then took his hands away. His grin was cruel as the hanging rope brushed her ear.

Then he backed down, just a couple of steps.

In his pocket he had more, thinner rope, similar to that binding her hands. He used this to tie her ankles. That done, he climbed up again. He was tight against her, both of them standing on the tiny platform. He leaned against her, forcing her shoulders back against the edge of the landing, and reached for the rope.

When he pulled up the noose and tried to put it over her head she jerked wildly, one way, then the other. He drew back his hand and, using his knuckles, slapped her face. Blood trickled from her nose. Breathing, already difficult, became impossible. Desperately she blew out through her nostrils. Her

4

breasts rose and fell jerkily. She sagged, braced herself with the heels of her bound hands on her knees, elbows straining outwards. Her chin was up, nostrils pinching then dilating, her eyes desperate. When her breathing settled it seemed that all resistance, all fight, had drained away with the trickle of blood. Again he forced her upright. Then he dropped the noose over her head, settled it around her neck and drew it tight so that the big knot was on the bone behind her left ear.

Then he sucked in a deep, shuddering breath.

'Listen,' he said, 'I told you what would happen. Warned you. Now it's over — all right? But I told you it won't hurt — and I was right. Don't do anything. Don't move a bloody muscle. I've worked it out. When the time comes you'll drop — and your neck will snap. You'll go out like a light.'

He stopped talking. His breath was hot on her face and she turned her head slightly, eyes again tightly closed. He leaned forward.

'Goodbye, Lorraine,' he whispered.

And he kissed her, very softly, very gently, on her damp forehead.

1

DAY ONE — MONDAY 31 OCTOBER

They were still playing five-card draw poker under the hot lights of the Sleepy Pussy night-club when I left at twenty minutes after midnight, drove out of the badly lit side street onto the main road and pushed the Quattro up to forty as it was buffeted by fierce cross winds.

An October storm that had flooded North Wales' rivers was dragging its damp coat-tails. Two weeks ago its full force had battered a clapped-out caravan and sent it bobbing merrily towards the Irish Sea. Two murderers were trapped inside, two wet and bloody private investigators were rescued by a woman with forethought and a couple of handy red and yellow canoes.

That investigation had ended successfully. Now I was faced with what was really nothing more than a minor irritation but, after a truly frustrating evening, I had been feeling miffed long before the unexpected and vaguely intriguing phone call.

With his hand clamped over the telephone's

mouthpiece, the Sleepy Pussy's barman had spotted me standing on my own, idly watching a woman in a headscarf reading the tarot cards, and asked if I was about to head home. He didn't know me; I didn't know him. I said yes. He asked me if I would pick up a man called Joe whose car had been stolen. He'd grinned as he told me I'd spot him easy, no sweat. 'Medium height,' he'd said, demonstrating by holding a hand level with his eyes. 'Wearin' jeans and a brown hoody, old Nike trainers, in this weather probably shelterin' in a fuckin' doorway.'

Unmissable.

Five minutes later I was on Breeze Hill pulling a cloud of spray through an area of cracked paving stones and boarded-up shops as, peering through the Quattro's slashing windscreen wipers at rain sweeping across the sodium lighting, I looked for what might as well have been the invisible man.

I was not exactly fired with enthusiasm. This was a chore I could do without. A telephone call two weeks ago had brought me tonight to the Brighton-le-Sands night-club in north Liverpool on what turned out to be an abortive attempt to sell toy soldiers I design and manufacture to a man who hadn't bothered to turn up. Now another telephone call had me searching streets I didn't know for a man I'd never met, and ferrying a soaking wet stranger to his warm bed was beginning to sound like one good deed too far.

Many a true word . . .

The stark truth in that idle thought didn't come screaming home to roost until almost twelve hours later, but when I did see the dark figure lurking in a shop doorway with a rusted iron grille and the man called Joe came splashing across the pavement to climb breathlessly into the car, I could already smell trouble. Maybe it was something about the way the wet clothing didn't quite fit his thin body, the cloying smell of Old Holborn from the roll-up he'd managed to keep dry, or the way he kept his eyes fixed on the windscreen as he thanked me out of the corner of his mouth.

This was a man getting soaked to the skin walking anonymous streets at midnight in lousy weather, there was no smell of alcohol — stale or fresh — and he was as twitchy as a smack-head with chorea. Where had he been? What had he been doing? And what kind of trouble did these contradictions whisper to me? Well, the kind at the very least to make a suspicious PI start asking questions.

'It's Joe, right?'

He nodded.

'I'm Jack Scott.' Another nod. 'Bad night to be out, Joe.'

For some reason that startled him. He flashed me a look.

'What's that supposed to mean?'

'Out. On the streets. Wet, cold, your car stolen.' I shrugged, glancing sideways as I probed. 'What was it, a night out with mates, the annual visit to your in-laws?' I'd caught the flash of gold, third finger left hand. He was married, or had been.

'A night out is right, first for a long time, but I'm short of mates so just leave it at that,' he said in tones that told me to back off.

'Fair enough. So, where d'you want taking?'

'Home.' For a moment nothing could be heard but the purr of the car's engine, the hiss of tyres on the wet road, and when I glanced at him I was shocked to see raw emotion on the thin face outlined by the hoody's cowl. Not young. Thirty, thirty-five, but dressed like a scally. He took a deep breath and his blue eyes had a wet shine as he smiled. 'Off Druids' Cross Road, opposite Calderstones park. Beech Crescent.'

I nodded. 'I know it well. That's a nice area.'

'It was,' he said enigmatically — and again he'd set me thinking.

At least I wouldn't be forced to detour. I

was already entering the Walton end of Queens Drive, and that venerable Liverpool ring road would take me most of the way to Joe's place. From there it was an easy and familiar drive to the Grassendale flat where Calum Wick painted my toy soldiers, plotted ingenius scams I chose to ignore, and who would by now be looking at his watch impatiently.

Joe had gone quiet. Very little more was said, traffic was light and I drove without thought. After a while my passenger sent his roll up sparking out of the window into the slipstream. A police car with flashing blue lights screamed past going in the opposite direction. I flicked on Radio Merseyside hoping for the news, but the time was all wrong and I got the latest rock band and switched off. And then we were as good as there. I indicated at the roundabout, turned off Queen's Drive into Menlove Avenue and a few minutes later we pulled into Druids' Cross Road.

I slowed, glanced enquiringly at Joe.

'The Crescent's on the right,' he said, 'but before that there's a narrow lane goin' up behind the houses . . . yeah, there . . . ' He leaned forward, pointing. 'Take it easy, right. Nice and quiet. The neighbours're old, they go to bed early.'

I grunted. Early? It was way past midnight.

I swung off the lighted road into an up-market back alley where wheel ruts ran either side of a central grass ridge and, as I drove by in low gear and without haste, the warm lights of expensive houses could be seen flooding across wet lawns bordered by designer shrubbery.

'Just here,' Joe said.

'Why the back way?'

'Because the patio doors're open.'

'Isn't that risky?'

'Not always, just tonight.' He smiled. 'I'm expected.'

He opened the door and stepped out into the rain, trainers slipping on wet grass, and I waited as he recovered his balance and wondered how a man wearing a hoody and dirty jeans and smoking roll ups held in a cupped hand could own a big house in an exclusive area of Calderstones. And why, tonight, the patio doors were open and he was expected. If this was his house, what the hell did that mean?

The car door slammed. Rain was drumming on the roof. Drips shaken from overhanging shrubs sparkled in the headlights like a shower of splintered glass as he opened a white picket gate and entered a garden that dipped steeply towards the rear of the house.

I watched him go then sent the Quattro rocking and sliding backwards down the lane's rain-slick ruts. I backed onto Druids' Cross Road, hesitated, then for the hell of it swung the wheel sharply with the intention of reversing slowly all the way up the sloping curve of Beech Crescent to what I judged was the front of Joe's house.

After thirty yards I was stopped cold.

A police car was parked in the area of darkness between two pools of subtle street lighting. No sign of the uniformed officers. I held my breath, eased my foot off the brake, knocked the stick out of reverse and dowsed all lights. Then, like a ghost, I coasted silently back down the slope.

I took it easy all the way down Druids' Cross Road. Back on Menlove Avenue I switched on the lights and stayed within the speed limit as far as the crossroads at Beaconsfield and Yew Tree Road. There I was held up by traffic lights, my fingers nervously tapping the steering wheel, my eyes locked on the rear view mirror.

The dash clock told me it was just after one. I switched on the radio. Once again I'd missed the news. Behind me a horn blasted. I looked up. The lights were on green. I lifted a hand in acknowledgement, turned into Yew Tree Road and headed towards Aigburth

Road and Grassendale.

And what I couldn't get out of my mind as I drove to collect Calum Wick for the journey to my home and workshop in Wales was the mystery of the scruffy man I'd dropped off in the lane behind the house he'd said was his, and the police car waiting patiently at the front.

Joe had said the patio doors were open, and he was expected. There was one obvious question I hadn't bothered to ask.

2

By nine the next morning rain had given way to sunshine and, as I walked under the oak tree and down the yard to my workshop, the high mists were clearing like strands of windswept cotton torn from the peaks of Glyder Fawr and Glyder Fach. Autumn was closing in. The clear air was cool and larded with the rank smell of damp vegetation, the swollen waters of Afon Ogwen were rushing across shiny black rocks under the stone bridge and the undergrowth on the slope down to the river was already thinning and taking on the colour of wet straw. A Land Rover trailed blue smoke down the main road towards Bethesda, the rattle of its engine carrying in the morning stillness. A green car was crowding it from behind, waiting for the chance to overtake that I knew would never come.

The workshop's doors were wide open. I stepped inside to be met by a wave of heat from the melting pot, the dull whine of the centrifugal casting machine as it slowed and stopped, the gratifying sight of gleaming tin-alloy military figures in ranks on the rough wooden shelves.

Immensely satisfied with the empire called Magna Carta that was my creation, I turned to the tall figure of Calum Wick. He was looking at me with amused speculation. The lenses of his wire-framed glasses were filmed with the talcum powder he was using to dust the inside of another black rubber mould. His hair was dishevelled, the wiry salt-and-pepper beard jutting as he used his chin to point.

'I take it you saw Willie Vine's car tootling down the road?'

'Tootling?' I grinned. 'I saw a green car.'

'Aye, well, in about three minutes' time you'll be getting a close up of a well known rusting Mondeo.'

'Vine's in Liverpool and you're hallucinating.'

'Maybe — but I've good cause because you never did get around to telling me what happened last night.'

'Fat chance. You snored all the way here.'

'So? Are you going to tell me?'

I walked over to watch him as he took the metal-filled mould out of the casting machine and set it aside to cool before removing the new figures. He put the two halves of the next talc-dusted mould together like a circular sandwich without a filling, placed it on the casting machine's turntable and dropped the

15

heavy metal plate on top. He stood holding the hinged lid, not closing it. He was watching me and waiting.

'So nothing,' I said. 'I went to the Sleepy Pussy, the new client didn't turn up, I left. That's it.'

'Pull the other one,' Wick said, and lowered the round metal lid. 'If I know you, that's just a wee part of it.'

The machine started with a whine, reached the selected speed and settled to a high-pitched drone. Calum dipped an iron ladle into the melting pot, poured molten tin alloy through the central hole in the lid, bent over to squint inside. He nodded his satisfaction. The machine continued to spin. Then he lifted the lid, the power cut off and the machine slowed and stopped.

And in the sudden silence we both heard the unmistakable sound of a car bouncing across the stone bridge and crunching up onto the yard.

★ ★ ★

DS Willie Vine, the Merseyside police officer with literary aspirations, was prowling my living-room elegantly, somehow managing to avoid tripping on the Indian rugs scattered across the vast slate floor while sweeping his

16

gaze along the packed bookshelves. DI Mike Haggard had flung himself onto the settee and was watching his detective sergeant with scorn. His jacket was open, white shirt crumpled, tie drooping from the unbuttoned collar. The usual king-sized cigarette was in his big fist, the usual glower darkening his broad face.

Calum was in the kitchen. The sound of water gushing and the rattle of percolator and mugs told me he was brewing coffee.

'Good news or bad? Which d'you want first?' Haggard said, switching his gaze to me.

I was standing with my back to the stone inglenook. The pale green curtains were moving like gossamer in the draught from the open window. I was soaking up sights and sounds: the oak tree with its yellowing leaves beginning to fall like weightless petals in the sunlight, the stone and gravel slope down to the old humped bridge, the hiss and tumble of the unseen waters of Afon Ogwen; looking, listening, relishing with a kind of grim determination the calm I knew was about to be shattered . . .

I heaved a sigh. 'Better make it the good.'

'Last night, some time after midnight, that expensive toy you drive was seen up a muddy track behind a house owned by Joe Creeney.'

'He was doing time,' Vine said without

turning. 'Fifteen years for manslaughter.'

'Take note of that 'was',' Haggard said. 'It was definitely your car behind his house, and the timing made it a couple of hours after he broke out of HMP Walton where he was seen getting in a metallic silver saloon. Could've been a Quattro.' He leered.

'If it was, and it was outside the prison, it wasn't mine. And isn't that the bad news?'

'The bad news,' Haggard said, 'is half an hour after you drove off, Joe Creeney murdered his wife.'

'So where were you,' Willie Vine said, still examining the books, 'between ten and ten-thirty last night when young Joe was going over the wall?'

'Kibitzing. Watching the poker players in the Sleepy Pussy night-club, Brighton-le-Sands.'

'Bollocks,' Haggard growled. 'You think a straight flush is a bog without a bend, two pair something you see bouncin' around on a couple of page three birds.'

'A phone call will provide proof,' I said, 'so stop showing off.'

Willie Vine chuckled appreciatively as he came away from the shelves, but there was a touch of steel in usually mild eyes.

'What about dropping Creeney off at his house? Are you admitting that?'

'I took a man called Joe home some time after midnight. His house was in Calderstones.' I lifted my shoulders in a slow shrug, at the same time pulling a 'you tell me' kind of face.

'The neighbour who bubbled you lives in a house on the other side of the lane behind Beech Crescent,' Haggard said. He shook his head. 'He was out in the dark lookin' for his black dog, if you can believe it — apparently it gets out several times a night, his wife was out chasin' it earlier . . . Anyway, while he was usin' a considerate suburban whisper to call this black mutt he saw headlights, poked his head over the conifers and got the car number. When his wife eventually phoned in — too fuckin' late to stop a murder — your name came up on the PNC. So . . . now you know as much as we do. The man you took home was Joe Creeney. He must've got in the house through a back door, and when the uniforms broke down the front door his wife was hanging from the fuckin' chandelier — or as good as.' He shook his head. 'What the fuck's goin' on, Ill Wind?'

He'd used the name he'd given to me during the Gault case. I thought that might be a good sign, a deliberate softening, a hint that he and Vine were resisting the urge to clap me in irons. I moved away from the

19

inglenook and dropped into a chair and the DI flicked his unfinished cigarette onto the logs in the dog grate. Calum ambled through from the kitchen, fingers poked through handles, a bottle under one arm. He put two steaming mugs and the bottle of brandy on the Ercol coffee table, handed a mug to me, sat down like a reclining telegraph pole and crossed his long legs at the ankles.

Willie Vine carried his coffee across to the window and stood gazing out at the view.

'First, what exactly is this?' I said. 'Off the record, two cops socializing, or an official visit with me being very careful what I say?'

'Day off,' Haggard said. 'There'll be a welcome in the hillsides — and DS Vine's doin' the driving,' and he looked pointedly at the bottle.

'I don't know what's going on,' I said, leaning forward to splash fiery liquid into his mug. I looked at Vine. He shook his head. I said, 'The barman in the Sleepy Pussy got a phone call. I was at the bar. He told me there was man called Joe whose car had been stolen, and could I take him home. I said OK. I found him waiting in a shop doorway on Breeze Hill.'

Willie Vine turned around, back to the window. He was frowning.

'That's what I thought,' I said. 'It doesn't

make sense. If the man I picked up was Joe Creeney and he was on his way home to Calderstones after breaking out of Walton, what was he doing on Breeze Hill? He was the wrong end of Liverpool, miles off his route. And why arrange to be picked up by me anyway, if a car was waiting for him outside the prison? That car could have taken him home.'

'But why go home anyway?' Vine said thoughtfully.

'Exactly. That's the first place your lot would look.'

'It's obvious why,' Haggard said, splashing brandy into his mug with a defiant glance at Vine. 'He had unfinished business with his wife.'

'So tell me more,' I said. 'What unfinished business? How did she die? What gave him away?'

'Lorraine Creeney heard a news flash sayin' Joe had got out, and phoned the police for protection,' Haggard said. 'She went to bed, we put a patrol car out front — '

'Joe Creeney told me he was expected,' I cut in. 'If Lorraine wanted protection, who was expecting Joe?'

'She was expectin' him, but she wasn't puttin' out the welcome mat — she wanted him kept away from the house.' Haggard shrugged. 'Anyway, some time after twelve your car was spotted up that track. A little after one there was a noise inside the house. Uniformed officers hammered on the door, got no answer and forced their way in. Joe Creeney was in the hall with a decorator's ladder. It's a fancy house with a wide hall and the stairs go up, turn on a small landin' then double back to reach the first floor. That leaves an open stairwell. Joe had tied a nice, bright orange rope to the first floor banister so it hung down in the well — between the stairs and the living-room wall. The way it looked he must've forced her up the ladder, put the noose around her neck with just the right amount of slack in the rope, then kicked the ladder away.' His grin was chilling. 'When the uniforms got to it the body was still warm, the muscles twitchin'. According to the doc, she died at one o'clock, minutes before she was found. Creeney got it right: her neck was broken, death was instantaneous.'

'Unlike the preparation.'

Haggard's look was sour. 'It took time to set it up, and I'm bettin' he didn't hurry. There's a connectin' door to the garage, the rope and ladder must've been in there.'

'All that going on, the police outside and nobody heard anything?'

'The man's wife was in the house, she was livin' on her nerves,' Haggard said, suddenly enraged. 'There was no noise, then there was. Christ, she was a decoratin' fanatic, passin' the time while Joe was in nick by remodelling the house. She could've come downstairs in her nightie and started rearrangin' the furniture, or splashin' silk emulsion on the fuckin' walls.' He shook his head, fumbled for a cigarette, changed his mind and got to his feet.

'Your mistake,' I said, 'was in watching the front door but not the back. 'Creeney told me he was going in through patio doors that had been left unlocked. If he could go in that way, someone else — the killer — could have got out.'

'No.' Haggard shook his head. 'He got in that way, but then he must've played safe. Those doors were locked from the inside.'

'And before you jump,' Willie Vine said, 'the back door leading out of the kitchen was also locked with the key on the inside, as was the front door.'

'Windows?'

Haggard sneered. 'The place was sealed like a fuckin' tomb. But just so you'll be happy, I can tell you the back garden and the lane were checked. It was raining. Great time for leavin' tracks. Your tyre marks were there, we could see where someone got out of the car and slipped on the grass, and his footsteps were clear all the way across the lawn and onto the paved patio. His footsteps. Goin' just the one way. And that's it. Nobody else went in or out the back way.'

'If Joe Creeney is going to wriggle out of this one,' Willie Vine said, 'there's a locked-room mystery to solve. That doesn't happen outside mystery novels. John Dickson Carr wrote a lengthy dissertation on the subject in *The Hollow Man* — published in the USA as *The Three Coffins*.' He flashed a glance at Haggard as the DI rolled his eyes. 'According to Carr, in Beech Crescent we're dealing with a hermetically sealed room — or as good as — in which various events have or haven't happened. Like, there was no murderer because the death was suicide, or an accident. Or the murder was committed by someone outside the room. Or there was a time element, the murder was committed earlier or later or there was some other twist — '

'Yeah, an' that's all clever stuff for those who go through life with their nose stuck in a book,' Haggard said, cutting in rudely, 'but it's not relevant. It's a locked room all right, but there's no bloody mystery because the only one locked inside is the killer. With the

24

implements he used to commit murder. And the killer's in custody. His name's Joe Creeney.'

'Exactly the point I'm making,' Vine said. 'Locked-room mysteries don't happen outside the pages of fiction. If Ill Wind's thinking of taking this on, he's wasting his time.'

'Yes, and there's something else, isn't there?' I said, looking at Haggard.

The DI took a breath, puffed his cheeks as he let it go.

'When Creeney ran out the door, he had blood on his face. He'd taken a knock on the snout. Later, smears of blood were found on Lorraine Creeney's elbow. Conclusion? She'd put up a fight.'

'And the blood on her elbow was fresh?'

'Sticky. And it matches Joe Creeney's group: B Positive.'

'DNA?'

'Awaiting results.' Haggard grinned. 'I'm taking bets.'

'Aye, well, all this erudite reasoning obviously leads to just the one conclusion,' Calum Wick said. 'It pains me to say it, but for once the polis have got it absolutely right. Nevertheless, I am extremely puzzled. If it really has to be Joe Creeney, what was wrong with a nice clean kitchen knife through the heart? Why all that elaborate bloody palaver with ladders and ropes?'

'Who knows?' Haggard said, his back to the inglenook, hands thrust in his pockets. 'He'd spent a year in the nick. Maybe he wanted her to suffer before she died.'

'Surely that would only be true,' I said, 'if she put him there?'

There was silence for a few minutes while four minds lingered on how well he had succeeded if suffering had been his aim. Haggard and Vine were experienced police officers who would have no difficulty imagining the terror that woman must have felt as the man who had broken out of gaol crept into the house, bound and gagged her and rigged a home-made gallows as she watched in horror. My own thoughts were hovering somewhere between gnawing guilt and intense anger at my stupidity. Without a second thought I had taken a man I didn't know to an address he gave me and watched him sneak in the back way. All right, so I'd had some misgivings — but I'd failed to act and now a woman was dead. And then realization kicked in.

'I don't know what part I'm supposed to be playing in this,' I said, 'but it's possible I was set up two weeks ago.'

Willie Vine had come lazily away from the window. Haggard was managing to look both bored and impatient. With the two detectives up on their feet I was feeling crowded. I stood up, ignoring Calum Wick's amused, knowing glance.

'We were here in the kitchen talking,' I said, 'the day after Danny Maguire and Georgie were taken away in handcuffs. I got a phone call. It was from a man interested in toy soldiers, sets of Papal Guards I don't produce. He was willing to commission them, exclusive designs, one-offs. I arranged to meet him.'

'In the Lazy Moggy,' Haggard said, and grinned at Vine.

'Right. I went there at nine-thirty. He didn't turn up . . . '

'What a surprise,' Vine said softly.

' . . . and just after twelve the barman took the phone call that sent me out in the rain looking for a man called Joe.'

'Forget it,' Haggard said.

'No. It explains my link to Creeney, and raises important questions.'

'Not about the murder. That's my priority, and as things stand it's over. Joe Creeney broke out of gaol and murdered his wife. Case closed, all over bar the shoutin' — and maybe findin' out who got Creeney out of gaol — and now here's you flyin' off on a fuckin' tangent. You were involved, but on the sidelines, and if someone's got it in for you — '

The phone cut him off. The cordless handset was on the coffee table. Ignoring it, I excused myself and raced through the kitchen to the office. I flung myself into the swivel chair and grabbed the phone.

'Jack Scott.'

'Good morning, Mr Scott. My name is Stephanie Grey. I'm a partner in the firm of Knott, Knott and Arbuthnot, solicitors. We've been asked by Caroline Spackman to represent her brother, Joe Creeney — if needed, and perhaps temporarily, but there are . . . complications that need looking into.' There was a pause. 'Your name came up.'

'I'm honoured, but puzzled. I've already spoken to the police — '

'You have!'

'Mm.' I didn't bother explaining, because I couldn't see where this was going. 'Joe Creeney escaped from gaol and was caught by uniformed police officers, in his house, alongside the body of his murdered wife. That sounds pretty straightforward.'

'If he did it.'

'There's no other explanation.' I hesitated, then took the plunge. 'You'll find this out anyway, so it might as well be from me. I was there, Ms Grey — '

28

'Stephanie.'

'Right. Well, I dropped Creeney off in the lane at the back of his house. He told me he was going in through open patio doors. Within half an hour his wife was dead. Seconds after that he was caught holding the ladder used in the . . . the hanging.'

'Caroline is quite sure Joe did not murder his wife.'

I took a deep breath. 'What does Joe say?'

'Joe Creeney is in no position to say anything, Jack. When caught he tried to escape, and was . . . restrained. He's unconscious, in Liverpool Royal Infirmary, and the signs are not good. He can't confess to murder, or protest his innocence, because he can't talk and is unlikely to remember what happened when he can — and that, really, is where you come in.'

3

By the time I came through from the office, Haggard and Vine were already bouncing over the bridge in the DS's old green Mondeo. Fading exhaust was drifting in the sunlight and, as the roar of the engine became a distant drone, I walked with Calum down my sloping yard to the workshop. A gift shop in Nova Scotia wanted five sets of kilted Black Watch grenadiers circa 1775. We cleaned the flash from thirty castings to make them ready for painting, popped them in a box lined with tissue and set off for Liverpool.

My appointment with the solicitor was at three o'clock. I dropped Calum at Grassendale with the raw castings, drove into town and parked in Paradise Street then made my way to Cheapside and the offices of Knott, Knott and Arbuthnot.

This was one of those business premises where time is measured by the slow swings of a long-case clock's brass pendulum, and hoary solicitors already crumbling to dust fight like tigers to keep away the man with the scythe. I remember walking into a bank in

Kirkwall on Mainland Orkney and talking to the cashier across a polished counter without bandit screens while rubbing a fingertip absently over black stains around recesses where inkwells once lodged. I had the same feeling here. My hand caressed polished banisters bearing ancient scars, my shoes slapped on brown linoleumed stairs under which ancient treads creaked and, in the upstairs corridor, I knocked on a deep-panelled door of immense weight that opened on brass hinges to admit me to a room where the opposing forces of mustiness and beeswax had long since declared a truce.

'Jack Scott.' Stephanie Grey was smiling as she came around the desk with pale hand extended. 'For Joe's sake, I'm delighted you could make it.'

I returned her smile, lightly squeezed fingers like smooth, cool bone.

'If you don't mind, I'll reserve judgement and tell you if I'm pleased to be here when I've heard the full story.'

'Full doesn't come into it; there isn't one. Just a conviction that something is amiss.'

She was as slim and straight as a witch's broom, with black skirts brushing the dusty wooden floor, one of those pink blouses you screw into a twist of wet rope rather than iron and lipstick so darkly red her mouth was like a parted wound as she smiled and I half expected to see blood glistening on white teeth. She noticed my confusion, and amusement danced in dark-ringed eyes. There was about her an aura of intelligence that to a lesser man might have been intimidating.

I smiled at my own arrogance that was as tedious as the history evident in piles of bulging manila folders heaped precariously on every available surface. She was watching me with a half smile of her own as she returned to her chair, one pale finger toying with a lock of shoulder-length black hair. I lifted some of the papers to the floor, grunting under their weight, and sat gingerly on a chair stiff enough to tame lions.

'So this is about Joe Creeney — and you mentioned complications,' I said, gently probing.

'I think those are now out in the open, aren't they? The evidence against Joe is overwhelming, but his injuries prevent him from speaking. As far as the police are concerned, he broke out of prison and murdered his wife.'

'That's the argument I used over the phone. It's so damning I'm wondering why I'm here.'

'It's not an argument; we've both been

quoting facts. But the facts are wrong.' She considered for a moment, her lips pursed. 'This might not help, but it's something you should know. Nine times out of ten a murderer will have a motive, but Joe Creeney had none, no reason to kill his wife. Twelve months ago he loved her enough to forgive her when he discovered she'd been sleeping with another man. Unfortunately, a confrontation that followed went wrong and he killed the man he thought she'd been seeing. That terrible mistake sent him to prison.'

'I'm impressed, but we need much more than his declaration of undying love. To strengthen the case against him it's easy to conjure up some more facts — and that's what the police and the CPS most assuredly will do. For example, we know a spell in prison affects a man: Creeney brooded for twelve months in a locked cell, love withered and died, he snapped, broke out and murdered his wife.'

'No.'

'I told you I've spoken to the police. The story I got from DI Mike Haggard was that between me dropping him off and Lorraine being found dead, Creeney rigged a makeshift gallows — '

'Somebody did. It wasn't Joe.'

Baffled, I shook my head. 'All doors were

locked from the inside. He was in the hall. His wife was hanging in the stairwell. Her body was still warm.'

'Yes, I know, and he was alone.' She nodded as if what she'd said added weight to an argument. It did, but on the wrong side of the scales.

'You see,' I said patiently, 'all you're doing is giving me more facts, more damning evidence that in the end will put Creeney in prison for life. You're not coming up with anything to suggest that somebody else could have killed that woman. Yet still his sister is convinced he's innocent. More, she's managed to convince you he didn't commit murder when we both know he was as good as caught in the act.'

Stephanie Grey leaned back in a swivel chair that was all buttons and padded leather buffed to a rich oxblood shine.

'What did Poe call it? The Imp of the Perverse?' She smiled. 'I don't know if I've got it right, but if I have then I think that's what lurks within me; if things are too neat, I get suspicious. So, because all the evidence points to Joe Creeney, my imp's prodding me with his fork and telling me there has to be another explanation for this killing.'

'Give me something, anything, to suggest you might be right.'

34

'Joe worked as a casual barman — '

'And could afford a house in Calderstones?'

'That came from Lorraine. Her father died and left her . . . well, comfortable. But what I'm getting at is that Joe was a barman, he spent a lot of time in night-clubs, on and off duty, but he's no killer.'

'He's killed before.'

'That was a mistake, an accidental killing that resulted in a conviction for manslaughter — and in any case, Joe had got it wrong.'

'How?'

Stephanie tutted, a mischievous smile lurking. 'I'm disappointed, Jack. You haven't been listening. What I said just moments ago was that Joe Creeney was there at the death of the man he *thought* his wife had been with.'

'Ah!' She was right, of course, I hadn't been listening, but that was because at that point she'd been talking about Joe Creeney's love for his wife and my thoughts had drifted and I'd once again seen his face — the wet shine in his eyes — as he sat in my car and told me he was going home. Had that been the face of a man planning cold-blooded murder?

'The man died,' Stephanie said softly, 'in an accident eerily similar to what happened

35

to Joe last night. Joe hit him, the man fell and banged his head. He died instantly. Later, Joe learned that he'd attacked the wrong man. He was distraught. That's what convinces me that if Joe was conscious now he could explain everything. Unfortunately, he chose the wrong time to make his second mistake: when the police burst into the crime scene, he bolted.'

'What, then fell and banged his head?'

'When the police broke in he was holding the ladder. Nobody knows what he was trying to do. Toss it aside perhaps so that he could get to Lorraine; use it so he could reach high enough to cut her down . . . ' She shrugged. 'What actually happened was that he went beserk. He threw the ladder at one of the policemen, then ran out of the open front door and leaped down the steps. The drive slopes; there's a rockery alongside the front lawn. The other policeman plays rugby. He tackled him. Joe fell awkwardly and cracked his head on one of those huge rocks.' She hesitated, frowning. 'I think the term for his condition is diffuse or axonal brain injury. If it is, the coma can last for weeks.'

'And meanwhile . . . ?'

'I expect you to prove Joe Creeney's innocence by finding the person who murdered Lorraine Creeney.'

'You expect?'

'Come on, Jack. You're the PI who found that knife thrower, Pedro and his Flashing Blades, when he'd been missing a full year. You dealt with his ghoulish killer in a derelict windmill. On another case it's said you took a bullet in the arm subduing a young woman bent on self-destruction.'

'Waste of effort. She died.'

'But you lived to soldier on.'

'You've done your homework.'

'Yes, and kick started the investigation.' She slid a sheet of A4 paper across the desk. 'This is a list of people you should talk to. Names, addresses, phone numbers. Joe's sister and brother. A man who shared his cell — '

My mobile interrupted her. It was a day for phone calls coming at the wrong time. I excused myself, stood up and walked away from the desk. The caller ID told me it was Sian. My heart thumped. I clicked on, listened. There was no sound.

'Sian? Sian, are you there?'

Pressed to my ear, the phone went dead.

I took a deep breath, switched it off and slipped it into my pocket. When I turned around, Stephanie Grey was watching me.

'Is everything all right?'

I went back to the desk, picked up the list and said yes. But of course, it wasn't.

Back at Grassendale I climbed the stairs to Calum Wick's flat overlooking the Mersey and walked into the big room that boasted a settee and leather easy chairs, Pioneer stereo system, wide-screen television with a Sky box and video over and under, a wall on which the Scot pinned his pictorial history of Liverpool, and a work table laden with soldiers of tin-alloy standing in massed ranks under an anglepoise lamp so heavily daubed it made Calum's spectacles look like polished Caithness glass.

The Black Watch figures were already primed, lined up, and drying under the anglepoise, the Scot watching over them like a bearded clan chieftain in wire-framed glasses. He had a coffee mug in one hand as he peered at me through paint-smeared lenses that did nothing to dim the query blazing in his dark eyes.

'One word springs to mind,' I said, sending my car keys bouncing across the leather settee. 'Impossible. I sat in an office straight out of *Rumpole of The Bailey* and the talk went round in decreasing circles and gave me nothing new. Everything Stephanie Grey told me matches what we got from Haggard and Vine — well, it would, wouldn't it, because that's where she got it? Yet despite all the evidence, Caroline Spackman has managed to convince her that Joe's innocent.'

'Stubborn and determined. A potent mix.' Calum rattled a brush in a jar of white spirit, dried it on a rag. 'I take it you listened politely, then told Stephanie the famous private eye was stumped, couldn't take the case and didn't want their money?'

'No.'

'Aye, that's what I expected: foolish and big headed — another mix to make strong men tremble.' He cocked an eyebrow. 'So now we get down to the hard graft, right? And, being sleuths of incomparable brilliance, we'll unmask the real killer in a matter of days and leave the police to mop up the bloody mess.'

'Perhaps not that quickly,' I said, 'but — as this is your day for aphorisms — hope springs eternal.' I smiled abstractedly. 'Joe Creeney murdered his wife, there's no other possibility — yet, strangely enough, Stephanie Grey's stubbornness is catching and I'm beginning to believe in the impossible.'

'The locked room situation adds to the piquancy, of course,' Calum said, getting up from the work table and switching off the anglepoise. 'But now get to the point and tell me what's really bothering you.'

It was hardly surprising that Calum Wick could sense my every mood. I'd first encountered the ex-SAS man, ex-potholer, more than ten years ago outside a rain swept spit-and-sawdust pub in Brixton. He had a fierce grin on his face, beneath the streetlights his black eyes glittered, and he was about to be beaten to a pulp by three huge Yardies. I was thirty-five, suntanned, fresh off the plane after five years in Australia. He was — well, he was Calum Wick, and in time I realized that was all I would ever know.

That night, shoulder to shoulder, we prevailed. The Yardies were vanquished, we retired from the scene to wash the blood of battle off faces and split knuckles in the ice-cold water of a cracked basin in an evil-smelling underground gents' toilet, and went on to become partners in a scam that involved ferrying expensive cars of dubious provenance over from Germany and selling them on through a bent Liverpool detective sergeant who had well-heeled contacts.

Neither of those activities could be called careers. Neither armed us with the skills needed to investigate violent crime. But before Australia and Calum Wick I had been a regular soldier, and over some fifteen years my tours with the Royal Engineers and SAS were complemented by a lengthy spell with the SIB — the army's Special Investigation Branch. When, disillusioned and conscience-smitten, I left Calum and his luxury car scam and began hitting the bottle, I was rescued and taken on by Manny Yates in his Lime Street firm of private investigators — an apprenticeship in investigation techniques which, when I walked out after five years, I thought I had put behind me.

But as the army had so often told me, I wasn't paid to think!

While working for Manny Yates I had discovered a talent for military modelling. It developed rapidly. In the mountains of North Wales I bought the isolated farmhouse known as Bryn Aur that became home and workshop, and set up business: Magna Carta — Military Miniatures for the Connoisseur, with Wick as a distant but irreplaceable colleague, because the man I had first met splitting his knuckles on the skulls of those massive Yardies had found in hands too delicate for such violent work a skill with fine paint brushes to which Magna Carta owed much of its success.

He painted toy soldiers. And when, in time, I found myself once again drawn to hunting down criminals of the very worst kind, he became an amateur private dick's assistant.

Somewhere along the way, Sian Laidlaw arrived on the scene.

Nowadays they would call Sian's childhood deprived: she had seen her Scottish seafaring father lost overboard in an Arctic gale when she was ten years old and illegally aboard his ship, had returned to nurse her dying mother in the Cardiff slums and, years later, with a university degree under her Shotokan karate black belt, moved north to become something of a legend among the high peaks of the Cairngorms.

I had met her in Norway — she taking a break from military duty, me on holiday and stepping gingerly onto skis for the first time since my own stint in uniform. Some months after that first meeting she had walked one day into my stone workshop at Bryn Aur and in the next two years had shared my home and occasionally my bed.

If I ever used the word relationship I'd say the one Sian and I had was on and off, but whatever name we gave to what we did have, we worked at it. After a spell instructing on an outward bound course for tired executives in stormforce winds at Cape Wrath — long after she had quit the army — she had returned to Liverpool and helped me with the Gault case but, behind the scenes, other more attractive propositions were looming. After Cape Wrath she had conducted a successful radio phone-in. That led to the offer of her own television series, to be filmed by Granada in Manchester. We were delighted, Sian anticipating less time spent in the field teaching overgrown office boys how to abseil down vertical cliff faces, me looking forward to more togetherness at Bryn Aur.

In a way it had worked out. We did spend more time together. But then the Sam Bone case took over, drew to a bloody close in Conwy harbour, and Sian was called to Manchester to discuss another series — this time overseas. And so I found myself nursing a gunshot wound at Bryn Aur — alone, once again without my Soldier Blue.

But a young executive called Nigel got the overseas trip put on hold and suddenly, a little more than two weeks ago and smack in the middle of the Danny Maguire case, the togetherness I had come to believe would never be permanent had seemed about to happen. Sian moved into Bryn Aur — the emotional decision as always made light of with wacky humour, this time something to do with sheltered accommodation. And so the Maguire case drew to a perilous close. Sian saved the valiant private eyes from a disastrous cock-up. The future had never looked so rosy.

Until last night.

★ ★ ★

'You made no comment when we got to Bryn Aur,' Calum Wick said, 'and said even less the next morning. I naturally assumed Sian had again been summoned by the moguls. Television work. More high jinks in wild, Godforsaken places.'

We were in his kitchen. Satan, the scarred moggy sans goolies, was curling sinuously around my ankles like a fat snake in a fur coat as I munched on a slice of two-cheese pizza and drank ice-cold Holsten from the bottle. Calum was minus the wire-framed glasses but the stains thereon seemed to have migrated to his beard, and thence to his shirt. The smears on his fingers could have been ketchup, Humbrol enamels or blood. Whatever they were, he seemed to like the taste.

'No,' I said, 'she'd said nothing. I suppose I noticed the Shogun wasn't behind the house, but it was late, dark, we were shattered, the penny didn't drop.' I shrugged. 'Then, when I went upstairs . . .'

'Empty bed, icy cotton sheets.'

'And chilling images preventing me from

44

sleeping. Where the hell is she, Cal?'

'For a start, you can ignore that mysterious phone call. You know what mobiles are like. Think adventure training, wilderness, mountains surrounding deep valleys. She didn't answer because where she is she can't get a signal.'

'So why not phone back?'

'Same reason. Or she's took busy. Look, she phoned — '

'Or somebody used her phone. And listened.'

'Who?'

'Same person that phoned me two weeks ago to set in motion a chain of events that led to murder.'

Calum pulled a face, licked his fingers absently and crossed to the stove to reheat the coffee. Satan had padded into the living-room. I pushed away my unfinished pizza and moved restlessly to the window.

'I agree there's something weird going on,' Calum said, 'but wouldn't it be foolish to see connections before we look deeper?'

'It would be even more foolish to do nothing.'

I swung away from the window. He had his back to the stove and was watching me with reproof.

'That wasn't what I said.'

'No. I know.' I smiled an apology.

'So?'

'So I'm wrong anyway. If an adult hasn't been in touch for a while, nothing is all we can do. We wait. Assume the best, not the worst. And in the meantime we look at the intriguing case that's been dumped in our laps and begin with what we've got. That's a list of names.'

The coffee was bubbling. I left him to pour and went through to the living-room. Satan lifted his head to blink sleepily at me from the settee, then collapsed. The list given to me by Stephanie Grey was on the coffee table. I sat in my usual chair, unfolded the sheet of paper.

Caroline Spackman (Joe's sister, married to Max Spackman). Declan Creeney, Joe's brother. Alec Creeney, his father. Cell mate, Damon Knight. Fiona Lake, Lorraine Creeney's sister. Names, addresses, phone numbers. Five of them, but they would lead to others.

I looked up as Calum came through carrying steaming mugs.

'Declan Creeney? Is that a name that rings bells?'

'Night-club owner.' He sat next to the cat, located a Schimmelpennick cigar, struck a match and looked at me over the flame. 'If I recall correctly, it was for the killing of one of

Declan's minions that Joe Creeney found himself on the wrong side of bars — iron ones, that is.'

'Minion as in?'

'Manager of some kind.'

'Would one of the clubs Creeney owns be the Sleepy Pussy?'

'Aye, it would.'

I rolled the list into a tube, leaned back and tapped it thoughtfully against my chin. Calum went over to the Highlanders, tested the primer on several of them with the tip of a finger, then sat down and clicked on the anglepoise.

'You know,' I said, 'when we were up that lane, in my car, I asked Joe Creeney why he was going in the back way. He told me the patio doors were open — he was expected.'

Calum, head bent, brush poised, peered at me over his glasses.

'Didn't Haggard tell us Lorraine Creeney called the police for protection once she knew her man was out?'

'Yes. So who was expecting him?'

Glass tinkled as he rinsed the brush. 'In the mind of a man who had been living with his imagination for twelve lonely months, I suppose she was.'

'All right, but why the back way?'

'You've been through this with Willie Vine.

Why go home at all? A prisoner doesn't go over the wall and stroll into the first place the polis will look.'

'But he did. So that's something else that's odd.'

Logic was pointing out to me, as had Haggard a few hours ago, that in the circumstances the only possible reason for Creeney to go home after a gaol break was to murder Lorraine. She had called the police, which suggested that she expected nothing less than that if he ever got out — but if I wanted to get close to the truth about Joe Creeney, then surely the man to talk to was at the very top of my list.

4

Declan Creeney lived some ten minutes from Grassendale, in a big house on the slope up Queen's Drive and close to the Woolton Road traffic lights. I parked the Quattro in the wide driveway, climbed out onto brick sets like multi-coloured parquet flooring curving around manicured lawns and was straining to hear the bell chime on the other side of the solid oak front door just before seven o'clock.

The door was opened by a tall man who could have been a middle-aged middleweight boxer maturing like inferior wine but still able to fill a charcoal-grey suit in the right places to make assailants in dark alleys turn and run. This, I assumed, was the brother of the man who had broken out of gaol, murdered his wife and was now in deep coma. There was no trace of concern on his face, unless it was for his own appearance. As he looked me up and down he lifted a hand to smooth black hair snatched back into a pony tail. A heavy gold bracelet encircled his muscular wrist, more gold glittered at the open throat of an embroidered dress shirt and his gleaming white teeth as he smiled had the wet

49

shine of expensive whisky.

'Jack Scott?'

I grasped the extended right hand, feeling the hard lump on the back where one punch too many had snapped a metacarpal.

'Declan Creeney,' he said. 'Come on in.'

The hallway was all thick carpet and deeply embossed burgundy wallpaper. Tall, smoked-glass mirrors reflected our progress. The warm air was larded with perfume that could have been sprayed from a bottle with an expensive label but was, I guessed, a block of something sticky evaporating inside a Glade air freshener.

I'd been right about the whisky. In a lounge where bay windows afforded views of the evening traffic on Queen's Drive a crystal decanter and glasses sparkled on an occasional table with a mock-onyx top. Same wallpaper, same carpets, the air that was perfumed with something either expensive or very cheap now spiced with stale cigar smoke. The decanter clinked. Spirit gurgled. Creeney handed me the glass, found his own and gestured to a chair.

'Take a seat. I'm on my way out, so you've got five minutes to tell me what this is about.'

'Your brother Joe,' I said.

He watched me settle into a chair as wide and deep as a settee and sip the whisky. I let

50

him see my approval, hoping to bring a measure of calm into a room crackling with tension.

'Joe was in gaol. He got out; now he's going back. What is there to talk about?'

'That sounds final.'

He lifted eyebrows threaded with the fine scars of wounds won in the ring or any number of back alleys. 'What happened to his wife makes it about as final as it can get.'

'You believe he murdered her?'

He'd been standing by the table. Now he sat down on the edge of a chair, frowning.

'Doesn't matter, does it? What I believe won't have much bearing on the verdict — if he wakes up, and if it goes to trial.'

'What Stephanie Grey believes might. Your sister's convinced the solicitor Joe's innocent. I've been hired to find the killer.'

'Yeah, you said something about that on the phone.' His faint smile was sceptical. 'I've read about you. Don't let previous results go to your head.'

'I might not be needed. If Joe does recover consciousness,' I said, 'there's a possibility he could clear himself without my help.'

Creeney hesitated for the blink of an eye, then shook his head.

'He was alone in the house. He'd brought rope and ladder in from the shed and used

51

them to string his wife up. Her body was still warm when the police walked in. He can't talk his way out of that.'

'Why d'you say shed? The police believe the ladder was in the garage.'

'They're wrong. I put it in the shed months ago.'

I looked into my whisky glass, then caught his eye.

'How do you know about the ladder?'

'I just told you — '

'No.' I shook my head. 'Not about where it was. How did you know it was used by the killer?'

For the space of several heartbeats there was a strange look in Creeney's dark eyes and I couldn't decide if it was disdain at my stupidity or because he was calculating how much or how little to tell me. Then he grinned.

'Come on! Lorraine's gone and I'm male, and family. Who d'you think was first to get a visit from the police, a lot of sympathy from a pretty woman PC?'

'When was this?'

'Last night. Well, early this morning. Fourish. They were lucky to find me in.'

'Why?'

'Isn't that bloody obvious? Ownin' night-clubs means I sleep mornings, do most of my work afternoons and nights.'

I thought of my own wasted night hours as I waited for a client who was never going to show up.

'Did you know I drove Joe home?'

His glass stopped halfway to his mouth. 'You what?'

'I'd been lured to your club, the Sleepy Pussy. On a pretext. I was wasting time there when your barman got a phone call. I picked Joe up on Breeze Hill.'

'What the fuck was he doing there?'

'Waiting for me.'

Creeney tossed back his whisky, grimaced and put the glass on the table. His hard black eyes were puzzled, darting here and there as if for enlightenment.

'But you'd never met him before last night — right?'

'Never heard of him.'

'Yet he breaks out of gaol, gets dropped miles from his house by the pillock who's helpin' him to escape then picked up by a man he's never met? Why?'

'It being your brother and your night-club,' I said, 'I was hoping you'd come up with an answer.'

'No.' He stood up, shrugged his shoulders to settle his jacket, located his car keys in a pocket. 'No, if anyone's got answers, it's you,

Scott. Because what it looks like is someone's using Joe's escape to hang something on you. If I was you, I'd be lookin' into my past.'

He moved towards the door, waving me ahead of him into the hall.

'Look, I'm sorry to rush you, but I'm already late.'

'Don't worry about it. A PI faces similar problems, and talking to you is just the beginning of my evening's work. But if you do think of something likely to be of help . . .'

I handed him my card, watched him pocket it, then stood back as he opened the heavy front door.

The door slammed behind us. He strode away across the brick sets, and must have pressed an electronic remote. The big double garage's doors swung open silently, revealing a sleek silver car. He turned and stood jingling his car keys as I walked to the Quattro.

'That bit about me being male, and family, and the police coming here,' he said. 'There was something else.'

'Yes. One follows the other: you automatically become a suspect.'

'The police know I wasn't at Joe's house last night. I haven't seen Lorraine for more than a week, but that's neither here nor there because nothing being said is causing me any concern. Joe's been doing time; I've been looking after his wife. For the past twelve months I've been honouring a pledge I made to him when he went down.'

'But?'

'You're looking into the killing because Caroline's got a bee in her bonnet; she thinks Joe's innocent. But if you were hoping to put me in his place, forget it. I left for work early, and for most of the night I was in the Copacabana in West Derby Village. That's not just another of my clubs, it's my watertight alibi. I'm not your man, Scott. I didn't murder my brother's wife.'

And then, for some reason, the good humour was cast aside and he deliberately spat on the fancy sets at his feet before turning away and walking into the garage. An unconscious habit? Or a crude way of telling me that my visit had been a waste of time? I shook my head as he used another remote to flash the silver car's lights and operate the central locking, and climbed into the driver's seat.

Well, he might not have murdered Lorraine I thought as I drove off, but West Derby Village wasn't too far away from Walton. Was it Declan Creeney, I wondered, who had picked up Joe Creeney in his silver car outside Walton gaol?

5

I drove from Queen's Drive down to Allerton Road, joined Mather Avenue then crossed the dual carriageway into the Tesco's car park. There I tried several times to reach Sian's mobile. No luck. Each time, I got her voicemail. On the last occasion I left a message.

'Ring me, Soldier Blue. I'm worried.'

With the phone back in my pocket I walked into the store, bought a bottle of Evian still water and paid at the cigarette counter. Then I drove out of the car park, turned left and headed for the Dingle.

Caroline Spackman lived in a tall, yellow brick house on Mill Street. I parked nearby, climbed worn sandstone steps with the smell of the Mersey in my nostrils and knocked on a door with light shining through coloured panels of Victorian glass. It was answered almost at once by a dark-haired woman in a shocking-pink flared housecoat and high-heeled slippers with gold straps. Dancing eyes flirted with me as I gave my name. I was invited into a hallway smelling of dust and Lemon Pledge and shut the door behind me as she moved away in a drift of California Poppy.

When I followed her into the front room it was to be introduced to a tall, dark-haired man wearing tailored jeans with leather belt, a draped single-breasted grey jacket over a shiny black T-shirt. He was tall and lean and as graceful as a ballet dancer as he moved away from a bamboo-fronted cocktail bar with beer bottle held in one hand so he could shake mine with the other. His eyes were glistening flint chips in a face as bleak as an Easter Island monolith. Surprise visitors to this Mill Street address would feel secure or terrified, depending on their business and Max Spackman's mood. I felt smug: I'd been invited.

'I feel so much better now you're with us, Jack,' Caroline said when we were all sitting down. 'I've told Stephanie and I'm repeating it now so we know exactly where we stand. Twelve months ago Wayne Tully died accidentally when he and Joe were going at it hammer and tongs. But Joe did *not* kill Lorraine. I just know it.' She smiled at me, and flicked a glance at Max. He rolled his eyes.

'She's a clairvoyant,' he said. 'She's so damn good we still haven't won the lottery — English, Irish or bloody European — and she cried her eyes out when the cat died unexpectedly.'

'Looking into the future's no help now,' I said.

'Success or failure would be nice to know about in advance.'

'We know enough,' Caroline said firmly. 'His track record speaks for itself.'

'Makes me sound like Red Rum,' I said, and smiled inanely into the silence.

'Her brother just phoned,' Max said. 'He thinks you're trying to pin Lorraine's murder on him.'

'I went to see him. I'm eliminating prime suspects.'

'What's that, yes or no?'

'Let's just say he's got an alibi. That means he was somewhere else. He told me he was at his club in West Derby Village.'

'Yeah, trying to get away from her.'

Caroline's snort was unladylike. 'Rubbish. You know that's not true.'

'I told you, he'd had enough and was trying to ditch her — '

'Whoa, hold on a minute,' I said. 'Are you talking about Lorraine? Are you telling me there was something going on between Declan and Joe's wife?'

'No, it's absolute nonsense.' Caroline stood

58

up. 'Would you like a cup of tea, Jack? A beer?'

'Tea would be nice.'

I got the feeling I'd get more information more quickly from Max, and tea would take longer to prepare. Caroline went out into the hall, high heels clicking, housecoat swirling. I heard a door open, the rattle of cups. I looked at Max.

'What Declan told me,' I said, 'was that he'd sworn to Joe that he'd look after Lorraine while he was in prison. What are you saying?'

'I'm saying that's what he did,' Max said. 'But a year is a year, and him and Lorraine were too bloody close for too long. What started out as taking care of turned into something more cosy.'

'Common knowledge?'

'Common sense,' he said. 'Knowing Declan, it was inevitable.'

'And you've known him a long time?'

'Yonks.'

'Could he commit murder?'

'Yes.' Then he shook his head. 'But not if he was somewhere else.'

'And you think he was?'

'I know it. I'm Declan's muscle, his head bouncer. He walked into the Copacobana just after eleven — '

'In West Derby?'

'That's it. And that's where I'm going when I've finished this beer.'

'And last night he stayed till when?'

He shrugged. 'Who knows? I was on my way out.'

'At eleven?'

'Just after.'

'And you were what — coming home?'

'You're joking,' Caroline Spackman said.

I'd misjudged her inquisitiveness. Bearing two china mugs she'd walked in behind me with eerie stealth. She'd been so quick I guessed the tea bags were still in the mugs, soaking in water straight out of the hot tap.

'Max didn't get in until gone one,' she said, handing me my tea, 'but don't ask me to verify, because I was tucked up in bed.'

'What she's forgetting,' Max said as she sat down, 'is that before I went to work I drove to Calderstones to see Lorraine. As a favour.'

I frowned. 'What time was that?'

Max pulled a face, shrugged. 'God knows. Eight, half past?'

'He picked something up for me,' Caroline said. 'Something Lorraine borrowed a long time ago, and I wanted it back.'

'A book on interior design,' Max said.

'Well, that fits,' I said. 'I heard that while Joe was away she was keeping herself occupied by redesigning — '

'Decorating,' Max said, and grinned. 'Pain in the arse. I was always there, lugging cans of paint, bringin' the ladder in from the shed, takin' it out — '

'Definitely the shed?'

He stared. 'Where else?'

'The police thought the garage.'

He shook his head. 'No. Declan stuck it out the back. It was awkward to move around, so I fetched and carried.'

'So let me get this straight. You went there on Saturday night to get the book, you knocked on the front door, stepped inside, chatted — then came away?'

'That's it.'

'You didn't go round the back? Into the garden, the shed?'

'Come on,' Max scoffed. 'I went in, got Caroline's book off Lorraine and drove away. Anyway, the police must've checked the back because that's the way Joe went in.'

'And he had to get the book from her last night.' Caroline said. 'She has a nice elderly friend who was planning to travel to Wales today, and Lorraine was going to follow her, stay for a few days . . . ' She looked at me, and I saw her swallow. 'Until this . . . happened . . . '

I waited. No details were forthcoming

61

about the friend. I wondered if it was a clue, something that could be the turning point that comes in every investigation, but it was too early in the case to decide one way or another even if I knew what Caroline was talking about. Leaving it, moving on, I looked at Max.

'So if you weren't coming home when you left the Copacobana — where were you going?'

Again the shrug. 'Declan's got several clubs. Copacobana, Sleepy Pussy. Night Shift. So I move around.' He grinned. 'Flex muscle, do a lot of bouncing.'

'Convenient though, isn't it? If you keep on the move nobody can say for sure where you are at a particular time. Copacobana thinks you're at Night Shift, Night Shift thinks you're at the Sleepy Pussy when all the time you could be somewhere else.'

'Yeah,' he said, 'me being family I thought we'd get around to Calderstones and murder.'

He stood up and put the empty bottle on the cocktail bar. Keys jingled as he reached into his pocket. When he turned around he was slipping his hands into thin, black-leather gloves.

'Max!' There was a warning in Caroline's voice. I watched him with detached interest.

Maybe thumping someone was his way of warming up before going to work.

Black T-shirt, black gloves. He'd seen bouncers on TV. All he needed to complete the picture was wrap-around aviator shades. The thought was bubbling beneath the surface when, lo and behold, he took a pair out of the jacket's top pocket and rested them on his nose.

'White stick?' I said innocently.

He sneered, patted his hip pocket, frowned, turned back to the cocktail cabinet, swept it with his eyes, hesitated.

Lorraine was watching him. 'Lost something?'

'What?' He shook his head. No . . . no, nothing. My hip flask. I remember now, it's in the club.'

'Lose his head,' she said, 'if it wasn't fixed on with one of those Frankenstein bolt things.' She chuckled, then shook her head at him. 'You never did find that glove, did you? That's your spare pair. When did it go missing — Saturday night? You had it when you left here.'

'I had it when I walked out of Lorraine's.' He shrugged. 'Probably dropped it getting into the car.'

'Someone will find it,' she said, 'and all your gloves have got your intitials on them in fancy gold letters.'

'To return it,' he said scathingly, 'they'd need to know what the M and the S mean.'

'Marks and Spencer,' I said helpfully.

As he turned to face me the light reflected off the black lenses of his shades. Was he glaring angrily? Were his eyes narrowed in a calculating stare? I thought of standing up to remove the sunglasses, and had difficulty supressing a grin.

'Think about this,' he said. 'From what I hear there's no way Joe didn't murder Lorraine; he was locked in, there was nobody else in the house. But that's just it, isn't it? There's always a way. And if I was a clever private dick trying to prove something, I'd go looking for the obvious.'

'The obvious being?'

'Joe was in prison because he killed a man. Wayne Tully. Wayne was a night-club manager. He had mean relatives, a couple of brothers also in the business, who swore to get Joe. They shouted it from the public gallery in court — and got slung out — and they were prepared to wait however long it took for Joe to finish his sentence. An' guess what? Suddenly Joe's out, and he's only done twelve months. So how did that happen?'

'He had help.'

'Of course he did. Joe was lyin' there in this

stinking cell, and he could see all that fresh air and freedom on the other side of the bars. So when someone walked in and offered him the chance, he jumped at it. But suppose it was a set-up. And suppose he walked straight into it with a little help from another friend.'

Max grinned.

'Me?'

'You drove him.'

'Yes, I did, and I'm still wondering why I was sucked in. But in the end, who took Joe home is unimportant. When he walked into that house, something bad happened.'

'And so we go round in circles because, like I said, there was no way it could have been worked by a third party. The way it looks, there was only one man could have murdered Lorraine — and that's Joe.'

'That's what you're saying — if I'm following you — but what exactly are you getting round to?'

'Whatever it was that happened last night,' Max said, 'you're looking in the wrong place, talking to the wrong people. It could have been a simple plan to get a man out of prison, or a plan within a plan — the second bit meant to send Joe back to prison for life — but it had nothing to do with me, and nothing to do with Declan. Brother, brother-in-law — forget it. Somebody else took their revenge. All you've got to do is find out who, and why.'

'Let's not forget the how,' I said, thinking of that locked house — but I was wasting my breath because Max Spackman was already on his way out.

6

When the front door had slammed behind Max I stayed long enough to finish my mug of lukewarm tea, place a business card on the table and drop sneaky questions into a pool of casual conversation. Waste of time. I was like a cack-handed Aborigine throwing boomerangs downwind: nothing hit the mark, nothing came back. Frustrated, but assuring Caroline I would do all I could to help Joe, I left her painting her toenails in front of the muted television and walked the fifty yards back to my car. As I drove off in the direction of town, cut right to Park Road then right again to point the Quattro in the general direction of my Liverpool base in Grassendale, I pondered on the fact that the visit to Caroline Spackman's had eliminated no suspects but widened the field considerably.

Declan Creeney's alibi still hadn't been verified, and the suggestion that he had been in a relationship with Lorraine Creeney that had turned sour provided him with a motive for her murder. Max Spackman had seen Lorraine on the night she was murdered — though the reason for that early evening visit seemed innocent enough. Later that night he had certainly left the Copacobana in plenty of time to drive to Calderstones and kill Lorraine, and he was unable or unwilling to say exactly where he had been when she was murdered. There was no motive for murder that I could see, though it was possible the earlier visit had ended in an argument that made him angry enough to return. And he was a hard man deeply involved in club life. Pointing the finger at Wayne Tully's relatives might have been a friendly tip, or a crafty way of diverting suspicion.

If I took it to be the latter — or even if I didn't — I had a feeling that first working through the list given to me by Stephanie Grey would be the best way of moving the investigation forward in logical steps. Steps that I knew would in any case scamper off in all directions. Alec Creeney was next on the list. If I went to see him it was likely that I would learn more about Joe, Declan and Max and perhaps get names of contacts. Or there was Fiona Lake, Lorraine's sister. From her I would get information with a feminine slant, discover the secrets of skeletons in cupboards Declan and Max were keeping locked, and watch the inevitable further widening of the field of suspects. Fiona had either a husband or an ex, and Liverpool club life was like a religious circle: you were born into it, married in or into it (but rarely out of it), and many of the people I would meet in the next few days would have strong opinions on the two murder victims — Wayne Tully and Lorraine Creeney.

If Joe was getting the blame for both, he would need a permanent police presence outside his hospital room.

Which brought me, in a roundabout way, to Joe's cell mate. Damon Knight would have inside information. Someone had helped Joe escape, and I'd be very surprised if he hadn't confided in the man he had been locked up with for perhaps twenty-three hours of every day.

* * *

I was lost in thought for the next couple of hours, first driving along familiar streets with no particular destination in mind, then sitting in the Quattro overlooking the lake in Sefton Park. High clouds drifted across clear skies. By the light of the moon the flat water became a sheet of glittering steel, the sleek outlines of moored rowing boats rakish black silhouettes, gently rocking. A tranquil scene, traffic a distant murmur, Classic FM playing something plaintive and nocturnal to create a background in tune with my thinking.

But around the lake there was darkness of a different kind. Shadowy paths snaked between thick shrubs blanketing the grassy slopes, and the occasional flicker of movement could have been looked on as innocent or sinister, depending on mood and point of view. I was a private investigator, not a detective working vice with the Merseyside police who might be excused for seeing everything as wicked until proved otherwise. Nevertheless, despite my detached status I suppose that at that time I was drifting towards the morbid. Murder on my mind. Sian out there, somewhere, with still no word.

When I did finally toss negative thoughts aside and make my way to Grassendale, there was a rusty white van parked outside the flat. Stan Jones had come a-calling, the middle-aged, white-bearded scally who, the first time I saw him, had a cigarette dangling from his lips as he was picked up and bounced on the bonnet of his own rusty white vehicle. We were in the middle of the Gerry Gault case. Calum had been doing the muscular bouncing and it had been some time before I learned it was all an act. Since then Jones the Van had, with Calum, wriggled out of a stolen car handling charge, been close to involvement in a Toxteth car-jacking, and on the past two investigations had assisted harassed PIs with sterling work as a mobile surveillance unit: one rusty white van, one mobile phone, one bottomless reservoir of patience.

I climbed the stairs, listened to sounds like the scuffling of hungry rats emanating from the room occupied by Calum's seedy downstairs neighbour, Sammy Quade, and walked into Calum's flat with the uneasy feeling of a man interrupting a meeting of Mafia godfathers.

Wrong, of course. Or had the scuffling I'd heard been my two recidivist friends scurrying to adopt poses of ineffable innocence?

'You're phone's ringin',' Stan said.

'He can't hear it,' Calum said, horizontal on the settee, eyes closed and an unlit Schimmelpenninck cigar jiggling between his teeth.

'He's not meant to,' Stan said. 'It's on vibrate, an' it's in his trouser pocket.'

'That,' I said, 'is so I don't get interrupted by Vivaldi's *Four Seasons* when grilling a suspect.'

Stan grinned. 'Bet you get some queer looks though when your pants start quiverin'.'

I sneered, threw my coat on a chair and dragged out my mobile.

It was DI Alun Morgan of Bethesda. His Welsh accent managed to sound both musical and mournful.

'I must be mad,' he said. 'Another blood-soaked body pops up, and who do I call?'

'In the words of Mike Haggard, 'him from the hills', 'the Ill Wind that blows no good' — and I think that should be 'whom'.'

'Yes, and it's a bad penny, more like. Maybe you should have been a copper.' He waited. I groaned obediently at the joke. 'But my philosophy,' he said, 'is to use whatever's available, however irregular, and when there are certain connections your sheer brilliance is invaluable.'

The final five syllables were beautifully enunciated, but this time my groan was a genuine protest. 'Not more connections. And if it's what I think it is, that means you've already spoken to DI Haggard.'

'Indeed. But that's pecking order, isn't it? I'm not saying you come last, mind . . . '

'All right, so where's the corpse and why should I be interested?'

'A block of what they call executive flats overlooking Conwy harbour. Several are used as holiday homes. A commotion was heard in one of them just a few hours ago. When uniforms broke in they found a woman on the floor with a single stab wound. Nasty, though. In the throat, not the heart, and she took a painful long while to bleed to death.'

'And the connection?'

'Liverpool, as you've already twigged, and I'll leave you to work out the rest.'

'Even great minds need something to go on. What's her name?'

'Rose Lane.'

'No, her name, not the address.'

'That's what I'm giving you.'

'Alun, please tell me you're joking. Rose Lane is in Mossley Hill, it's a leafy thoroughfare linking Mather Avenue with Elmswood Road.'

'This Rose Lane's a murder victim. Rosamund, if you want the first name in full, Lane as is, and genuine. She got that one from her husband, of course, but I guarantee her maiden name was something like Budd which would have given her school friends an abundance of ammunition.' His chuckle was dry, his next words suddenly very serious. 'Her address is Redcliffe — that's the house name, and it's in Ash Crescent. In case you're wondering, that's Calderstones.'

But already my interest had rocketed from mild to intense.

'Ash Crescent backs onto Beech Crescent,' I said, looking across at Calum. 'Both are cul-de-sacs, one convex, the other concave. The two snuggle together like spoons, with just a narrow lane running between the back gardens.'

'Exactly,' Morgan said. 'We know all about that — what do they say, we're up to speed? — and now that lane has a murder both sides of it.'

'One a hanging, with a suspect in custody. The other a stabbing.'

'So when discussing locations, would it be outrageous to believe these murders happened too close to each other for coincidence?'

'Twenty-four hours and fully sixty miles apart? Yes. You've established Rose Lane's Liverpool connection,' I said, 'but she was murdered in North Wales. You're not seriously suggesting the two murders are linked?'

'Let me put it this way. I'm a Welshman through and through, and perhaps there are dark forces and mystic powers within me that in your modern, pragmatic Liverpool coppers have long since atrophied. Something's amiss, I can feel it in my water. Thanks to me, you know the women were close neighbours. All you've got to do now is find whatever it is connects the two murders.'

74

I quickly brought Calum and Stan up to date, thought for a moment, then keyed in the numbers. The phone rang once, twice — then it was picked up.

'Creeney.'

I switched off.

'He's there. At home.'

'Him being there,' Calum said, 'tells us nothing.'

'When I went to see him he was in such a hurry he could give me just five minutes of his time. That was around seven o'clock, and he was on pins. Why? He's been in the nightclub business for years, so what was special about tonight? And if special, why home so early?'

'It's last night that was special,' Calum said. 'Last night someone phoned one of his clubs and arranged for you to pick up his brother. That links him to a gaol break. Bad for business.'

'Good's more like it,' Stan Jones said. 'The punters'd have a field day.'

'Maybe,' I said, 'but what if his mind was on murder — and I'm not talking about Lorraine's. And if it was — if he was going after this Rose Lane intent on silencing her — did he have time for the round trip?'

'Even I could get to Wales and back in a couple of hours,' Stan Jones said, 'and you've seen my van.' He pulled out a tobacco tin and began rolling a cigarette. 'But what about this other feller, Max? If he's king of the bouncers he's already halfway to bein' a killer.'

'And what about wild flights of fancy?' Calum said. 'You're both flapping about trying to pin a murder on two men going peacefully about their business. Granted that business might have shady connections — but what the hell has this Rose Lane done to attract their attention?'

'She saw something.'

'To do with Joe Creeney?' Calum rolled his eyes. 'How, for God's sake? Her house backs onto Joe Creeney's place, but so what? You heard Haggard. Every door in Joe's house was locked from the inside. Examination of the grounds and the lane showed that the only person passing that way was Joe — on his way in. You're not seriously suggesting that from where she lives this Rose Lane could see into the front hallway of Joe's locked house and identify the mysterious killer as either Declan Creeney or Max Spackman?'

'Things are moving so fast I don't know enough to suggest anything,' I said.

I found the telephone directory, looked up the Copacobana and punched in the numbers. I got the bar, asked for Max Spackman and over a woman's shrill voice screaming *Like a Virgin* through the karaoke machine was told he was manning the door. I waited, wondering what I could say; to be exact, wondering what I could say that would ruffle this cocky bouncer's plumage.

The phone clattered.

'Max?'

'Yeah.'

'Jack Scott. I've had some news.'

'Go on.'

I thought quickly, found a straw to clutch and placed it delicately on the camel's back.

'It's Joe. He's coming out of his coma.'

'Is that right?'

'I spoke to Stephanie. The police are hoping to get a confession from him within twenty-four hours.'

'That's not news, that's a fuckin' miracle. This is the second phone call I've taken. The first was from the Royal. Joe Creeney didn't regain consciousness, and he never will: he died an hour ago.'

★ ★ ★

'Stephanie?'

'Yes?'

'Jack Scott. Have you heard?'

'About Joe? Yes, I have. I've just been talking to Caroline. She's upset, but resolute.'

'I'm getting a bad feeling. What are you saying? Where does this leave me?'

'Exactly where you were, but with a clear field. You see I've also spoken to DI Haggard. Merseyside police consider the case closed. Unlike us, they see no reason to look for another killer.'

'Unlike us? I like that. So far the only reason you've given me to press on is Caroline Spackman's refusal to believe in Joe's guilt. Against all the evidence.'

'Circumstantial.'

'Irrefutable.'

'Fabricated.'

I chuckled. 'Willie Vine would love this word play. But are you serious? Fabricated?'

'Of course.'

'By a killer who disappeared in a puff of smoke?'

'By a killer, yes.' She paused. 'Have you heard of John Dickson Carr?'

'Twice in two days.'

'He was a literary prestidigitarot who used misdirection to make simple murders look complicated or impossible. Got it? Misdirection? Joe didn't kill Lorraine. The evidence to prove it is there. I want you to get out, talk to people and find the bits and pieces that make up that evidence, then put those pieces together in some sort of order and unmask the killer who is laughing himself sick at his own ingenuity and police stupidity.'

★   ★   ★

'Laughing himself sick?'

'That's what she said. She did her best to be tactful, but we all know who he's laughing at: us.'

'You.'

'All right, me.'

'Which we will proceed to put right.'

'We?'

'Us.'

Stan Jones was watching and listening with an expression in his eyes that was miles away from the scally image he projected with surprising energy. This is the man with a beard like wire wool and a smouldering roll-up in the corner of his mouth who rides in a rusty white van to theatres showing plays by Beckett, takes the *Telegraph* for its cryptic crossword and reads *War and Peace* when involved in boring surveillance work. Calum accepts him and uses his talents because he's streetwise and wily. I accept him, well, partly because he's accepted by Calum and perhaps partly to prove to ever-sceptical Stan that the work I do is never a doddle.

And I felt a rush of adrenalin at the thought that this time we were involved in something that would challenge the intellect of Jones the Van — who, Calum tells me, also reads the classics in bed, frequently by candlelight because he's run out of cash for the 'lecky' meter.

'An' seein' as Sian's gone AWOL,' Stan said now, 'that 'us' and 'we' you've been battin' backwards and forwards like Chinese ping-pong players includes me?'

'It does,' I said, 'and I have your first mission.'

'Mission,' Stan said in awed tones. 'Like in secret fuckin' agent?'

'You'll be working on *The Assassin Identity*, or — '

'*The Creeney Protocol*,' Calum offered.

'How about *The Jones Supremacy*?' Stan said, deadpan, and he winked at Calum.

'Call it what you like,' I said, 'but we're going back to the beginning. Joe Creeney killed a man called Wayne Tully because he thought Tully was, erm, bedding Lorraine.'

'Bedding?'

'Polite term.' I grinned at Calum. 'But according to Stephanie, Joe was wrong and it was someone else doing the — '

'Bedding,' Calum said, and nodded sagely.

Stan pinched out his dog-end and put it in his pocket. 'So what's this mission, then?'

'Dig up the Wayne Tully story. Locate his relatives. Bring me names and addresses.'

'Do I get a cyanide pill. You know, in case of torture, stuff like that?'

'Stuff like that?' I shook my head. 'And here's me thinking you were blessed with the vocabulary of a self-taught man.'

'Yeah, but the stuff I'm talkin' about is stuff I know.'

'Convince me.'

'Wayne Tully's old man lives in Colwyn Bay.'

I blinked. 'As in North Wales?'

'As in one phone call and you've got his address.'

I tossed him my mobile. 'Go ahead.'

'Yeah, but my sources are — '

'Unsavoury?'

'Sacrosanct.'

'OK, take the phone into the kitchen.'

He went. I heard a cat miaow, the scrape of a chair.

I looked at Calum. 'Sacrosanct?'

'I told you, he's a reader. First War and Peace, now The Da Vinci Code. He's found some kind of religion.'

'Jones the Pious. Mm. Has a certain ring to it.'

Whatever he was to be called, he came back within minutes. The address he gave me for Karl Tully, Wayne's father, was one I recognized from my infrequent visits to Colwyn Bay. Stan was grinning as he walked out and clattered down the stairs to his van, Jones the Informer, off to dig up more dirt. But we'd changed plans. With Karl Tully located, Stan was now going to find out what he could about Joe Creeney's cell mate, Damon Knight.

I had one more task before I went to bed. Through solicitor Stephanie Grey, Caroline Spackman was my employer. I rang her, offered her my sympathy, and assured her I was doing all I could to find out who was behind the murder that had, indirectly, led to her brother's death. I even told her where I was going the next day.

It was only when I rang off to face Calum's look of disbelief that I realized giving out information like Smarties might not be the safest way to proceed.

7

DAY TWO — TUESDAY 1 NOVEMBER

I set off early the next morning, crossed the River Mersey at Runcorn, took the coast road from Queensferry and was driving past police headquarters, Eirias Park athletic track and through the east end of Colwyn Bay at a little after nine o'clock. Karl Tully lived on the west side of town. I parked on the main road alongside Rydal College rugby fields, skipped across the road through the early morning traffic and walked back to the block of flats on the corner of Marine Road.

Built of modern brick and set in attractive lawned grounds, they were clearly ideal for elderly people looking for maximum comfort, minimum work, and proximity to local shops, libraries and transport. I'd called Tully before leaving Grassendale and he'd told me he lived on the top floor where the salt air could be appreciated when the wind was in the right direction and wide windows afforded oblique views of the rugby grounds. I pressed the bell, he buzzed me in and moments later the introductions were over and I was gazing through the slats of vertical blinds at those sun drenched playing fields.

'Beats Liverpool's acres of concrete,' he said at my shoulder.

'Horses for courses. A lot would disagree with you. I'd guess Declan Creeney's one of them.'

'He would, wouldn't he, poncing around with the filthy rich on Queen's Drive. But that didn't help his kid brother, did it?'

'News travels fast. And that sounds like my cue. What about Joe, Karl? Was he as bad as they say? He killed once, twelve months ago. They say he had good reason, but it wasn't good enough to keep him out of prison. And what about now, this latest murder? Did Joe break out of prison to kill again? To murder his wife?'

Tully scowled. He was probably in his seventies, tall but bent as if his spine was giving way under the weight of massive shoulders, with watery pale eyes in a face as grey as fissured pumice stone under a shaven skull tanned by the sun. He motioned me to a chair, then sat down facing me across a glass coffee table with the sun shining in my face and on his broad back so that eyes devoid of humanity were lost in pools of deep shadow.

'Why ask me?' he said. 'They say he did; they say he was caught at it — the silly bugger. And they say it was you that picked him up and drove him home so he could do it.'

'I was roped in as taxi driver, and my part in it went no further. But I came here to talk about you and your family. I've been told threats were shouted in court when Joe was sent down. He couldn't have enjoyed prison, but with your mob still after him escape must have been like leaping out of the frying pan into a situation where he could get badly burned.'

'My mob?'

'Maybe that's disrespectful. But you have got other sons, and I've been told it was them doing all the shouting.'

'So what? Joe gets out of gaol, murders Lorraine because she'd been playin' away and cracks his skull when doin' a runner. All in the same night. Christ, he was dead before my lads got word he was out.'

'So you say — '

'What — you callin' me a liar?'

'I'll put it another way: what if you've been misinformed? What if your boys heard about the break before it happened? — it must have been planned. And if they did know about it in advance, what possibilities does that open up if I tell you Joe Creeney did not murder Lorraine?'

My meaning wasn't difficult to follow. Karl Tully grunted, uncoiled from his chair and crossed to a cocktail cabinet under a black-and-white photograph of dinner jacketed men with squashed noses cosying up to a glistening boxer wearing a shiny Lonsdale belt. He poured amber fluid from a decanter into two glasses, passed me one, sat down on the leather settee with his face out of shadow. It was deliberate. I was now seared by the naked menace in eyes that blazed.

'Let me work this out,' he said. 'You're a private dick hired by Caroline Spackman because she believes little Joe never killed his wife. Now you're pluckin' names out of thin air, and who better to latch on to than a couple of angry lads who've seen their brother beaten to death with a lead pipe — '

'Seen?'

'They weren't there, but isn't hearin' about it bad enough?'

'Wayne cracked his head when he fell.'

'Yeah, only he didn't fall.' Tully's tone was scathing. He tossed back his whisky, clattered the glass on the coffee table alongside a bowl inside which cornflakes clung like wet cardboard. Leant back. Steadied his breathing. 'Wayne didn't fall, he was knocked down,' he said. 'He was dead before he cracked his head. My opinion — but who

86

cares, what's the fuckin' difference? Dead is dead.'

'Your boys care, and for twelve months their hands were tied. Then one wet night Joe's back on their side of the wall and on his way home to his wife. And so your boys get what might be their one big chance, an eye for an eye: they lose a brother, Joe loses a wife and walks in to a nightmare.'

'Wrong.' Tully shook his head. 'This is not the Colombian fuckin' drug mafia, dynasties slaughtered for stealing a couple of ounces of white powder. The way we work it's strictly hands off families — '

'Ah,' I said. 'So now, at last, it's 'we'.'

Tully's snort was derisive.

'Bollocks. You know bloody well Joe Creeney sweated for a full year then broke out of gaol so he could get rid of all that shit inside his head that was drivin' him crazy. He killed his wife. End of story.'

He climbed out of the chair. His big fists were clenched, his fierce glare was daring me to argue, and I sensed that if I didn't leave willingly he'd send me the short way down to the lawn in a shower of broken glass.

I rose, shrugged, thought of shaking one of those big hands and decided against it.

'The odds are you're right. Joe Creeney went to pieces, arranged a break and murdered his wife. That's the way the police see it, and so far all I've got is madcap theories. You've heard one of them, and refuted it, but I'd still like to ask your boys where they were on the night Joe's wife died.'

'Feel free.' He was grinning like a shark, and I knew he was looking ahead with relish to the reception I would get.

That in itself was food for thought, but the one thing I couldn't get out of my mind was that in the half-hour or so I spent talking to Karl Tully, Joe Creeney's name came up but Karl never once said outright that Joe had killed his boy. Wayne was beaten to death with a lead pipe, Karl said. He didn't fall, Karl reminded me, he was knocked down — but despite the fury blazing in his pale eyes, never once did he place the blame for his boy's death squarely on Joe Creeney's shoulders.

★ ★ ★

I walked out with two names, two Toxteth addresses and four phone numbers — land lines and mobiles — but before heading back to the big city I decided to call on DI Alun Morgan. He had ended his phone call to Grassendale with a challenge: find out what connected two murders that occurred sixty miles apart to victims who lived close enough to each other for the fairies at the bottom of their gardens to link hands. I knew a lot about Joe Creeney's death, but almost nothing about how Rose Lane had died. Now was the time to put that right.

Alun was based in Bethesda, and I had many times visited his house cum office nestling just off the A5 in the lee of Carnedd Daffydd. The easy way from Colwyn Bay was a fast drive along the A55 coast road to Bangor then inland on the A5 through the Nant Ffrancon. So I took the easy way, but instead of stopping at Alun's house I continued for a mile or so up the Nant then swooped down the single-lane road and across the Afon Ogwen to my home and workshop beneath the soaring peaks of the Glyders.

Two murders were begging for my attention but I still hadn't heard from my Soldier Blue, and I had suddenly remembered Calum and I being worried about her during the Sam Bone case and walking into a silent Bryn Aur unaware that Sian was fast asleep upstairs.

I drove there with anticipation and a dry mouth, but this time I was out of luck. The Quattro bounced over the hump-backed stone bridge and up the stone and slate yard and as

I pulled in under the oak tree I could see at once that there was no metallic-silver Mitsubishi Shogun parked behind the house. Clouds had covered the sun. The air was swiftly cooling and I could smell rotting autumn vegetation and the dank of the river as I walked towards the house. The spare key was in the sludge and the wood lice crawling beneath the stone pot of now woody geraniums, and when I turned the key in the door to cross the quarry-tiled porch over-looked by silent toy soldiers standing in stone niches lining the steep stairs and enter my big living-room I knew at once that I was alone in an empty house.

And yet . . .

I tossed the car keys onto the chesterfield, felt sudden nervous tension tighten my shoulders as I let my eyes stray over white walls and bookshelves, stone inglenook fireplace and red-shaded wall lights, the thin Laura Ashley cotton curtains that allowed light from the small window to spill onto a floor where bright Indian rugs were scattered over huge slate slabs. Shiny slabs now marked, as clearly as black fingerprints mark a white linen tablecloth, by the sole of a cleated trainer too large for Sian's feet.

Just the one footprint. How could that be? Even a man hopping on one leg leaves a trail.

But this single print was almost hidden by the coffee table and I visualized someone with a yellow duster tied round the head of a broom, diligently wiping prints from the tiles, but in haste or because of bad light missing just this one. Sian . . . removing the evidence?

What alerts you when you enter your home and realize that your privacy has been violated? With me it's always an unfamiliar smell in a room that's as comfortable and familiar as an old slipper, a rogue scent that alerts the senses like milk bottles bearing the sudden stink of petrol during a peaceful demonstration. Doesn't matter how faint it is. And an unfamilar smell had been there when I walked into the living-room. It had stopped me dead. Raised hackles. Made me step to one side out of the exposed doorway and sent my eyes flicking left and right while my head stayed unnaturally still as if any unnecessary or sudden movement would invite . . . what? Attack?

I grinned mirthlessly into the heavy silence, sucked in a slow deep breath that to my straining ears sounded as haunting as winter winds hissing across naked moorland, and metaphorically got a grip of my knickers.

It took me a couple of minutes to search the rest of the house. I scooted up stairs and along passageways, sniffing like a bird dog, and decided from lingering scents and small signs of disarray that a stranger had slept in the spare room, Sian in the main bedroom. That last bit was debatable; Sian had been sleeping in my bed ever since a warm homecoming during the Danny Maguire case, that investigation had ended two weeks ago and so her presence there was well established.

Nevertheless, as I finished the search and sat down behind my desk in the office I admitted that no signs of forced entry led to the inevitable conclusion that Sian had let him in. Unless, of course, he knew about the spare key hidden in the shadows. And anyway, why was I assuming it was a him, a he? Why not a woman with big feet who'd got to know Sian on one of her adventure training courses and been invited back for drinkies?

I swivelled, sniffed, shook my head. No. The scent I could still detect was male perfume. A cheapy: Lynx, Gillette Arctic Ice, something along those lines, something sprayed on liberally enough to soak into the walls.

Again I grinned, and now the tension was seeping out of my muscles as the bright side of what I'd discovered began to warm the cockles. The stranger was male, but by God he hadn't shared Soldier Blue's bed! And while yesterday I'd been scared witless by the sight of Sian's name staring at me from the LCD of a silent mobile phone, I now knew that she had walked into this house, and walked out again, at some time in the past twenty-four hours.

For all I knew she might be shopping in Bangor or Beaumaris, yet even as the thought crossed my mind it was dismissed. A woman expecting to come back leaves traces: clothes on the bed, toiletries in the bathroom . . . soft indoor shoes or slippers in the porch ready for her return.

There was nothing.

And I caught myself wondering, as I locked up and walked down the yard to my car, if the peculiar goings on that both Sian and I seemed to be experiencing could be linked not only to each other but to the two murders that themselves might be connected.

About the latter, I was hoping soon to find out much more.

★　★　★

'Have you ever heard of the Lysander?'

I looked into Alun Morgan's sharp grey eyes and saw amusement lurking as he waited for me to answer the question he had lobbed in my direction like a bowler delivering a googly.

'Wasn't he a Greek general who lead the Spartan armies in the Peloponnesian War?'

'He may well have done that, and won,' Morgan said, skilfully fielding my return, 'but the Lysander I'm thinking of is a plywood boat.'

'Right. And this has relevance?'

'Connectivity.'

'To?'

'Murder.'

I'd arrived at the DI's house with clouds gathering and the wind gusting hard enough to flap his trousers as he emerged from the front door on his way to a late lunch in Bethesda. I drove him there in the Quattro and the conversation was taking place in the timber and stained-glass lounge of his local pub. Trees tossed madly on the other side of the car park. Raindrops as hard as airgun pellets rattled the windows.

'Murder as in the death of Rose Lane?' I said, sipping my half-pint of shandy.

'And more,' Morgan said. 'The Lysander links Rose Lane to a bearded man who lives in a tatty caravan off the beach at Red Wharf Bay. There's another link you'll be interested in — but that can wait.'

'I could be ahead of you — but go on, tell your tale.'

'The Lysander,' Alun Morgan said, 'was a trailer-sailer designed in 1963 by Percy Blandford. You could build it in a large domestic garage using marine ply. The original was gunter rigged for sailing on rivers and estuary waters, but I've seen cutter and gaff rigged variations. Davey Jones specializes in Bermudan rigged versions strong enough to cross the Irish sea in bad weather.'

'Davey Jones?'

'Middle-aged, long hair going grey and a liking for fancy shirts and jeans and leather sandals worn barefoot summer and winter. A craftsman producing exceptional work with the minimum of tools. Lives on the aforementioned Red Wharf Bay.'

'And where does Rose Lane come in?'

'The flat where she was murdered was her holiday home. Just hers; her husband is Barry Lane. He's an ex-boxer, fighting name Rocky Lane, but long retired and sliding in and out of dementia. Walks the dog, stares at the tele. Having a flat overlooking Conwy harbour got Rose interested in sailing, that led her to old Davey's boat-shed on Anglesey, and she ended up paying him for her very own seventeen-foot Lysander that he put together with hammer and nails in less than a month.'

He paused, looking at me expectantly across the rim of his glass.

'I've heard from reliable sources,' he said softly, 'that Rose was never one for sailing single handed.'

'Ah.' I nodded, thinking about the second link he knew would interest me and going over a recent conversation with a murdered woman's sister-in-law. What was it Caroline Spackman had said? — Lorraine's friend was planning a trip to Wales, and Lorraine would have followed her if she had lived. For friend, I thought, I need look no further than close neighbour Rose Lane. And my only objection to that obvious connection was that, if the trip had been planned in advance — before Lorraine died — it could not have been motivated by criminal activity Rose had witnessed. She lived behind Lorraine Creeney's house, but had almost certainly seen nothing. I was at once elated and disappointed.

'If the reliable source gave you a name for Rose's sailing partner, would it have been Lorraine Creeney?'

'Absolutely,' Alun said. 'Lorraine Creeney was a frequent visitor to Rose's flat. It was a joyful life on the ocean wave for two adventurous females now dead, murdered within twenty-four hours of each other in two entirely separate incidents.'

'Separate incidents without any connection,' I said, and I told him about Rose and Lorraine planning the trip to Wales, and where I had heard about it.

'Annoying, but not unexpected,' Alun said. 'It would have been understandable if Rose had seen something relating to Lorraine's murder and left town because of it, but not all that helpful when you think about it: now that she's dead there's no way she could tell tales even if she had seen someone put the rope around that woman's neck.' He shrugged. 'As it is, we've established a connection between two women, but it's a connection to boating not murder and does us no good at all.'

'If we can believe Caroline Spackman.'

'You were there. What's your opinion?'

'It came out in a mild verbal altercation between Caroline and Max. If either of them had something to hide, it would have been Max.' I shook my head. 'No, I don't think she had reason to lie.'

'So bang goes the link.' He shrugged. 'And good riddance, too, because now we can look hard at several local leads. Davey Jones is already in for questioning, because he was seen leaving Rose's flat that night. And I've heard a rumour that an actual eyewitness has come forward. Oh yes, don't tell me, I know what eyewitnesses are like, but even a bad one can let something useful slip by pure accident.'

There was a gleam in his eye at that thought. We finished our drinks, Alun went to the bar for a quick word with one of his acquaintances, and I crossed the windswept car park and slid quickly into the Quattro. As I started up and turned on the heater I recalled leaving Karl Tully's flat with high expectations of learning something interesting from Alun Morgan. It hadn't turned out that way. All I'd achieved was the removal of one potential witness — Rose Lane. The sprightly elderly lady from Ash Crescent had sailed her boat for the last time, but had left nothing drifting in her wake that would help me to solve Lorraine Creeney's murder.

I was in no mood for light conversation as I drove Alun Morgan home, then headed for the coast road and the journey back to Liverpool.

★ ★ ★

That was what I intended, and that was the way it turned out, in the end. But first there was an unexpected and unpleasant delay.

Dropping Alun Morgan at his home had

taken me only a couple of miles in the wrong direction, but instead of driving back through Bethesda I went in the opposite direction with the aim of switching to the A470 at Betws-y-Coed and joining the A55 at Glan Conwy. A longer drive, but a pleasant one. No problem. And, as it turned out, my change of plan was never going to have a bearing on the outcome because whoever was following me must have done so doggedly for some time, played a patient waiting game then raced ahead to set the trap.

Between Llanrwst and Tal-y-Cafn the road dips and dives, with long straight stretches rising and falling across a series of switchbacks with the railway line and river on the left, wooded hills on the right. It was as I came over one of those rises — with the road ahead and behind me unusually clear of traffic — that I saw the car parked at the side of the road in the dip, the young woman in a bright red fleece with blonde hair streaming in the wind as she waved me down.

I pulled in behind the small white Fiat — a Punto, I think — parked on the grass verge on the wrong side of the road right on the edge of the trees. When I climbed gallantly out of the Quattro she was all smiles and breathless relief.

'That's brill,' she said and went on, in

impressive estuary English, 'Thanks a lo', I think I've go' a puncture or somethin' an' I can' fix i',' while leading the way gaily around the side of the car that was listing on the wet grass.

No puncture. At least not that I could see. The rear wheel was high and dry, the front wheel had settled in soft wet mud causing the car to tilt. So what had happened? Had she felt something go while driving, and pulled in — on the opposite side of the road? Or had she pulled in for some other reason, and assumed a puncture when the car began to sink?

I looked up. She'd walked around the front of the car and was leaning forward with her hands on the warm bonnet as she watched.

'You're sure it's a puncture?'

'Yeah. Or somethin'.'

I looked again at the front wheel. It was buried in mud up to the bottom edge of the silver trim. Beneath the mire, I supposed, the tyre could be flat. I hesitated, looked at the uninviting mud, hung onto the door handle with one hand and bent down for a closer look —

And a tree fell on me.

I groaned and slumped to my knees. My face smacked against the car. Red light flashed and there was a rushing in my ears.

Another tree hit me on the back of the head. A wave of blackness engulfed me. I floated weightlessly. Then my hair was snagged by a giant claw. Searing pain snapped open my eyes as my scalp ripped. I floated backwards. A cold metal vice clamped on my wrist. Through the roaring I heard a voice scream. Then my arm was jerked almost out of its socket, I slid backwards, backwards and, as I kicked feebly and tried to cry out, another tree hit me and I went on sliding all the way into the black hole that was oblivion.

★　★　★

'You OK now?'

'Mm. Yes. Thanks.'

'What about driving?'

'I'll be fine. Army trained.'

The dark-haired man chuckled. 'Like Foggy. A trained killer. Didn't do you much good, did it?'

I was sitting on the back seat of his BMW, door open, my feet planted on the wet grass, elbows on my knees and wrists dangling. Weakly. I felt like a wet rag.

'Tell me again what you saw,' I said, 'before you go.'

'Well, I came over the hill, making for the coast, and I could see this white car and a big bloke and a blonde girl trying to drag you into the woods. She had hold of your hair. He looked as if he was pulling your arm off. I kept my hand on the horn and swung over to pull in behind your car. And that was it. They saw me coming, dropped you and drove off.'

I managed a grin. 'You could have gone after them, but thanks again for stopping.'

'What was going on?'

'Robbery, I suppose. She was the bait, I was the sucker.'

'They prey on decency. I used to pick up hitch-hikers, but not any more.'

And so I returned shakily to my car and my rescuer went on his way. As I climbed in I saw lying in the grass the heavy broken branch that had been used to club me. Neatly round, no jagged projections so no blood in my hair. Just a couple of tender lumps, and a headache fierce enough to split logs.

Eventually I started up, eased back onto the correct side of the road and pointed the Quattro towards Glan Conwy. Once again I had plenty to think about. I'd told Caroline Spackman about my trip to Colwyn Bay, and it was possible she had told Max. But from the window of his flat, Karl Tully had almost certainly watched me drive away, and a phone call would have put someone on my tail. Then again, someone I had not yet spoken to could have followed me all the way from Liverpool. It had been done before.

My head was pounding. Thinking was bringing me nothing but nausea and a desire to scream, and just about the only decision I did make on the drive back to Liverpool was to be much more careful when dishing out Smarties. Yet even that resolution was soon forgotten. When I parked on the edge of the Mersey outside Calum's flat I was behind a metallic-silver Shogun, and from an upstairs window I was being watched by a frowning Sian Laidlaw.

8

'How's your arm?'

'My arm?'

'Gunshot wound, remember? Sam Bone's noisy little pistol, the yacht in Conwy harbour, a nasty graze that was aggravated when you tumbled out of Danny Maguire's floating caravan?'

'I'm losing track of injuries. Getting better at private eyeing, but much worse at ducking.'

'So it seems. There's mud on your knees, and you were chalk white when you got out of the car.'

'Shock. I thought you were miles away, never dreamt you were so close . . . '

I'd walked through the door and she'd run to me and was snug in my arms, her subtle perfume making my poor battered head swim as she leaned back and examined my face with concerned eyes that didn't quite meet mine.

'Ducking suggests someone bashed you on the head,' she said. Her eyes danced as she smiled and looked away. 'And here's me thinking it was serious.'

'It all depends,' I said, 'on what you're

talking about and how you define the word.'

I lowered my head quickly to brush her cheek with my lips as she gently slipped her arms from around my neck.

'I'll make coffee,' she said, drawing away, 'while you tell me exactly what that's supposed to mean.'

I followed her into the kitchen, sat down by the table as she filled the percolator with cold water and set it on the stove.

'Where's Calum?'

'He went out to see Stan when I got here. That was less than an hour ago.' She glanced over her shoulder, then turned away as she juggled with mugs and spoons and sugar basin. 'If you've been to Bryn Aur, you must have just missed us.'

'I stopped on the way home, fought off assailants, crawled in some convenient mud.' My face felt stiff. I rubbed it with my fingers. 'You said 'us'. That would be you and the man with big feet. Did you know you missed a footprint?'

'I was cleaning, not destroying evidence.'

'Who is he?'

'Mark Deeson.'

'Do I know him?'

'You know of him. I saved his life.'

'Ah. Cape Wrath. Hypothermia, the young executive who didn't want to lose touch. He spoke to you during the Gault case, I recall, and we had a difference of opinion in that pub out Hale way while a marvellous woman pianist soothed us with sublime jazz. What happened this time? Did he come to you, or you to him?'

'He walked in when I was eating breakfast.' She turned to face me as the percolator began to bubble. 'He was very persistent. He wanted me to go with him.' She paused, watching me. 'His manner warned me refusal wasn't an option, Jack.'

'And you a trained killer.' I was echoing the words so recently thrown at me, but I couldn't keep the relief out of my voice because what she was telling me pointed at coercion rather than connivance.

'Being a trained killer is an ego boost, but not always that much use when it comes to the crunch,' she said ruefully. 'I know the moves, Jack, but the thought of being responsible for someone's death gives me the willies. If I was up against a man who was truly evil, well . . . maybe . . . ' She shook her head. 'But Mark's certainly not like that.'

'As far as you can tell. You saved his life at Cape Wrath, now this, just a few hours as his unwilling companion.' I watched her shrug. 'You were there at Bryn Aur when I left for the Sleepy Pussy on Sunday, gone by

Monday morning when I returned with Calum. Where did this Mark take you?'

'A cave in the mountains.' She saw my look, and smiled ruefully. 'Honestly. He wanted to impress me, to show me that he really could survive in the wilderness. But he went about it the wrong way. He had a gas heater, a camp bed with down sleeping bag, a two-burner stove and a shiny new Land Rover hidden in the trees . . .'

She turned away again to pour the coffee, and I thought for a moment and said, 'Why didn't you answer your mobile? I called several times. Calum guessed you couldn't get a signal. Was he right?'

'Partly. But Mark's a big lad. He didn't want me to talk to anyone, and I wasn't in the mood for ducking punches or thrashing about on the ground.'

'But you did call me.'

'When he was out using the chemical toilet. Would you believe it, a Porta Potty in the bushes?' She chuckled at the thought, and handed me a steaming mug. 'But he climbed back up the slope sooner than expected and saw the phone and I told him I was checking the time.'

'So now the obvious question. Why? What did he expect to gain?'

She sat down opposite me, frowning,

nursing the warm mug, a little girl looking for comfort when all around her there was uncertainty. Or was I underestimating her? Did her obvious nervousness have another cause? My own mood was like a yo-yo. Ten seconds ago I'd been up, now I was down again because somehow, without conscious thought, I really did know where this was going and I was sick with foreboding.

'He wanted to impress, I know that,' Sian said. 'I *thought* that. But after a while . . . '

She sipped her coffee. I waited, saying nothing, watching the thoughts race behind her troubled blue eyes. She tugged at her blonde pony-tail, slipped off the elastic bands; toyed with them.

'We slept in the cave just the one night, Sunday. Monday we were back at Bryn Aur. I put him in the spare room.' She smiled briefly as she saw my nod, and I knew she accepted that like a clever little PI I'd followed their trail through the house and what she was telling me was nothing new. 'Today,' she said, 'he went back to his cave, and I suppose he broke camp and headed for home.' She looked up at me. 'It was a job well done, wasn't it, Jack? He'd got what he wanted, and he didn't even have to ask.'

I nodded.

'Do you know what I mean?'

'Mm.' I smiled. 'I never did see you as a TV personality, and I don't think you were pleased with your image. Radio was OK, but TV . . . ' I shrugged. 'Reality shows are forcing others to dumb down, which makes the call of the wild, for a woman of your calibre, that much more attractive. This pillock dragged you off into the woods and showed you what you've been missing.'

'Absolutely. I miss the excitement. The sheer joy of the outdoors — even when it's bloody freezing and my knickers are damp and my hair's all knotted with twigs and spiders' webs. I miss seeing eager faces around the camp-fire, watching young executives struggle in after a successful — or, more often, unsuccessful map-reading exercise; the debriefing around a roaring fire in the nearest pub when a course ends and they begin to realize what amazing feats they've achieved.'

'What you've helped them achieve.'

'Yes. That especially, that more than anything.'

I nodded slowly, looked at her over my coffee mug. She met my eyes. Hers crinkled at the corners and I wasn't sure if it was in joy or pain.

'So it's back to old times,' she said softly.

'Good ones or bad ones?'

'That depends, doesn't it?'

109

'On me?'

'On us.'

'We're adults.'

'Are we? I'm going back to playing soldiers. You spend your time making them.'

'When I'm not chasing the baddies.'

'Talking of which,' she said, 'you've been bashed over the head so it's game on. What do I need to know?'

'Nothing,' I said, 'if you're no longer part of the team.'

'Oh, Jack,' she said reproachfully. 'One of the good things about my return to the wilderness is that what I do makes me better at what you do. Not better than *you* are at what you do, but better than I would be at what you do if I didn't do . . . Oh, God,' she said, her eyes glistening, 'you know exactly what I mean because you always do, so come on, tell me what's been happening, everything, from the very beginning — and let's get at them.'

★ ★ ★

When Calum walked in I was sitting at his work table with one hand holding a bag of Bird's Eye frozen peas to my aching head, the other turning a shiny Black Watch Grenadier under the bright light of the anglepoise. On

110

the other side of the coffee table, Sian was stretched out on the settee with a black moggy curled up at her ankles and her ears hidden beneath fluffy pink earphones. She'd borrowed Calum's Walkman. The 'phones looked more attractive on her than on the tall Scot, but the combination of her pink ears and my weird green headgear stopped him in his tracks.

'Jesus Christ!' he said, 'have you two gone completely round the bloody twist?'

'*Music has charms to sooth a savage breast*,' I quoted. 'Sian has jettisoned her television career, rekindled the flames of enthusiasm and is about to burst. I've got a sore head.'

'War wounds?'

'A sucker punch. Painful, but acceptable because it proves we're on the right track.'

He cocked his head at that, tossed his leather jacket at Sian's feet, slipped out of tan Timberland boots and dropped into a chair. I put down the finished toy soldier, clicked off the anglepoise and carried the bag of peas back to the fridge freezer. My hair was wet. I found a towel, thought about coffee; filled the percolator, put it on the stove, took three china mugs from the cupboard: Sian was back, we would drink our coffee in style.

When I returned to the living-room, Sian

111

had removed the earphones and was talking softly to Calum. From the earnest look on her face I knew she'd swiftly told him of her plans to return to the wilderness; from the smug look on his, I knew he'd been expecting it for some time, and approved. I could understand why. In the hour between our heart-to-heart talk and Calum's return I had told her everything that had happened since an unidentified person phoned the Sleepy Pussy and sent me out to find Joe Creeney. And I knew that while listening to Calum's Walkman she would have been mentally sifting and filing the evidence, tirelessly searching for clues that would lead us to the identity of the killer.

She would have been doing it more diligently, I suspected, than during any of our previous investigations into ghastly crimes — and with good reason. Sian had told me, in tones that were ferociously intense, that she wanted this killer found and dealt with. That was the way she had put it: not brought to justice, but *dealt with*; and the menace in those words disturbed me greatly. To make naked threats — even euphemistically — was unlike her, yet in this case understandable. When, in recounting of what had happened, I had reached the point when the police burst into Joe Creeney's house and found his wife hanging in the hall, she told me that she had met, and liked, Lorraine Creeney. Some weeks ago she had been in town with DS Meg Morgan; they had popped into Marks and Sparks for morning coffee and struck up a conversation with two women. One of them was Lorraine Creeney. The other ... well, that doesn't matter. There'd been instant rapport between all four, phone numbers had been exchanged, and there had been talk of an evening out at some time, the theatre followed by dinner.

It would never happen.

I sat down.

'Time for a council of war.'

'Which suggests,' Calum said, 'that this attack on your person has convinced you we are right, the police wrong?'

'Yes. Either I was in the wrong place at the wrong time and was set upon by thieves, or it was a planned attack. That first bit's rubbish. The intention was to remove me. Someone doesn't want me to find out what really happened to Lorraine Creeney.'

'Lorraine Creeney,' Sian said, 'could have been murdered by a stranger.'

'No.' I shook my head. 'The murder was planned — witness the weird routine with ladder and rope, the locked doors. The plan was to incriminate Joe Creeney, and I'm sure it was set in motion long before Joe got out of gaol.'

'So there was this fiendishly clever plan to send Joe back to prison for life, it would have worked perfectly if he hadn't died instead, and now the real murderer realizes we're on his trail?' Sian said. 'Who arranged today's attack? Caroline Spackman?'

'Doesn't make sense. I can't see someone hiring me to find out who killed Lorraine Creeney then hiring someone else to stop me. That suggests that if the information did come from her, Caroline unwittingly talked to the wrong people.'

'Max, or Declan Creeney,' Sian said.

I nodded. 'They're the obvious ones, but what if they're innocent? They too could have passed on the information without intent, and that gives us suspects by the score.'

'Aye, but think closed circle,' Calum said. 'The classic detective story always deals with a finite number of suspects with motive and opportunity. That happens in real life, too. Unless we're talking random murder, why should this be any different?'

'I agree,' Sian said. 'This murder screams of family connections, and I believe we should be looking at the Tullys. One way or another, Joe Creeney caused the death of Wayne Tully. His brothers swore they'd get him. If they were impatient but couldn't get him because he was in prison, his wife was an obvious target.'

The coffee had been bubbling for some time. I went through to the kitchen, came back with three filled mugs and placed them delicately on the table. When we'd tasted and savoured fine coffee by Mr Taylor of Harrogate — I'd added soft Demerara sugar and a dash of Bailey's Irish Cream — I returned to the puzzle.

'Let's deal with Caroline first. We know she was the only person I told about the trip to Wales. If she told others, we can easily find out by asking her. Moving on, the other possibility is that the trip to Wales was discovered in some other way.'

'What does that mean?' Calum said. 'Are you saying Declan or Max or whoever the hell is guilty could have stuck a tail on you, and had you followed?'

'Yes. And, as Sian said, that does point squarely at the Tullys. Yes, I could have been followed from Liverpool, but I spoke to Karl Tully in Colwyn Bay. I told him I wanted to talk to his two sons. He agreed — but he could easily have set somebody on to me to prevent that happening.'

For a few minutes we were silent, sipping hot, sweet, creamy coffee as we mulled over what we'd discussed. Satan uncurled, dropped to the floor and padded into the kitchen. Sian followed, and I heard the sound of a tin-opener, the rattle of a feeding bowl on the floor.

When she returned and sat down I could see by the glint in her eyes that my Soldier Blue was her old self, looking forward to a life packed with adventure but also totally absorbed in my intriguing puzzle.

'I was thinking about what you said, about this murder being planned some time before Joe got out of gaol,' she said. 'And I'm trying to make sense of it. Joe was already in gaol. If someone wanted to keep him there, a murder could have been planned inside the prison.'

'That's a bloody good point,' Calum said. 'Why engineer a gaol break to frame a man for murder, when there'd always be the risk of him scarpering?'

'Not so strange, if you think about it,' Sian said. 'Someone wanted Joe Creeney back in gaol, but they also wanted Lorraine Creeney out of the way.'

9

'She's good,' Calum said.

'At complicating a simple investigation, she's the best.'

The Scot chuckled. 'Bad enough working out how Joe Creeney could be framed for murder inside his locked house. Then along comes this clever wee lass with a spring in her step and suddenly we're looking at not one problem, but three. Why was Joe Creeney sprung? Who wanted him framed? Who murdered Lorraine Creeney, and why was she in the way?'

'That's four.'

'Aye, maybe — but I've still got a terrible fear that complicating the motive for a multi-faceted crime has made getting to the finishing line much more difficult.'

We were finishing breakfast. Sian had left Calum's just before midnight, heading for the spare room in DS Morgan's Calderstones' flat. Meg Morgan was Alun Morgan's sister. She had for some time lived with Joe Leary, a taciturn detective with an abrasive personality whose rank changed in inverse proportion to the seniority of the inflated egos he'd pricked. The last I'd heard he was down from inspector to sergeant and treading gingerly on eggshells.

I slotted two more pieces of wholemeal bread into the toaster, poured coffee and returned to the table.

'According to Mike Haggard,' I said, 'Lorraine Creeney was murdered some time after one on Sunday night. Max Spackman is pretty sure Declan Creeney had become much more than Lorraine Creeney's minder, but whatever was going on had turned sour and he was trying to ditch her. Max's wife, Caroline, rubbished the idea. But if Max is right, and if Lorraine wouldn't go quietly, attempts at dumping her might have led Declan to murder. Could he have done it, that night, given the timing? Well, we know he walked into the Copacobana in West Derby Village just after eleven, because Max Spackman saw him. But we don't know how long Declan stayed because Max himself was on his way out — and we don't know where *he* went.'

The toast popped up. Calum brought it across to the table and busied himself with knife and butter. He slid my plate across, his eyes thoughtful.

'Lorraine was murdered at around one o'clock Sunday night. Two hours after that magic eleven. We can assume both had the opportunity. We *know* both knew where the ladder was stored. But according to Sian, shouldn't we be ignoring them and concentrating on the Tullys?'

'Already done. Karl Tully gave me his sons' phone numbers and addresses: Frank and Len, both of them living off Princes Road. I phoned Frank after you'd gone to bed. He told me to call at his place off High Park Street any time this morning. Friendly enough, but his voice got tight when I told him what was going on — and if it *was* Karl who changed his mind and tried to stop me seeing them, that suggests they've got secrets he'd like to stay hidden and I'm already wasting time.'

Calum nodded. 'I checked with Stan last night. He's meeting a laddie he hopes will tell him something about Joe's cell mate. The other names on your list were Joe's father — '

'Alec.'

' — and Fiona Lake, Lorraine's sister.'

'Mm. I'll talk to Fiona later and take along the tender, understanding member of our team.'

Calum grinned. 'Leaving me to . . . ?'

'Pack the Black Watch figures and send

them winging to Nova Scotia. Then wander down town and have a word with Manny Yates.'

'The sage of Lime Street, the private eye's private eye with a brilliant mind concealed under a gelled comb-over. As you well know, talking to Manny of the bursting red waistcoat will lead to a liquid lunch in the American Bar. Will you be joining us?'

'That,' I said, 'depends on whether I emerge unscathed from my confrontation with Frank and Len Tully. Somebody clobbered me. If it was them, I could be gone for some time.'

★ ★ ★

My mobile chirped as I climbed into the Quattro and, as I took the call, in my mind I was transported to a back-street night-club where not too long ago a crazed taxidermist had used his Sinatra impersonation to croon his loopy valedictory.

It was Frank Tully. He'd changed the plan, and laid bare inexplicable impatience. Had Frank been the would-be assassin who leaped out of the woods wielding an oaken club? Were he and his brother that anxious to finish me off? I would soon find out, for they were both on their way to the King of Clubs in

Pelham Grove off Lark Lane. Frank politely asked how long I'd be and what I would be drinking. I looked at my watch, told him ten minutes and Holsten Pils and he said he'd have an ice-cold bottle on the table.

★ ★ ★

At midnight on any Saturday a vivid imagination could turn George Kingman's sleazy night-club into the run-down business venture of an underworld king whose crown had slipped. Nailed to dirty brick walls that had been pointed during World War 1, the neon crown that would paint those Saturday night skies red was reduced by a grey November day to a tangle of wonky glass tubes. The entrance was covered by the grubby curtain I remembered well, and when I parked with my nearside wheels crunching greasy discarded takeaway trays in the littered gutter and pushed my way through into a passageway with cerise-emulsioned walls illuminated by a single bulb in a four-sided shade of glass playing cards — all kings of clubs — my shoes squeaked on cracked brown linoleum, and warm air larded with the fumes of stale beer and fresh cigarette smoke threatened to slice off the top of my head.

Two terraced houses had been knocked into one. An RSJ supported a load-bearing wall through which a wide opening had been hacked to give access to a main room carpeted in cigarette-burned green cord. At the far end, away from George Kingman's glittering bar but close to the small platform where a knife-thrower had committed murder and the ghost of taxidermist Oliver Dakin would forever cling languorously to the chrome-plated microphone, two men in jeans and rugby shirts sat smoking at one of the round tables.

'Best behaviour, lads,' George Kingman called. 'Private dick on the premises.'

He was sitting on a high stool on the customer side of the bar reading the back pages of the *Sun*. Running to fat, he wore his grey hair in a grade-one cut and his white shirt was opened all the way to the wide leather belt holding up his black trousers. Heavy gold necklaces nestled in crisp body hair. A bottle of Vat 69 stood close to a thick wrist encircled by more clunking gold. His face was shiny with sweat.

George grinned at me as I walked by. 'How's it goin', Shamus? I hear you've opened a taxi service for escaped cons,' and behind the bar the black-suited heavy I knew as Solly growled a dirty laugh that set the optics tinkling.

I dragged out a chair and sat at the Tullys' table. As promised, condensation was misting a bottle of Holsten Pils. No sign of a glass. I took a long swig, felt the ice-cold lager hit my forehead and awaken the painful lumps on my skull, and smiled bravely.

'Thanks for coming,' I said, and looked from one to the other. 'Which is which?'

'Frank, Len.'

The man who'd spoken jabbed his own striped blue shirt then jerked a thumb sideways. Both men were dark, and as tall as their father. These were night-club men, as was Max Spackman, but there the similarities ended. Spackman was a posing bouncer who would hide behind wrap-around shades as he sent a drunk tumbling down a night-club's stairs with blows from bony fists protected by black leather gloves. Both of these men would leave gloves to the sissies. They'd club you to the ground with bare fists but without warning, then stamp on your face. Something in the blankness of their gaze warned me they'd do it from behind and by stealth, if necessary, and again I remembered the girl leaning on the bonnet of a white car and a man who had crept silently out of the dark woods.

'What I'm trying to do,' I said, 'is learn

more about the night twelve months ago when your brother died.'

'Why?'

That was Frank.

'Caroline Spackman has asked me to look into Lorraine Creeney's murder. The police are out of it: Joe Creeney was caught *in flagrante delicto* — red handed — Joe is now dead, case closed. I'm hunting the real killer.'

'That murder was last Sunday, so why go back to Wayne?'

'They say your brother's death was probably Joe's fault. He went to see him thinking Wayne was knocking off Lorraine, but that he didn't intentionally kill him.'

'If the intention was there to scare Wayne to bloody death,' Len Tully said, 'then when he dies hasn't the intention been fulfilled? And isn't the man who goes there with intent guilty of murder?'

Well spoken, and knowledgeable. A barrack-room lawyer?

'Apparently Joe's legal advisers didn't think so,' I said. 'He pleaded guilty to manslaughter.'

'Yeah,' Frank said, 'but if you're investigatin' the death of Lorraine Creeney we still don't know why you're going back to Wayne's murder — so what's goin' on?'

They were drinking Jack Daniels with Red

Bull chasers, or maybe the other way round. This was ten o'clock in the morning and they'd probably been awake all night, the bourbon was a downer, the Red Bull an upper, but far from going cross-eyed they were making me feel tired with the sheer weight of their energy. I watched them toss back a couple of drinks, light two more cigarettes and pin me to my chair with baleful, brooding glances beneath which malevolence lurked, and suddenly realized I didn't really know what I wanted from them. Concentrating on the Tullys was Sian's idea (unanimously accepted) because she thought they were the men most likely to have murdered Lorraine Creeney, but short of asking Frank and Len outright if they had done it I couldn't see how I could find out if we were on the right track.

Besides, I thought, sipping my warming lager, Karl Tully had as good as ruled out an eye for an eye killing. So why had they agreed to talk to me? Why had Frank Tully been unable to hide the tension in his voice on the phone, and changed the venue so his brother could come along for the ride?

They were still staring. I looked at Frank and raised an enquiring eyebrow.

'That's such a good question,' I said, 'I'll pretend I asked it. You tell me what's going on. Tell me why you agreed to talk to me.'

'Because you're working for us,' Len Tully said. 'We're checking on progress, the state of play.'

I pursed my lips and raised both eyebrows. No mean feat, and a testament to my astonishment.

'Care to explain?'

'You're trying to find out who murdered Lorraine Creeney. We figure the person who murdered her is the same person who murdered Wayne. You find Lorraine's killer, we've got our man.'

'That brings us back to Joe Creeney,' I said, now frowning. '*He* killed your brother because he thought she was knocking off his wife. It was a bizarre accident, but he was to blame. Joe's dead, your man is dead.'

Len shook his head with what looked like the edge of impatience. 'Joe wasn't even there when Wayne died. Wayne lived in Fazakerley. Joe was miles away when he died.'

I took a deep breath, expelled it. 'Hang on a minute. The story I got is that Joe went to confront Wayne, there was an argument, a blow was struck, and Wayne fell and fractured his skull.'

'Wayne was found, and pronounced dead by the attending doctor, at eleven that night. There was a tip off, anonymous, and the police picked up Joe Creeney in his brother's club, the Sleepy Pussy.'

'And?'

'We know for sure Joe had been drinking there since six.'

'Makes no difference, surely? All it means is that the argument happened before six, turned violent, and Wayne had been lying on the floor unconscious for five hours.'

'No.' Frank's voice was hard. 'Wayne was at the local chip shop at half past nine. With me. So he was definitely alive and kickin' three hours after Joe downed his first pint.'

I shook my head. 'If you're right, then all this — and especially the alibi — would have come out when the police questioned Joe. A couple of phone calls would have given them the proof. Joe would have been released that same night.'

'It didn't come out, for a very good reason,' Len said. 'The police got a tip off, arrested Joe Creeney, and he called a solicitor. And then it was the other way round, out of police hands, out of the solicitor's hands. Because the solicitor didn't advise Joe, it was Joe who gave her instructions. He told her he was there when Wayne died, *he* was to blame, and he was pleading guilty to manslaughter.'

'Christ!' I said softly. 'Why the hell would he do that?'

'What policeman's going to go looking at alibis,' Frank said, ignoring my question, 'when Joe Creeney's fingerprints were all over the crime scene, and they'd got a confession?'

'And you've got an answer for the fingerprints?'

Len shrugged. 'Maybe Joe had been at Wayne's place before, some other time. Who knows when? Who cares? He went down, and a killer walked. We didn't find out about the timing being wrong, about Joe being in the Sleepy Pussy — '

'Until six months later when someone spoke up,' Frank said.

'And by then,' Len said, 'the trail was cold.'

'There's something else you should think about,' he said. 'Wayne wasn't knocking off Lorraine Creeney, that's a fact. So what *was* he doing to get up someone's nose? Why was he murdered? And why did that man wait a year to murder Lorraine Creeney?'

'I'll do my best to find out,' I said, 'now I'm working for you.'

'Looking for Lorraine's killer,' Frank said.

'The self same man who murdered our kid brother,' Len emphasized.

They were serious. Their faces were hard, their eyes relentless as they contemplated the sweetness of revenge. But that was now, and I wondered what they had been doing since uncovering the truth — or the lies?

'You told me someone spoke up and you realized you'd been hating the wrong man — but have you found out anything else, anything useful?' I looked from one to the other, saw tight lips, heads shaken negatively. 'You knew Joe was innocent six months ago. You've got contacts who told you the timing was wrong, but for six months before that it must have been common knowledge around the clubs. Your brother was what — a club manager?'

'He managed the Copacobana,' Len said. 'He died on his night off.'

'You said it yourself: the man who murdered your brother probably murdered Lorraine Creeney. If you'd gone to the police six months ago, Lorraine might be alive today.'

'Fuck the police,' Frank Tully said. 'We've come to you.'

'Here's my card.' I flipped it onto the table between their empty glasses. 'If anything comes up let me know — anywhere, any time.'

On the other side of the room Solly switched on a vacuum cleaner. George Kingman was wiping tables with a damp rag, then moving on to the next as ash from the stubby cigar dangling from his lip fell on the wet table he'd just cleaned. He was hard at work wasting his time, and suddenly I knew exactly how that felt.

'What you've told me creates a strange dilemma,' I said above the racket.

'Caught between a rock and a hard place,' Len said. 'Caroline Spackman's asked you to find the man who killed her sister-in-law, and you'd love to do it because you've got this rep as a brilliant PI. The trouble is, when you do find him — that man is as good as dead.'

10

As I got into my car and drove out of Pelham Grove to head down town it was dawning on me that a simple investigation was an oxymoron. Desperate criminals fight to keep their freedom. No investigation to unmask killers staring at the certainty of life in prison would ever be simple. Sian had complicated matters only by stating the obvious: she'd come up with nothing new, but had placed the obstacles we faced under the glare of the spotlights. The Tullys, on the other hand, had complicated by simplifying. If Joe Creeney had nothing to do with the death of their brother, Frank and Len had no reason to murder Lorraine. Two suspects had reduced the likelihood of their guilt, but in doing so they had opened up a plethora of interesting possibilities.

If the Tullys were telling the truth, Joe Creeney had pleaded guilty to manslaughter when he had a watertight alibi. Why would he have done that? There were only two reasons that sprang immediately to mind: Wayne Tully had been murdered by someone very close to Joe Creeney, or by someone who had some sort of hold over Joe — perhaps someone he feared. And it was always possible that they were one and the same person.

Joe had pleaded guilty to protect, or to survive. He had been willing to go to prison for one or both of those reasons — but twelve months after he was locked up something had happened that changed everything. But what? Did he get word that the person he cared for was now safe, no longer likely to be under suspicion for the killing of Wayne Tully? Had he or she died? Or had he learned that the person with some kind of hold over him was no longer a threat?

The answer to those questions would tell me if the man really involved in the killing of Wayne Tully was still out there, and possibly — although not certainly — could lead me to Lorraine's killer.

Town was quiet, the skies still overcast, and the winds that had buffeted a Bethesda pub had blown themselves out. I drove into the Mount Pleasant high rise car-park, locked the car and set off on the short walk to Lime Street, reminding myself as I did so that the purpose of the investigation was to discover who murdered Lorraine Creeney. Which brought me back to my oxymoron: a simple investigation. I was looking for a killer who had slain with sufficient guile to create an impossible crime, and to find him it seemed that I would have to go back twelve months to another killing and follow a trail that had been cold even before the Tullys picked it up. And even that, I thought ruefully, was fully six months ago.

I was still pondering on the day's compounding of difficulties that still lay ahead when I turned into the American Bar.

* * *

'I know what he knows,' Manny Yates said, nodding at a distant Calum Wick as I sat down, 'an' when I know what you know I'll put it all together, untangle the various strands and get a result.' He grinned around his Schimmelpenninck cigar, blue smoke curling around his glossy comb-over. 'Wisdom will prevail, my son. The Lime Street dick does it again and solves another baffling case for his bumbling acolytes — right?'

'In your dreams,' Calum said, returning from the bar with cold lager for me and three packets of salt and vinegar crisps. 'Getting a result is a nonsense expression — there's *always* a result, one way or another — and I'd say we're looking at a worried man.'

'Oh, it takes a worried man — '

'To sing a worried song.' I finished the line

for Manny, and waited for him to finish a spluttering laugh that sent grey ash tumbling down his red waistcoat. 'The Tully boys,' I said, 'have probably removed themselves from the list of suspects and set the case back twelve months. Joe Creeney had nothing to do with their brother's death.'

'Who says so, and so what?' Calum said.

'They say so — and what d'you mean, so what?'

'In the first place I mean you're a gullible fool if you believe anything you're told without double checking.'

'They'd be even bigger fools to tell me lies that could be easily disproved.'

'Not if there's an ulterior motive that will stop you proving or disproving.'

'You don't trust them?'

'Do you?'

'I can't see any reason not to — yet.'

'Fair enough. But in the second place I mean, so what, why should we be remotely interested in Joe Creeney's previous crimes?'

'This will become much clearer,' I said, 'if I give you a condensed version of everything I know.'

I told them the full story as we munched crisps and washed the corrosive smears of grease from our lips with the tipple of our choice. Midday office workers came and went. Glasses and money jingled, conversation was a comforting murmur shattered by the occasional burst of laughter, and through the open doors the Lime Street traffic rumbled and exhaust fumes drifted like unseen marsh gas to sting our eyes. My two companions were all ears. I was laying before them a puzzle, and just as talking over problems can clear the air, so the mysteries shrouding two cases of murder became less complex in the sharing, the way forward easier to plot.

'If the Tullys are keen to top the man who killed their brother,' Manny said when I dried up, 'they're likely to have fed you some helpful information. So we can accept that Joe Creeney had nothing to do with their brother's death, but that doesn't mean they're right about two murders bein' committed by the same man. I mean, what have they got to go on? They were six months late findin' out about Joe. Unless they know something they're not lettin' on, I'd say they're guessin'.'

'Aye,' Calum said, 'and they'd be doing that because, like Jack said, they've had six months to go hunting and don't like admitting they've made no progress.'

'True.' I looked at Manny. 'But I think they're right. Joe went to prison for someone else's crime. On the night he goes over the

135

wall, his wife is murdered. There *has* to be a link. Maybe, just maybe, it's not the same killer — but there *must* be a connection.'

Calum reached across the table and plucked a cigar from Manny's waistcoat pocket. 'You believe that because you don't believe in coincidence — right?'

I nodded.

He struck a match, the flame illuminating his greying beard, the sharpness of his eyes. 'If that's true, then you must also believe that the murder in North Wales is linked to the murder of Lorraine Creeney — despite the conclusions to the contrary reached by you and DI Alun Morgan.'

I thought for a moment, and knew he was right.

'Alun's questioning a man who was seen outside Rose's flat, but, you know, I do think he's on the wrong track. I *don't* like coincidence, so my mind's stubbornly telling me there *must* be a connection. I'd ruled it out because Rose was already going to Wales before the murder. But so what? Rose Lane saw something, the arranged trip to Wales conveniently got her out of town — but she still paid for it with her life.'

'Rose Lane?' Manny was rubbing his hands with glee. 'More fancy names — I remember her husband, Rocky — and now it's *three* murders. So go to it then. You've given us the facts, now let's hear some deductions.'

I watched him sit back, red waistocoat threatening to burst, his eyes as bright as its shiny black buttons. Calum was leaning forward with his elbows on the table, cigar jutting from white teeth. He was looking at me, but the distant look in his eyes told me that although he was prepared to listen I would not have his full attention. Each point I raised would send him scampering off along a trail of possibilities. He would have answers before I'd posed questions — always supposing I could think of any.

'Deductions may be thin on the ground,' I said, 'so the best I can do is highlight the details and invite intelligent comment.'

'Get on with it,' Manny growled.

'First, a fact: Joe Creeney goes to gaol for the manslaughter of Wayne Tully. Second, something that *might* be true: six months later, Frank and Len Tully discover that Joe Creeney was in the Sleepy Pussy at the time the crime was committed. If true, he went to prison for a crime he didn't commit. To be willing to make that sacrifice, the killing must have been done by someone close to Joe, someone who had some kind of hold on him, someone he feared — or all three.'

'Which puts us back with Declan Creeney,

Max Spackman,' Calum said, 'and just about anyone with enough strength to swing a length of lead pipe.'

'Not forgetting Lorraine Creeney herself,' Manny said — and he snapped a match, lit another cigar and gazed at us from beneath hooded lids.

'Beautiful,' I said softly. 'What a bitter sweet solution. Wife murders lover, husband steps in, takes the rap, 'a greater love hath no man' . . . '

'And neatly cuts the link between first and second murders,' Calum protested.

'Unless,' Manny said, 'Lorraine committed suicide. She couldn't take it; she'd killed a man, Joe was in prison because of her . . . '

I shook my head. 'That would be even better, because it would eliminate a phantom killer who managed to get out of a house with all the doors locked on the inside. Unfortunately, Lorraine *couldn't* have killed herself, her wrists and ankles were tied.'

'Not difficult to do, with the wrists in front of the body — as they were,' Calum said, quivering like a pointer. 'Wouldn't have to be tight, either. And it's one way for the wee lass to make bloody sure she couldn't change her mind.'

Manny shivered. 'Steady the buffs.' He grinned fiendishly, at the same time shaking his head. 'Will you listen to yourselves. *I'm havin' you on,* you daft pillocks. I'm demonstratin' how easy it is to dream up outlandish possibilities and completely lose the thread. Sure, Lorraine could've killed Wayne. Sure, she could've jumped off that fuckin' ladder. But I'm bettin' she did neither — so, go on, what comes next?'

'A year after he was locked up,' I said, 'Joe Creeney got out of gaol. Someone picked him up and dropped him in Breeze Hill. I was in the Sleepy Pussy when the barman got a call, and he asked me if I'd pick up a man called Joe — '

'Asked for you by name?'

'No.'

Manny shrugged. 'More coincidence. Go on.'

'I dropped Joe behind his house. He told me he was expected — I recall later wondering why I hadn't asked by whom.'

'Whom,' Calum said, and wiggled his cigar as he grinned at Manny.

'When he'd gone I thought I'd take a closer look at his house, but the police were out front. So I slunk away, headed for Grassendale — and you know the rest.'

'And you've asked each other the obvious questions,' Manny said. 'Why did Joe get out of gaol, how was it worked, and who by?

Sorry, by whom? Also, why was he dropped miles away in Breeze Hill and why the fuck, after all that effort, did he go straight home?'

'Which brings us to Rose Lane, and a murder in Wales,' I said softly. 'Calum and I discussed this. There's no way she could have witnessed the murder — so what the hell was it she saw?'

'If her house was behind Joe's,' Manny said, 'she must have seen something at the back of the house, or in the garden.' He scratched his head with the hand holding the cigar, this time dropping ash on his shoulder. 'Where did Declan say he put the ladder?'

'In the shed.' I looked at Calum. 'That's what she saw. She saw the killer taking the ladder and rope into the house — '

My mobile rang.

I stood up and wandered away to the rear of the room with the phone to my ear. It was Frank Tully.

'I've got a name,' he said. Then I thought I heard him mutter 'shit', and the sound of feet shuffling.

'What name?'

'Yeah, that's right.'

I could hear him breathing. I said, 'Are you still in Kingman's club? You're on the pay phone, and someone's listening — right?'

'Probably, yeah.'

'Is this the name of the man who killed your brother?'

'Exactly. It's runnin' in the three thirty. We can watch it on TV if you come round.'

'I'm in town, but I'll leave now. Will Len be with you?'

'No. He doesn't like racin' or the tele.'

'OK. Go on home, I'll see you there.' And then, for no reason that I could think of, I said, 'Watch your back, Frank.'

11

Funny how links appear out of nowhere. Gwydir Street, where Frank Tully lived, cut through from High Park Street to South Street and was one of a whole row of streets as Welsh as a Max Boyce show in Tiger Bay. It was also just a couple of blocks away from Admiral Street police station where Mike Haggard and Willie Vine were based — though why I should be taking the broad leap to include that connection as I drove out of town I had no idea.

'Pelham Grove to Gwydir Street,' I said, 'Frank will get there before us — but only just.'

'Aye, he will,' Calum said, 'but does it not strike you as strange that for six months Frank and Len have been treading water and suddenly they can name the killer?'

'What I'm wondering is why they've bothered to call me. I'm the middle man. If they know the killer's name, why not go after him?'

'Because there *is* no bloody him. It's them. They're crafty bastards, guilty of Christ knows what, and they want the nosy PI out of

142

the way. My God, you left them just a couple of hours ago knocking back some deadly cocktail — '

'Jack Daniels and Red Bull.'

'Right, and so they down some more to stiffen their resolve and decide, OK, we made a hash of things in Wales but if we invite him round on some pretext we can make damn sure we finish the job. Whack him over the head, this time much harder. Slice him up. Stuff the bits in a black bin bag.'

'You think I haven't thought of that?'

Calum chuckled. 'Aye, just ignore my twittering. I'm thinking aloud, wondering, like you, what the hell's going on.'

'Well,' I said, 'we'll know soon enough.'

We'd been driving along High Park Street. Now I turned into Gwydir Street, scanned the houses looking for the right number, and pulled into the kerb behind a purple Skoda Estate I remembered seeing outside the King of Clubs.

I sat looking at the house that was strangely silent — then smiled and shook my head at the daft thought; had I ever looked at a house that was strangely *noisy*? I heard Calum's door click open and the car rocked as he got out. I did the same, and we stood together on the pavement like a couple of insurance salesmen adding up the commission.

'If he rang you from Kingman's,' Calum said, 'he's only just got here.'

'He's left the door open.'

'*Someone*'s left the door open,' Calum corrected. 'Come on, nothing ventured . . . '

Hesitancy draws attention, boldness goes unnoticed. I knocked once, called, 'You there, Frank?' and walked in.

Calum clicked the door shut. We stood in cool gloom, scarcely breathing, listening hard to a clock ticking, a tap dripping, the humming of a refrigerator.

'Frank?'

Nothing.

'Wait there.'

Calum brushed past me. He went into the living-room. I heard him go through to the kitchen. Cool air touched my face and I shivered; he'd opened the back door. When he returned, he shook his head.

I tightened my lips.

'I'm not looking forward to this,' I said, and started up the narrow stairs with Calum at my heels.

The carpets were thick, our footsteps soundless, our nervous breathing and the rustle of our clothing deadened by encroaching walls papered with absorbent flock that was an acoustic nightmare. Since my shout before we walked through the front door I had spoken six words, those in a whisper. Calum had said nothing. Now I felt the urge to clear my throat loudly, to call something, anything — yet I knew even as I clenched my teeth that any sound I did make would fall on dead ears.

We found Frank Tully in the front bedroom.

His phone call had been genuine, but it had brought down on him a terrible retribution and was the last he'd ever make. Whoever had got there before us had clubbed him to the floor, moved the bed to one side and stood over his unconscious form as they looked critically at the height of the ceiling. Then they'd bent Frank's legs at the knees, used the victim's shoelaces to lash his feet back against his thighs to reduce his height, and hanged him from the heavy metal light fitting with a length of orange nylon rope.

This time there was no long drop. Frank Tully's neck had not snapped. The rope had tightened around his neck and, as the air was cut off and his face turned purple and his eyes bulged, he had bounced and jigged at the end of the rope and it had been too much for the screws holding the light fitting and it had ripped out of the ceiling.

The heavy metal had crashed down on his head and sprayed blood. For my own peace

145

of mind I like to think that killed him before he suffocated.

★ ★ ★

Once we knew Frank was beyond help we walked quietly out of that room of death, shut the door behind us and went downstairs. It was not one of those situations where the premises needed searching. Frank had information for us he was unlikely to have written down, and the time between his phone call and our arrival meant that the killer must have walked in on his heels, walked out minutes before we arrived.

In the darkened hallway, where we had been alternating nervous talk with uneasy silence, I voiced my frustration.

'Five minutes, if that. The difference between being handed the killer's head on a plate, or walking away with nothing.'

'Not quite. Whoever did this left a clear message.'

'The orange rope?' I nodded. 'He's telling us he murdered Lorraine Creeney. Which means Caroline Spackman was right: her brother was innocent.'

'And there's more, maybe not a conscious or deliberate threat by the killer but certainly one implied by his actions: this is what will happen to you and me if we don't back off.'

'Len Tully, too, if he's not very careful. I wonder where he was when Frank phoned me?'

'There, perhaps — all you got from Frank was that Len wasn't going to be here with him. My guess is he doesn't know anything of what's been going on — Frank's phone call, this . . . ' He waved a hand vaguely. 'But you do realize the importance of Frank's phone call — I mean, beyond the startling fact that he was about to give us a name?'

'Oh yes. Frank was given the name of the killer while he was in the King of Clubs. So, optimistically, the information came from Solly, or Jimmy Beggs . . . maybe even from George Kingman himself. Looking on the gloomy side, it's more likely to have come from someone we don't know, a stranger — but no matter what, it's one hell of a breakthrough because whoever gave him the name was in George Kingman's club around lunchtime today.'

Calum had been nodding slowly in agreement. Now he pulled out his mobile.

'Give me that number,' he said. 'On the off chance Len was there with Frank . . . '

The Post-it note given to me by Karl Tully was in my pocket. I handed it to Calum. He thumbed in the first number, listened, tried the second — shook his head.

'Land line keeps ringing, mobile's switched off.'

'Mm. We'll keep trying.' I thought for a moment. 'You know, the killer as good as admitting he murdered Lorraine still doesn't tell us how he worked it. I think it's time we looked at the crime scene.'

'Which might be difficult if we report this to the polis. They'll reopen the case, and Joe's house will be sealed off.'

'If?'

Calum grinned. 'Maybe that should have been 'when'. I mean, I know we're going to report it, eventually — but we can do it anonymously and choose the time, can we not?'

'Putting off the call is risky,' I said. 'Someone must have seen us here. Noted the car number.'

Calum winked roguishly. 'Time of death's always imprecise. When confronted we don't deny we were here, but point out that when we left Frank he was alive and kicking — '

'And planning on hanging around for a while?'

'Something like that,' Calum said with a grin, 'if you're in the mood for black humour. Come on, let's go and get that key.'

148

★ ★ ★

I thought it would be a bad idea to let Declan Creeney know what we were doing so I rang Caroline Spackman, found out she had a front door key to Joe's house, and drove to Mill Street to pick it up at about 3.15. It was almost a quarter to four by the time we got to Beech Crescent, way too early for office workers to be returning home, but just in time for the women ferrying children home from school to gaze imperiously out of their silver Suzuki Vitaras as Calum and I entered Joe Creeney's house.

'So much for keeping a low profile,' I said, as I shut the door.

'They'll think we're cops,' Calum said. 'I flashed my open wallet at a tight-looking blonde as we came in.'

'What's inside it, your bus pass?'

'Oh, now that is very bloody droll.'

'But this,' I said, 'is very pleasant indeed.'

The hall was roughly square, and as large as Calum's living-room. The floor was expensive herringbone parquet, the carpeted stairs Mike Haggard had described climbing the inside of the right-hand exterior wall and turning sharp left at the top. A passage between the stairs and an inner wall led to the rear of the house — probably the kitchen. Set into the inner wall there was a heavy panelled door.

Daylight seeping through venetian blinds covering a small window bathed the stairs in cold light, but late in the afternoon of a grey day the square of coloured glass set at head height in the front door left the hall in eerie semi-darkness. Calum clicked on the light. In the sudden glare from three bulbs in fancy glass shades the floor shone with a rich, polished lustre, and I noticed a small oak telephone table with padded tapestry seat, a corner display unit fitting into the angle between the exterior wall and what I supposed was a downstairs cloakroom.

On the telephone table next to the phone there stood an aerosol can of beeswax furniture polish draped in a crumpled yellow duster.

'She wasn't splashing silk emulsion on the walls as Haggard suggested,' I said quietly. 'With the police sitting outside her front door she was busying herself with housework to take her mind off the shocking news about her husband Joe.'

'And not too long after that,' Calum said bitterly, 'she was being forced up a stepladder in that passage and probably sqeezing her eyes shut as some bastard dropped a noose over her head.'

For a moment there was silence as we both visualized our worst nightmares and found their horrors as nothing compared to what had been done to Lorraine Creeney. Then I shook myself mentally and the soles of my shoes squeaked on the glossy wood blocks as I crossed the hall to the panelled door and turned the brass knob.

As expected, I found myself in the main living-room, and my eyes were immediately drawn to the big patio doors and beyond those the lawned garden sloping gently up to the back fence.

'That's the way Joe came in. He told me those doors would be unlocked.'

'So he came in that way, stealthily crossed this room and crept silently out into the hall,' Calum said, walking past me and skirting the huge sofa to look out at the garden. 'Maybe he went up for her then, maybe later. According to the police, he brought ladder and rope in from the garage. According to Declan Creeney, he must have brought them in from there.' He pointed to the top of the garden where a Cuprinoled 8′ × 6′ shed stood under the drooping branches of two graceful silver birch trees.

'Declan knew about the ladder. So did Max.'

'And others we don't know about.'

'According to Manny,' I said, 'whoever it was, Rose Lane probably saw him do it.'

'Him.' Calum said.

'That's right. The mysterious him. But not Joe.'

'That's what we believe, and it's what the latest killing strongly suggests, but there's no way we can prove it because Rose Lane will take her evidence to the grave.'

'Unless,' I said, 'she told her husband.'

'Who apparently drifts in and out of dementia.'

I bent to pick up a heavy wooden tray I'd knocked with my foot. As I straightened up my other foot slipped on a white cloth lying crumpled on the polished floor, and I almost fell. I saved myself by grabbing the edge of the open door with my free hand. As I did so I saw a stain on the door's edge. Head height. Dark.

Paint — or blood. And what was the significance? I shook my head, dismissed it and swore softly as I bent to lean the tray against the wall and draped the cloth across it.

'People who scatter rugs on polished floors deserve to break a leg.'

'That, my man, is a tray cloth.'

'A stray cloth more like,' I said, and looked around without much hope of spotting any clues.

'We could check all the doors and windows,' I said, 'but I don't see the point. If the police say they were locked, that's good enough, and we're left with the insoluble problem of how the real killer made his escape.'

'There's always the possibility that when winding us up Manny had stumbled on the truth.'

I stared at him. 'What — Lorraine committed suicide?'

Calum was frowning as he came away from the patio doors.

'Think about the alternative. Not only would a killer have to make his escape leaving doors and windows locked on the inside, the time of death tells us *he must have been here, committing murder, when Joe walked through those patio doors.*'

'Then there would have been a fight.'

'Damn right there would.'

'But there wasn't. The police heard nothing until the disturbance that forced them to break down the door. When they did, they found Joe alone with his dead wife.'

Calum dropped into one of the big easy chairs. I wandered around looking at sideboard and roll-top desk and cocktail cabinet and walls hung with original oil paintings and a plasma television with a screen as big as a shop window, and I thought of dramas I'd seen on the box and Jonathon Creek stories with impossible twists and I told myself, think laterally, you'll reach just the one possible conclusion.

'The other alternative is that Joe let him out, and locked the doors,' I said. 'He might even have let him in — he told me he was expected. What if he really did snap in gaol. He got out to murder Lorraine — and he had help all the way.'

'Nice try,' Calum said. 'Apart from raising the question of why he'd lock himself in the house with his dead wife, he couldn't have let this mysterious helper out the *front* way because the police were sitting in a Panda. And if you remember, Haggard told you the *back* of the house had been checked. The only person to cross that garden was Joe Creeney — on his way in.'

'Yes,' I said gloomily, 'and when the police did break in he tried to run, didn't he . . . ?'

I was still bemoaning the destruction of another brilliant theory when the front door bell chimed so loudly in the quiet it chopped a good five years from our lives.

★ ★ ★

Declan Creeney knew where Lorraine kept the booze, and he made straight for it. The cocktail cabinet crashed open, the decanter stopper squeaked, amber liquid splashed into crystal glasses and he handed them out with a splash of Canada Dry and a fierce scowl.

'What the hell are you doing here?'

'Investigating.'

'Where'd you get the key?'

'Does it matter?'

'My brother and his wife are dead, the case is closed and you're trespassing.'

'So what are you doing here? Removing the evidence?'

He frowned.

'What bloody evidence?'

'Oh, clothing you left in Lorraine's wardrobe. Your razor and toothbrush from the glass shelf in the en-suite, pyjamas from under her pillow . . .'

He was standing, glass in hand, his back to the garden. The light put his face in shadow. I couldn't see his eyes.

'You been talking to Max?'

'Is he right?'

He snorted. 'Depends what he said. I've already told you I was looking after Lorraine for Joe. Now they're both dead and I'm the executor.'

'Ah!' I nodded sagely. 'A licence for the

155

unscrupulous to print money: this house must be worth a packet.'

'What the hell do you want?'

Calum stirred. He'd remained sprawled in the deep easy chair, sipping his Chivas Regal. Until the Scot's sudden movement alerted him, I think Declan had forgotten he was there.

'For starters,' Calum said, 'we'd like to know where you were around the time your kid brother was going over the wall.'

'Talking business with my manager in the Copacobana.'

'Aye, you were there at eleven because Max saw you, but he was leaving when you got there. Are you telling us you stayed? You didn't maybe go out for a wee while — say some time before midnight?'

'Piss off.'

'Charming.' Calum grinned across at me. 'Didn't someone tell us the Copacobana was where Wayne Tully used to work?'

'Manager,' I said, 'according to his brothers. With an eye for the ladies.'

'Joe got it all wrong,' Declan said, shaking his head. 'He thought Lorraine was playing away from home, got his sights set on Wayne Tully as the super stud and went to see him at his house in Fazakerley. Big mistake. They came to blows, and you know the rest.'

'Everybody got it wrong. Joe didn't go near Fazakerley. He was drinking in the Sleepy Pussy.'

I'd expected that to shock him, but he rode the punch without blinking. Was he a poker player *par excellence*, or was my startling news already history?

'Oh yeah? The plea was guilty to manslaughter. Entered by his solicitor, at Joe's insistence.'

'He was protecting someone,' I said, 'or saving his own skin.'

'Crap. If he didn't do it, who did?'

I smiled, and probed the opening. 'How about you?'

'I was somewhere else at the time.' He grinned. 'Ask Joe's solicitor.'

'Who's he?'

'She. You know her well. It was Stephanie Grey.'

12

I dropped Calum at his flat in Grassendale. He was about to make an anonymous phone call to the police to report a murder. I was heading for the Dingle to return Joe's key to Caroline.

Before I left I once again tried Len Tully's numbers. No use. One rang without response, the other was still switched off.

Declan Creeney's words were still ringing in my ears, and the thought that accompanied them as I cruised along Aigburth Road was that Stephanie Grey had been sparing with the truth. Oh, she'd mentioned manslaughter, but had said nothing about Joe asking her to enter a guilty plea. You know the feeling: when you catch someone telling even the mildest of lies you begin to wonder how many more there have been. Trust goes out of the window — the more so in this case because the investigation seemed to be getting more complicated by the hour and the news of Stephanie's involvement had come from Declan Creeney.

A man who, for the first time, I was seriously considering as a suspect.

I turned off at the Dingle, powered up Beloe Street and was close to Caroline Spackman's house in Mill Street when I recognized something about the car in front of me. A white Fiat Punto. A tall man in the passenger seat, the driver a blonde woman wearing a red fleece.

My scalp prickled. I slowed down, let it pull ahead. It didn't go far. As I eased into the kerb I watched it pull across the street and stop outside Caroline's house. The blonde young woman got out and waited on the pavement for the man to come around the car. Max Spackman.

I lowered my window. Spackman and the young woman were talking animatedly. Then he grinned, they embraced and, as she ran back to the car, I heard her call, above the noise of the traffic, 'Bye, Dad.'

My poor brain could take no more. When she had driven off and the front door had slammed behind Max I dug an envelope out of the glove compartment, slipped Joe's key inside and sealed the flap. When the coast was clear I climbed out, ran across the street and poked the envelope through Caroline's letter box. Very quietly.

Then, feeling more than a little dazed, I drove home to Wales.

13

My decision to drive into Wales was not quite spur of the moment. Calum had posted the parcel containing red boxes of Black Watch Grenadiers, they were on their way to Nova Scotia and he had an empty work table. I had several non-urgent toy soldier orders from dealers in the USA, but they were for figurines I didn't have in stock so I planned to spend Thursday morning in my workshop casting those sets.

While Calum and I had spent Wednesday talking to suspects, conferring with our Lime Street mentor and making gruesome discoveries, Sian had been severing links with Nigel at Radio Merseyside and her producer in Granada's Manchester studios, and making joyful telephone calls to several hard-bitten ex-army characters she had worked with on adventure training courses.

I had spoken to her via mobile phone: she was spending another night at Meg Morgan's flat. Tomorrow, Thursday, she would finalize the arrangements for a survival course for IBM executives she was to co-lead in western Scotland early in the winter.

She also agreed to phone Fiona Lake, Lorraine Creeney's sister, and fix up an appointment. If she could make that for Thursday, she would get it over with and perhaps have something helpful to contribute to the three-way discussion I thought was urgently needed.

Calum, too, was hoping to have more news: Stan Jones was not just asking around about Joe Creeney's cell mate — Damon Knight — he'd made arrangements to visit the man. This, too, would be done tomorrow. Stan was meeting Calum when he got back from the gaol, to pass on any information he'd managed to extract.

Promising stuff. I was uplifted by the thought that positive action was almost certain to bring in fresh leads, and arranged a get together at Calum's flat when I returned to Liverpool.

As I was also planning on spending some time with DI Alun Morgan, the return trip would be late Thursday afternoon or early evening. The prospect of seeing my Soldier Blue brought with it the usual comforting glow that stayed with me all the way to Snowdonia, and was still warming me in my lonely bed in Bryn Aur when I dropped off to sleep.

At eight in the morning the mist was a chill white blanket hanging over the tumbling river and clinging like melting snow to grey-green foothills. I could smell the tang of wood-smoke from a nearby farm, somewhere on the rocky heights a sheep baaed plaintively — it had my sympathy — and droplets of icy condensation spattered my bare head as I walked under the sprawling oak tree, jogged down the slope, and unlocked my workshop.

Three hours later I was outside in watery November sunshine, sitting on a scarred and wonky wooden stool and drinking hot coffee out of a mug as I contemplated through the open doorway the glittering rows of newly cast metal figures standing on shelves. Troops of the 1st Virginia Battalion and the 14th Brooklyn who had fought each other in the bloody Battle of Gettysburg were standing in ranks waiting to be armed with their 1859 Sharps breechloaders. They would wait a while longer; time was pushing on, and during a short break I had phoned to arrange my meeting with Alun Morgan.

We'd agreed to meet in Toad Hall, a hotel with an elevated outlook over the Colwyn Bay promenade. Two hours after packing away my tools I walked in and joined the Bethesda detective at a table by the window. He was looking mildly chuffed.

'Make my day,' I said. 'Davey Jones has been released without charge. He didn't murder Rose Lane.'

'Indeed. He has, and he didn't. So it was straight back to Anglesey yesterday, where I've no doubt he spoke to his solicitor about wrongful arrest and police harassment.'

'Then why chuffed?'

'You first. Tell me why Jones being released pleases you.'

'Mm. Well, last time we talked we ruled out a link between Rose Lane and the Liverpool hanging. I had found out her trip to Wales had been arranged before Lorraine Creeney died, which meant she hadn't fled because she saw something frightening or disturbing. However, Manny Yates — '

'Ah yes,' Alun said. 'The Lime Street dick.'

'Manny,' I repeated, 'with the unblinkered view of an outsider, was able to suggest what Rose *might* have seen, and I belatedly realized that the prearranged trip came in very handy. Although it didn't save her life.'

'Lucidly explained, if a trifle long-winded,' Alun said, 'but all sad and rather pointless when I tell you the eyewitness I mentioned has been interviewed and we have now arrested a middle-aged woman.'

163

'A *woman*!'

'Brunette, shoulder-length hair, wearing a pink blouse — all clearly seen, as was the fatal thrust of the knife, by a disabled woman watching through powerful binoculars from her flat in Deganwy. The rest, as they say — '

'Is wishful thinking.'

'However. The one clue we found at the crime scene was some saliva in the form of spittle, soaking into the carpet — '

'Spittle? A clue?'

'DNA, you see. Wasn't around when you were working with the army Special Investigation Branch, but I'm sure knowledge of it's filtered through to you by now — '

'Yes, all right, so you got a sample of DNA from this spittle and because it didn't match Rose Lane or Davey Jones's you're hoping you'll have better luck with this suspect — what was her name again?'

'Ann Rice.'

I picked up my beer and sat back as a waitress brought eating irons, serviettes, and two cheeseburgers dripping hot grease onto white plates. She left with a bright smile. I sipped my ice-cold Holsten and glared at Alun.

'From across Conwy harbour,' I said, 'your witness couldn't possibly recognize a face — or much else. And you say she saw the

164

knife thrust? Come on, surely that's not possible! She saw a woman visitor, middle-aged, dark hair, pink blouse; saw her waving her arms around, not stabbing a victim. Then she read about the murder and her imagination took off, and she put a face to the pale blur she'd seen at the other end of a telescope when you and I know it could have been *anyone* — '

'You mean someone from Liverpool. All right, I'm willing to listen. Have you got a convenient female suspect there matching that description?'

'Well . . . '

'Doesn't matter,' Alun said. 'This Ann Rice lives in a flat on the same floor as Rose, and her fingerprints were found in Rose's flat. Other residents have heard her making threats; despite Lorraine Creeney and Rose Lane being married women, Rice always thought the relationship was unnatural.'

'Yes, but a knife in the throat?'

'She used to be a nurse in Bangor. She was dismissed for cruelty, or something worse; the details elude me.' He sliced his cheeseburger in half, took a bite, wiped grease off his chin. 'Anyway,' he said, swallowing, reaching for his glass of mild, 'why the obsession with a link between murders? If you think Joe Creeney did not kill Lorraine, then find the real killer.

165

Trying to prove that person also murdered Rose Lane means twice as much work — doesn't it?'

'Or two avenues to explore, with double the chance of finding the killer.'

'You can always live in hope. She could be working for your elusive Liverpool hangman. A hired assassin in a pink blouse, from Liverpool with love, I can almost hear Shirley Bassey . . . No, I think that one was Matt Munro . . .'

There was more of the same. I took it because I had no choice, Alun relished poking fun at me almost as much as he was enjoying his greasy cheeseburger washed down with warm beer, me with a fixed grin that turned sheepish as I quickly came to realize that he was absolutely right: who needed a Welsh murder, when we had two of our own?

But even that apology for a grin was wiped out. Alun's mobile phone rang. He took it out of his pocket, apologized and walked away to answer it with his back to me.

Not for long. He said a few words, then turned to face me. His grey eyes were as cold as Ffestiniog slate.

'Jack Scott?' he said, walking slowly towards the table. 'What's he done now?'

He listened, nodded; pulled out the chair he had abandoned and sat down.

'Typical, isn't it?' he said softly. 'Not responsible, I'm sure, but withholding information is an offence in itself — and it's becoming a habit.'

He watched as I practically wriggled in discomfort, listened some more, then nodded.

'At his workshop, I shouldn't wonder. If I'm up that way I will — how would Willie Vine put it? — advise him of your displeasure.' He laughed at something Haggard said, his expression wooden. 'If I see him here in Colwyn Bay . . . well, his own displeasure should be something to see.'

He switched off.

I shook my head. 'If that was about the killing of Frank Tully, it was reported.'

'But not by you.'

'Calum phoned in.'

'Did he?' This with a raised eyebrow. 'That call must have got lost in — what do they call it, cyber space? — because Tully's body was discovered by a next door neighbour who saw two shady characters enter the deceased man's house. When they drove away — looking furtive — he went to investigate.' His smile was fiendish. 'But not before jotting down the number of the car, an Audi Quattro, silver — '

'Thanks, Alun.'

'For?'

167

'Procrastinating. Holding your horses.'

'Acting like a bloody fool by withholding information from one of my own?'

I spread my hands. 'Calum really did report it.'

'Anonymously, no doubt, and without touching on the delicate matter of how the hell you found a body that, by all accounts, was still bloody warm.'

'No. But that would have come later.'

'Sooner, more like it. Haggard phoned me from Vine's car. They're on their way to pick up Calum Wick.'

And, although I couldn't be absolutely certain, as the Bethesda DI turned away with a gleam of amusement in his grey eyes I thought he gave a broad, conspiratorial wink.

★ ★ ★

Seagulls were crying overhead, and the cool salt breeze was driving in from the Irish sea when I walked back to my car, phoned Calum and got straight through.

'Where are you?'

'Home.'

'Get out now. Haggard and Vine are on their way.' Then, recalling for the umpteenth time that the tall Scot did not drive, I said, 'When you've put distance between you and the flat, phone Sian, tell her where you are, get her to pick you up. It's just after two. Let's meet at four in The Gallant Trooper, Frodsham. We'll regroup, debrief, analyse, weigh all the options — OK?'

'I'll try to remember,' Calum said drily, 'if I make it. I'm at the window, and Vine's grotty Mondeo is screeching to a halt.'

He must have taken the phone away from his ear to demonstrate because I clearly heard the rattle of a dying engine, the double slam of car doors, the sound of running footsteps.

Then, abruptly, he switched off.

14

A cold drizzle was falling when I drove into Frodsham, slid out of the Quattro in The Gallant Trooper's car-park and ran through pools of warm yellow light spilling from windows set in white stone walls under an overhanging slate roof.

Late afternoon had not yet become early evening and the lounge was almost empty when I walked in. Wall lights revealed the unevenness of rustic stone and glittered on polished brassware. A log fire hissed and crackled. Dancing flames splashed light and shadow across stone floor and beamed ceiling.

No sign of Calum, or Sian.

Apprehensively, I stood back in the shadows near the door and let my eyes roam. Back against the glittering optics the barman was polishing a glass and watching me with amused curiosity. One man, perched on a bar stool drinking what looked like gin and tonic with a slice of lime, had heard me come in and was twisting to look over his shoulder.

'Through there,' the barman called, and he nodded towards a doorless opening alongside the fire.

'Sorry?'

'If you're Jack Scott, your table awaits.' He shook his head. 'You're late, so the others started without you. There's a menu on the table.'

Relief washed over me, making my head swim. I lifted a hand in thanks and walked through to a dining-room that was a miniature version of the lounge complete with crackling fire, more wall lights, and half-a-dozen small refectory tables.

Flushed by the heat of the fire at her back, Sian was as pretty as a serving wench in white blouse and flared burgundy skirt. I bent to kiss her lips, moved a stray wisp of blonde hair with a trailing finger and whispered in her ear.

'No Shogun. I imagined you in a cell, on bread and water, not all this . . . '

'Remember the boy scout motto,' she said. 'It's tucked away under the trees, unseen but ready.'

I squeezed her shoulder, and grinned across at Calum as I sat down.

'The damned elusive Pimpernel. Was it a clean getaway, or a mad scramble?'

'I made it downstairs to Sammy Quade's room before the cops came through the door, left when they gave up and drove away.' He shook his head. 'I believe someone once said, when dying, that on the whole they'd prefer Philadelphia. God knows who it was, but forget the irony: having spent a wee while in Sammy's lair I can echo those sentiments with sincerity: I'd rather have been *anywhere*.'

Sian chuckled, and reached across to squeeze his hand.

'The poor lad was a bilious green and shaking like a leaf when I picked him up on St Mary's Road.'

'Lily-livered, that's his trouble,' I said. 'Doesn't bode well for the stern tests that lie ahead.'

'Sounds scary. We'd better leave the details until you've eaten,' Sian said.

And so we did.

I downed steak-and-kidney pie baked with a pastry that flaked as I cut it and was light enough to float on the warm air. Boiled potatoes glistened with butter. Garden peas were topped with a sprig of mint. The red wine was dark and warm and, as I tucked in, Sian and Calum left me to it, my Soldier Blue striding lithely off to the cloakrooms with her ankles trim in backless wedges, Calum to buy his usual Schimmelpenninck cigars at the bar. He was out of luck. He came back to the dining-room with nothing but a grimace of disgust. I pushed my plate away with a sigh and we sat nursing the wine until Sian rejoined us.

'First thing,' I said as they looked at me expectantly. 'There's a man called Len out there who might know the name of our killer. Trouble is if Len *does* have that name, he'll hunt the man down — and so far we can't reach Len.'

'Not by phone,' Calum said. 'But you know where he lives, so why waste time?'

'Because . . . ' I shrugged, said quietly, thoughtfully, 'If Len kills the killer, it's *almost* a case of everyone's a winner — right? Len avenges the death of two brothers; Lorraine Creeney's real killer pays for his crime, and we've succeeded without really trying.'

'So why 'almost'?' Sian said.

'Because that last bit's not *quite* true. The use of orange nylon rope in two murders by hanging strongly suggests it's the same killer — but that's a long way from proof; from knowing that Frank's murderer also murdered Lorraine; from knowing *how* he did it, *if* he did it.'

'So, once again,' Calum said, 'why the hell are we wasting time?'

'We're chasing a shadow. We can't get Len on the phone, and we could drive to High Park street and still not find him. If we do find him there's still the chance that he might not know the killer's name, and that would be more time wasted. So let's use up an hour or so pooling what we do know in case there's something we're missing. I'll go first — OK?'

They exchanged glances, then nodded.

'Right. I can tell you that, in Wales, Alun Morgan has arrested a woman for the murder of Rose Lane. That seems to rule out any links to Lorraine Creeney's murder, but, as Alun pointed out, it's good news because it allows us to concentrate on one murder.' I looked at Sian. 'Has Calum told you how we came to find Frank's body, and what emerged from our talk with Declan?'

She nodded. 'For what it's worth, I don't see anything sinister in Stephanie being Joe Creeney's solicitor. Quite the reverse. When Lorraine was hanged and Caroline Spackman wanted to reach you, she went to a solicitor known to the family.'

'Mm. Probably.' I shrugged. 'But what about you? How'd you get on with Fiona Lake?'

'Ah, yes, Lorraine's sister, the young widow.' She smiled reflectively.

'Widow?'

Yes. Her husband got drunk and a club bouncer tossed him down some steep concrete stairs. He broke his neck.' She looked at me. 'Don't start seeing connections.

This was, oh, four years ago, no links to Declan Creeney, different club, different town.'

'Where?'

'Chester.'

'Mm.' I shrugged, letting it slide. 'So, back to how you got on.'

'Not very well. Nothing really useful emerged, and before I left I almost killed her.'

'Third degree?' Calum said. 'Spotlight, rubber truncheon?'

'Aerosol spray. I went to freshen up, used the perfume you bought me last week — and the poor woman had an asthma attack.'

'I didn't know Calum had bought you perfume,' I said, loftily.

'I thought it was a can of mace,' he said, and winked at Sian.

'Might as well have been, the effect it had,' she said. 'Anyway, the point is the only thing I learned from Fiona was that asthma runs in the family, Lorraine had it — and that's my single lousy contribution.'

'For lousy, read ghastly,' I said. 'Step once again into that dark hallway where the stage is being set for a woman's hanging. Bad enough for someone with your experience to be forced to watch, but if Lorraine suffered from asthma she was already in trouble before the noose was placed around her neck . . . '

'Ugh.' There was real anger blazing in Sian's blue eyes, two bright spots of colour in her cheeks. 'You know, if this bloke Len really does have the killer's name, why don't we just step aside and let him take his revenge?'

'Because that's not the way we work, and it's a decision you would always regret.' I smiled at her. Then, swiftly moving on, 'Cal, what have you got?'

'What I got comes from Stan Jones, and amounts to another big fat zero. Stan visited Damon Knight in prison. The man knew nothing of any jail break, and Joe's only visitors during his twelve months inside were the people you would expect: Declan; his sister, Caroline; his wife, Lorraine; and one you perhaps might not expect, our busy solicitor, Stephanie Grey.'

'But not Max Spackman?'

'His name didn't come up.' There must have been something in my voice, because he was watching me closely.

'I asked,' I said, 'because there's something I haven't told you. I found out that Max's daughter could be the young woman who lured me to my fate; it's possible she was the young woman driving the Fiat Punto when I was attacked.'

'Which sounds promising but needn't necessarily point the finger at her, or the rest of the family,' Sian said.

'Unfortunately, no. Caroline seems genuine. Max may know nothing about murders or me being waylaid. His daughter could have been roped in, got scared when everything turned sour. The man who attacked me could have been anybody, following orders, glad to pocket a few quid.'

'So we know more,' Calum said, 'but we're no further for'ard?'

'More confused.'

'Frustrated?'

'Mm. I can't rule out that link to the murder in Wales. And the one person I know I should talk to is Barry Lane, Rose's husband.'

'Dodgy. Isn't he likely to be . . . unreliable?'

'Maybe not. His mental condition might rule out deviousness.'

'So is that a plan?'

'Part of one. Like, steering clear of Haggard and Vine. Finding Len.'

'I thought you said chasing him in the hope that he has a name could be time wasted,' Sian said. 'And that this session was to look for anything we might have missed — ' She broke off, head cocked. 'Jack . . . Hello . . . '

I nodded. Smiled. But she knew I hadn't been listening. I'd been distracted. My attention had been caught by movement on the other side of the room, and now I was watching intently as my mind raced out of control. An elderly couple had finished their meal and left. A waitress had arrived to clear away their dishes. Now she was cleaning the table. Ordinarily she might have used a damp cloth. But these were small refectory tables, and they seemed to be genuine timber — possibly elm. So she was using polish. Pledge. Applying the spray with a bright yellow duster.

And suddenly bits and pieces of what I had seen, heard and experienced in the past few days began to come together. Somewhat hazily, but becoming clearer with each second that passed, I was beginning to see how a fiendishly clever killer might have worked a locked room mystery.

I had the answer — almost. Not close enough for me to start crowing. Not even close enough to share my thoughts with Sian and Calum because my mind resembled a flat table on which the pieces of a complicated multi-coloured jigsaw had been scattered by a careless hand. One edge was forming, and a couple of corners, but those are always the easy bits.

Before I could fill in the centre and complete the picture, I had to turn theory into fact.

15

It was still raining when we left The Gallant Trooper and splashed to the cars, pushing ten o'clock when Sian's Shogun was skimming along the A561 leading us back to Liverpool. Behind her I cruised with a feigned air of nonchalance, tootling — as Calum would say — down Speke Boulevard with sodium lighting splashing metronomically on the Quattro's rain-wet bonnet and windscreen and my passenger blinking nervous yellow eyes as he kept a watch for prowling police cars.

We had committed no crime — well, nothing serious — because Calum had confirmed that he did indeed anonymously report the death of Frank Tully. Nevertheless I had watched Alun Morgan's face as he took the call from Haggard, and I didn't trust the Liverpool DI or his eloquent, elegant sergeant, didn't need their harassment when I had ingenious theories to prove. So, working on the principle that one person could more easily evade the deadly duo than three, two bolt holes had been arranged and two-thirds of the team were going to ground.

Before leaving The Gallant Trooper, I had phoned my mother. She is a white-haired, graceful widow who insists her sons and everybody she encounters call her Eleanor. When, towards the end of the Sam Bone case, I had trailed a suspect all the way to one of Gibraltar's marinas, Eleanor had been there on The Rock in a sun-drenched house hung with purple bougainvillaea being wined, dined and probably bedded by a diplomat turned lotus-eater called Reg.

I had tried to phone her, but she'd been out then (she told me later she and Reg had been in Tangier) and I'd not seen her since, but now she was back home in her Calderstones flat and, with Calum sneaking off to meet Stan Jones and thereafter to abscond in the scally's rusty white van to places wisely unspecified, I had booked a bed for Sian. She would enjoy a nightcap with Eleanor — gin and tonic or Horlicks — then snuggle down on a bleached wood futon in a room of low bookcases and soft carpets where she could watch widescreen TV as she drowsed or be lulled to a deeper sleep by soft light from the red table lamp glowing in a warm atmosphere tastefully scented with Chanel Number 5.

That cast me as Lone Ranger, and I had work to do.

On wet nights the neon lighting above The King of Clubs transforms glistening pavements and gutters into rivers of blood. I parked directly beneath the glowing coils of the hideous crown, shivered as the November air coiled its icy fingers about my neck then crossed the cracked paving stones and pushed through the greasy curtain and on into the main room. It was as if I had waded through blood to be thrust like a knife into a hot and throbbing heart. Strobe lights pulsed green and red, turning lazily dancing couples into twitching marionettes. On the platform a stereo system, balanced on two chairs near the dead mike, boomed like a headache. The effect of sound and light was to make the walk to the bar at once weightless and an effort, like trying to catch butterflies in an underwater dream.

Solly was behind the bar, dark suit shiny and crumpled, lumpy white face glistening. He looked up when I'd floated halfway across the tatty green carpet. I mouthed, 'George?', and he jerked a stubby thumb towards the ceiling. I turned, made my way back to the linoleumed passage then climbed the stairs and clumped along the passageway to the front office.

George Kingman was slumped behind his enormous desk, glass in hand, an unlit bulb dangling from dusty black flex directly above his head. It was his habit to leave all the lights off and sit bathed in the glow from the huge crown that was nailed to the brick wall outside the uncurtained window. It was like gazing at the scene through red cellophane and I could see no change, no improvement, from my first and only other visit. The stained office table was still littered with papers, ashtrays overflowed, sepia prints of racehorses in dark frames still hung at crazy angles from rusty nails, the *Playboy* centrefolds from lumps of Blu-Tack stuck to the grey wallpaper.

'I was expectin' you,' George said wearily. 'Or maybe dreadin' seein' you. Christ, every time you walk in here, someone snuffs it. Next thing is Cassidy and Sundance waltz in and threaten to close me down, then that blows over and before I can draw breath we're off again, musical fuckin' chairs with the one left standin' gettin' the chop.'

'I hate to spoil your day, but the blind piano player's just struck a chord.'

I picked an old *Liverpool Echo* off a chair, looked for a space to put it when there were no spaces, then dropped it on the floor and sat down. George was watching me warily.

'What blind piano player? What's that

supposed to mean?'

'I can't locate Len Tully.'

'Try the undertakers. He lost his kid brother, so now he's arrangin' a funeral.'

'If he's not careful it could be his own.'

'Then you know something I don't.'

'No, *Frank* knew something. Somehow he'd got hold of a murderer's name, and it got him killed. If he passed that name to his brother, Len could be in danger.'

Kingman drained his glass, heaved himself out of the swivel chair like the incredible hulk suffused with blood. His huge shadow fell across the filing cabinet as he reached for the bottle of Vat 69 I knew was standing in the half-open drawer. He held it up by the neck and waggled it at me, the black bottle glinting like red wine. I shook my head. He bent to splash whisky into his glass, took a cigar out of the packet lying on the desk and lit it with a paper match from a book bearing the club's name. When he sat down sweat was filming his brow and glistening like watery ketchup in the close cropped grey hair. He puffed smoke. His gold ring clinked against the glass.

'After you left,' he said, 'Frank and Len sat there drinkin' and talkin'.'

'Just the two of them — or was there someone else?'

He frowned, shook his head. 'The place was empty. Solly was outside takin' a delivery from the brewery. Jimmy Beggs was somewhere around . . . '

'So Frank and Len were over there getting smashed on JD and Red Bull, talking — and what?'

'An' nothing. That's it.'

'And nobody spoke to them?'

'I told you.'

'Yes, but I want that confirming: the whole time they were here, nobody spoke to them, nobody approached them?'

'They ordered drinks.' Kingman sneered. 'Len lifted a finger, Solly took 'em to the table.'

'But no talk?'

'Jesus Christ!' Kingman said. 'How many fuckin' times — '

The thump of music from downstairs was vibrating the floorboards. There was the sudden sharp crash of breaking glass. A woman screamed shrilly, then began to laugh.

'So they talked, brother to brother. What kind of talk was it? Where they cracking jokes, planning a week in Majorca — arguing?'

'They were *always* fuckin' arguin'.'

'What was this one about?'

'Who knows? I caught snatches. One'd say they should've, the other'd say they shouldn't, stuff like that, like, you know, then they were on about so what do we do now, up to you, blah, blah, fuckin' blah.'

'And then Frank got up, didn't he? The pay phone's by the bar. He went over there and used it — maybe got change from Solly.'

'Christ,' Kingman said, 'was he callin' you?'

'Cagily. Telling me one thing, but meaning something entirely different.' I let Kingman take that in, then said, 'Someone was watching him.'

'I told you,' Kingman said. 'The place was empty.'

'How about Solly? When I was here he was using a vacuum cleaner, sucking cigarette burns off that green stuff you call carpet. He was also behind the bar. That's why you put the phone close by; you like to know what's going on, listen to private conversations.'

'Bollocks. And I told you where Solly was.'

'Taking a delivery.' I nodded. 'Where were you?'

'When Frank phoned you? I was up on the platform fixin' the mike, only I couldn't, which is why tonight there's music but no singer.'

'But you saw Frank go to the phone?'

'The rogues I get in here it pays me to know what's goin' on.'

'So who was listening to him?'

He puffed on the cigar; touched the glowing tip to an ashtray that was like a landfill site; tossed back an ounce or two of Vat 69.

'Yeah, well, the place *was* empty an' then your boss walked in.'

'My *boss*?'

'Employer.'

'What — Caroline?'

'Steph.'

'Steph?'

Kingman grinned. 'As a shamus,' he said, 'you'd make a fuckin' good echo.'

'You don't mean Stephanie Grey, the solicitor?'

'Why not? She pops in now and then. Ear to the ground, finger on the pulse. Probably picks up a lot of stuff she can use in court, stuff people tell her, stuff they let slip . . .'

'And she was listening to what Frank was saying? She could hear what he was saying?'

'Did I say that?'

'No,' I said wearily, 'you didn't.'

'What I was *about* to say was, it was *Len* trying to hear what Frank was sayin'.'

'*Len*?' I said, then held up a hand as the echo rang in my ears and Kingman shook his head and grinned.

'He was fumin',' Kingman said. 'He tried to get close, grabbed Frank's shoulder. Frank

186

pulled away, turned his back.'

'And then?'

'Finished the call. The two of them walked out.'

'Did they say where they were going?'

'We know where Frank was going,' Kingman said.

'To his death.' I nodded. 'And now his brother's missing.'

Kingman grinned, and winked. 'Maybe you should talk to your friendly solicitor.'

16

Len Tully's parting shot when I left the brothers that afternoon had been to warn me that when I found the killer, that man was as good as dead. If Frank had been telling the truth on the phone, they had beaten me to it. He and Len had come up with a name, but it was Frank who had died — so what had gone wrong?

According to George Kingman, they had started arguing when I walked out. They were alone in the club. Nobody had spoken to them. Yet soon afterwards, Frank had used Kingman's pay phone to tell me he had the name of the killer.

If he had the name then, he had it earlier when I was talking to them. The only conclusion to be drawn was that it had been the intention of at least one of them to give that name to me when I walked into the King of Clubs but, between phoning me and my arrival on the scene, something had changed.

I got there, talked to them, nothing useful came out of it and I left. Some time after I drove away it had been Frank who picked up Kingman's phone. According to Kingman,

Len had been desperate to find out who his brother was calling, what he was saying; Frank had been just as determined to keep his brother at bay. Again, there were only a couple of possible reasons for the disagreement: Frank was scared, he wanted out, and was desperate to give me the name and wash his hands of the whole affair. Len had bowed to Frank's wishes and spoken to me, but what came out of that meeting had done nothing to change his mind. He wanted revenge: he had the name, and he was going after the killer.

There was one other terrible possibility. Len Tully had not only hanged Lorraine Creeney, but he had also, twelve months ago, murdered his own brother. If he had done that, he had also murdered Frank. And if I was right on any of those counts — perhaps even on more than one — where was Len now?

DAY FIVE — FRIDAY 4 NOVEMBER

It was twenty past midnight when I turned the Quattro off High Park Street, the pitted tarmac drying in a freshening breeze and Len Tully's house in darkness when I pulled up with the tyres whispering against the kerb. I switched off the engine, sat in warmth and darkness studying windows like blind dead eyes. Weak light from the street lamp immediately outside the gate crawled gamely along the short path towards the front door. Beyond curtains drawn back from window panes stained with the dust of passing traffic, I caught the shine of furniture and what might have been light reflecting in a wall-mounted mirror. When I wound down my window I heard the whine of a car racing along High Park Street, the soft singing of the wind in overhead cables.

I climbed out reluctantly, opened the creaking gate and walked up the path. When I tried the bell, there was no response. Several loud knocks threatened only to alert the neighbours. I turned my back to the door, looked up and down the street — a number of lighted windows, all upstairs — bathrooms or bedrooms. As I watched, one light went out.

Len's front door was the kind with big frosted glass panels divided by a deep wooden crosspiece. On the doorstep there was a heavy rounded stone up against the wall. In days gone by residents would have used it to secure a note for the milkman, or to hide a spare key.

I found another use for it. One swift blow

shattered the glass panel close to the lock. I dropped the stone, slipped my hand through the jagged hole and let myself in.

My feet crunched on broken glass. I stood listening to my heart thumping and my pulse hissing in my ears; reached behind me to click the door shut; leaned back against it with a feeling of despondency I could not explain.

Light filtered through the frosted glass, throwing my faint shadow across a tiled floor. The front-room door was on my right, half open, and I could see the corner of a desk. A flight of stairs to my left climbed into deeper shadows, and the passageway in front of me would lead to a back room and kitchen. Len could be anywhere, but he had not shown himself and my straining ears could detect no sound.

I opened my mouth to call out, then hesitated, biting my lip. I had rung the bell several times, hammered on the front door, used a stone to shatter a panel of glass. If Len was in the house, why hadn't he answered the door, or come pounding through to investigate as broken glass tinkled? What was he doing? Was he standing behind the front room door with a shiny number nine iron clutched in both hands, waiting to crack the skull of the mindless scally who had broken into his house? Was he even now whispering into the telephone, calling the police?

Or was he doing none of those things because, too late yet again, I was trailing with painful slowness in the footsteps of a killer?

My skin prickled at the thought. I felt my nostrils flare, instinctively sniffing the still air for the odours of death. I closed my eyes, saw Frank Tully in rugby shirt and jeans, a grotesque grimace on his white dead face and his body jerking and jumping as he hung from his own bedroom light fitting.

I thought briefly and enviously of Calum, up to Christ knew what capers with Jones the Van, of Sian snuggled down with a gin and tonic in Eleanor's cosy flat. Then I took a deep breath, let it out in an explosion of self-disgust, and commenced the search.

In the next few minutes, feeling like a timid and fearful child forced to play hide and seek with all the lights switched off, I opened doors, looked into shadowy rooms, peered under beds and behind limp shower curtains, cast sidelong glances filled with trepidation at light fittings, and confirmed what I had expected: I was alone in the house. The gallant PI had ventured forth, and got nowhere.

Downstairs again, in the front room where weak street lighting glinted on polished furniture and a desk-top computer monitor, I thought for a moment then sat down in a swivel chair in front of the pine desk and once again tried to reach Len on his mobile. It rang . . . rang . . . and then it was answered.

'Yes?'

A woman. Voice indistinct. She must have been standing in the open air, for the wind was whipping across the phone's mouthpiece to roar like distant surf in my ear. Through it I thought I heard a car engine start, a door slam, the snap of what could have been dry twigs and a man cough, spit, then hoarsely ask a question.

'If that's Len coughing, tell him it's Jack Scott. I need to talk to him.'

'Not now.'

And the phone went dead.

I tried again. It was switched off.

I stared at it, nonplussed.

As I did so, I was conscious of an eerie light at my shoulder. I swivelled the chair. The computer monitor had come to life. It must have been in suspend mode. If you've got a computer, you'll know the routine. You leave the room to make coffee, and when you come back the screen's blank.

While talking on my mobile, my elbow must have touched one of the keys. Now the Windows XP screen was telling me Len Tully was logged on.

To begin, click user name.

Was it worth my while looking closer?

I reached for the mouse, left-clicked on the name, and the screen switched to the desktop background. Shortcut icons were dotted about a bright, clear photograph. For one stunned instant I thought it was a tacky still from a violent computer game. Then realization hit me so hard the breath caught in my throat. I rocked forward in the chair, staring at the screen. My hands gripped the edge of the desk. In that frozen, ghastly moment I could actually hear neck hairs scratch against my collar as they stiffened with fright.

A murderer had taken a photograph.

He had tilted the camera sharply upwards. I could see stairs leading to a landing, the very top of a stepladder being used as a crude gallows. A woman I knew must be Lorraine Creeney was standing on the tiny platform. She was wearing a pink, three-quarter length nightgown. Twists of thin cord bound her ankles and wrists tightly enough to bite into flesh. Already swollen, her naked feet and hands were a mottled purple. A crimson gag, knotted behind her neck, was dragging her mouth out of shape. Her cheeks were wet with tears and her eyes, pools of terror, were looking inward at imagined horrors that brought a cold sweat to my brow.

It was a still photograph, but something about the thin nightgown and the position of the naked knees revealed by the camera angle told me that the poor woman was trembling uncontrollably.

My God, what else could she do!

For about her slender throat there was looped a vivid orange hangman's noose. When the murderer had carefully put away his digital camera he would step forward and kick the stepladder from under her. She would drop like a weighted sack. Her neck would snap.

As I gazed in horror at that dreadful scene it was as if I was experiencing one of those moments when the house of cards comes tumbling down, when ideas patiently moulded into workable theories go fluttering out of the window like terrified starlings. And yet . . . why should they?

In The Gallant Trooper I had watched a waitress cleaning a table and visualized a sequence of actions that might have explained how a man other than Joe Creeney could have murdered a woman in a locked house. Stored in my mind for verification, clarification, feasibility or viability — call it what you will — that theory still held good: in the picture on Len Tully's computer desktop I was not seeing a ladder soon to be kicked away by the man taking the photograph, but a scene carefully set, a trap cunningly laid.

With fingers that trembled I reached forward and depressed the key that would put the computer into hibernation. I waited, sickness welling in my throat, for the seconds it took for the command to be obeyed, for that terrifying image to turn black.

Then I turned again to my mobile phone. For a moment my numbed mind refused to work. I cursed softly, thickly, thumbed clumsily through my electronic phone book and keyed in DI Mike Haggard's home phone number. Then I went to the front door, opened it, left it ajar and went in search of some strong spirit and a cool glass to make the waiting more bearable.

For it was a toss up, of course. I'd telephoned the police, but I'd also called Len Tully. And when some time later a car did draw up, doors slammed, footsteps trod unhurriedly up the path and the front door squeaked open to let in a gust of cool night air, I still didn't know who had come a-calling.

17

'You didn't say what was going on.'

'It's sensitive, and it wasn't you I spoke to.'

'It was my wife, for God's sake. She passed on the message.'

'And here you are.'

'Yeah, and if she hadn't and I wasn't I'd have got to you eventually.' He scowled. 'Phone call or no phone call.'

'I know that.'

'All right,' he said, 'so what do you want? And what the hell are you doin' in this house?'

'Your job,' I said. 'I've found out who murdered Lorraine Creeney.'

'We worked that out a week ago. If you've got anything more it's a half-baked theory that won't hold water. And yeah, I know,' he said with a weary glance at Willie Vine, 'that's a few more mixed fuckin' metaphors but it's late and I'm tired and Ill Wind's dragged me out of bed — '

'We're both tired,' Vine put in, 'but we're still capable of separating wheat from chaff.'

'Chaff is right,' Haggard said, glowering. 'Creeney killed his wife. Creeney's dead. Any other theory's garbage.'

Less than a minute earlier DI Mike Haggard had been an exhausted, red-eyed bull powering through Len Tully's front door, with Willie Vine tagging on behind like someone anticipating fireworks. The front room door had been open. They'd seen me sitting in front of the computer, sagging a little with relief at the sight of them. Haggard had charged in with jutting jaw, thought about a cigarette, changed his mind and swept his coat back to place hands on hips and glare.

He'd said his piece, asked his question, but the answer I'd given him wasn't enough. He was still glaring. He wanted more.

I said, 'Look at this, and change your mind about Joe Creeney.'

I faced the monitor and pressed the key to bring the computer out of hibernation. Waited in tense silence for the *logged on* screen. Used the mouse to click on *begin*. Swivelled away from the computer, stood up and backed out of the way.

'In the early hours of Sunday morning I dropped Joe off at his house,' I said quietly as Vine slipped into the chair, Haggard peering over his shoulder at the screen. 'You know that, you know what time it was because my car was seen. Joe crossed the garden in darkness, and we know he went into the house through the patio doors. Once inside he had time to take a photograph — but what could he have done with the camera? The police heard noises, they broke in. Seconds later, Joe was dead. If he'd taken the photograph, the camera would have been on him, or in the house. It wasn't — right, Willie?'

I looked at Vine for confirmation. He nodded, then turned back to the monitor.

'So the only way the camera could have left the house and that photograph ended up inside this computer,' I said, 'is if someone else was there, in Joe's house *before* he arrived.'

'Why before?'

Haggard had turned away from the computer, his face wooden but an ugly gleam in his eyes. Vine had picked up the mouse and opened the *My Pictures* folder. He was looking for the original photograph, the original digital file.

'It's a flash photograph,' I said. 'It was late. The street lights are dim. If the police had been outside, I'm sure they would have seen the flash. That suggests it was taken before they arrived.'

The DI grunted. 'Forget the uniforms, an' what they should've seen. Of course it was before Creeney got there. When Joe was caught holdin' the ladder, his wife's heart had only just stopped pumpin'. When that photograph was taken, she was clingin' on to some kind of life.'

'And with more than two hours to live,' Vine said. He swung the swivel chair to face us. 'I've found the file downloaded from the camera. It was taken on a Samsung digital compact at 10.45 p.m. on Saturday, 29 October. Lorraine was forced up that ladder two hours before she died. Why?'

'Because whoever was in there,' Haggard said, 'was preparing everything for Joe Creeney to kill his wife. Makin' it nice and easy for him. Only they couldn't be sure what time Joe was breakin' out of goal, so they played safe.'

'Why would she stand there all that time?' Vine said. 'Would she have the *strength* to do that?'

'Bound hand and foot, that's why,' Haggard said. 'And Christ, yes, she'd find the strength. If something like that happened to me I'd hang on by my fuckin' *fingernails*.'

It was a solemn moment, but quite a picture. Vine's lips twitched. I met Haggard's gaze and he shook his head and turned away, patted his pockets and this time went ahead and lit one of his king-sized cigarettes.

'So, speaking hypothetically,' I said, 'you're saying that Joe Creeney had a lot of help. Prison break, getaway car. And then one of his helpers set things up for him so that all he had to do when he walked into his house was kick away the ladder?'

'He had help on the inside, and on the outside,' Haggard said. 'And then — accordin' to this picture — yes, he had help inside the house.'

'So — still talking hypothetically — the person inside the house arranged that grisly tableau, took a photograph for his family album at 10.45 — and then what?'

'Waited for Joe Creeney, and together they killed Lorraine.'

Haggard and I turned to stare at Willie Vine.

'Couldn't have,' Haggard said. 'Uniforms were parked outside from eleven until they broke down the door at one. Joe was alone.'

'Supposing the assistant was still there, and left *much* later?' Vine suggested. 'Like, seven or eight in the morning, when all the fuss had died down.'

'Bloody hell,' Haggard said. 'You could be right. We knew we had the murderer, so what was the point in tearing the house apart? And all the time we were in there his mate could've been hidin' in the attic.' Then he grinned. 'It's clever, I'll give you that. It explains how the bugger took the photograph then got clean away — but does it matter?'

'We deserve a kick up the backside for slack procedure,' Vine said, 'but in the end, no, it doesn't. I've no doubt there's an accomplice out there, and I know we'll get him — '

I pointed at the computer. 'Len Tully.'

'Or his brother. Or neither of them.'

'If not them, why's the photograph here?'

'Maybe it's not just here. At this moment there could be a thousand copies on the internet. Ten thousand. But Mike's right. It doesn't matter who took it, when it was taken, or how many photographs are out there because in the end, with or without help, it was Joe Creeney who killed Lorraine.'

'Yes,' I said. 'I'm sure he did.'

Haggard puffed at his cigarette, and grinned happily.

'So we're right and you're wrong. You're admitting Creeney was guilty?'

'No, I'm not,' I said. 'Joe's wife died by his hand — he *did* kill her — but in the end he was guilty of neither manslaughter nor murder.'

★ ★ ★

Registering disbelief, they asked for an explanation. I told them I'd have to gather my thoughts. Haggard seemed to think that could take some time. I assured him he was right.

Then his eagle eye spotted the empty whisky glass I'd placed alongside the computer. He grabbed it, poked his nose inside and with a roll of the eyes sent Willie Vine for two more and the bottle. Willie returned, splashed liquid into glasses, then sat in front of the computer and idly traced mousy patterns on a small yellow mat. Haggard and I dropped into easy chairs. We all savoured our drinks, swilling the fine spirit around our teeth like expensive Listerine.

The burly DI raised the subject of Frank Tully's murder (as I knew he must), gave me a bollocking for fleeing the scene of the crime, didn't press for details of hows and whys but enquired about the current whereabouts of Calum Wick and Sian Laidlaw and turned sullen when I refused to tell him. And in the empty silence following my unsatisfactory answer I found myself wondering what the hell we were doing sitting with our feet up drinking whisky in Len Tully's home.

I put it to them.

Willie Vine said, 'If we wait long enough, Len might walk in with his wrists held out and say something original like 'It's a fair cop'.'

'If we wait even longer,' Haggard said, 'Ill Wind might say something that makes sense.'

'I really would explain,' I said, 'if it wasn't so complicated.'

'No,' Haggard said, 'you'd explain if it was simple. Complicated's beyond you.'

'Complications are the grist to my mill, and the cause of your frequent complaints. But putting complicated issues in terms simple enough to be understood can be . . . er . . . complicated.'

'Get on with it,' Haggard growled.

'It goes like this. You two have either lost your marbles, or you're too tired to think straight. It's barmy to suggest our mysterious photographer was Joe's accomplice. In the picture you're painting he erected the makeshift gallows, put the victim in place and took a photograph, waited for Joe, they murdered Lorraine — and his accomplice ran upstairs and hid in the attic. Leaving Joe to the police. Why would he do that?'

'It went pear shaped,' Haggard said. 'They weren't expectin' a police car to be parked outside the house. Joe walked in, the shit hit the fan and he was too slow reactin'. Who knows? Maybe the other feller was already halfway up the stairs, checkin' the rope, plantin' a farewell kiss on the woman's cheek — '

'Your men had been outside for two hours. The plan would have been aborted.'

'We know someone other than Joe was there, because of the photograph,' Vine said. 'If he wasn't an accessory to murder — which I think you've ruled out — and if Joe killed Lorraine — which you've admitted — what the hell was he?'

'The man who took that photograph was an evil bastard, and he had a truly cunning plan to frame Joe Creeney. He put that woman up the ladder at 10.45, and he took a photograph.' I nodded towards the computer. 'It's in there, on record, camera, time, the lot — beyond dispute.' I looked at Haggard. 'And when he'd done that, he walked out.'

'Two hours before Creeney got there.' Haggard snorted. 'Leavin' instructions on a postcard for the poor sod: walk in, kick the ladder into touch, listen for her neck to snap, bugger off sharpish. Only the police were there — '

'He arranged for the police to be there. He told Lorraine to call them. It was part of the plan.'

'So give us the rest.'

'I can't. I've got ideas, but I'm still working on how this person arranged the death of

Lorraine Creeney.'

'Share those ideas, or you're withholdin' information — '

'*Short* of information. I told you I think I know how it was done, but I'm not sure. I need to talk to people. Ask questions.'

'Yeah, and so do I. You've overstepped the mark, Jack, tellin' us we're not thinkin' straight and losing our marbles, and what *I'm* sayin' is if the cap fits, wear it' — all this outpouring done with a glare at his poker-faced literary DS — 'because far from me being barmy the scenario *you've* painted has convinced me the man who took this picture *was* Creeney's accomplice.' He sneered. 'Think about it. According to you, this feller set the scene so he could frame Creeney, then walked out. Now think back to Monday, an' the talk we had in Welsh Wales. You told me when Joe Creeney got out of your car and walked towards the house, he said he was expected, and you wondered who by. I said it was his wife, but I was wrong. He was expected by his fuckin' accomplice — only Joe was late, there'd been a hitch, you name it, I'll buy it, and so his oppo walked out still confident Lorraine would die by Joe's hand and the two of 'em would meet up later when the deed was done. You say frame up, I say planned murder by an escaped con and his crafty accomplice.'

His phone rang. He stumbled to his feet, dug it out, walked away listening. Then he grunted into it, and snapped it shut.

'Damn, damn, *double* fuckin' damn.' He glared at Vine, at me. 'Let's go — both of you, now.'

Vine was already moving. 'Where?'

'Heswall.'

'Another killing,' I said, out of my chair and following the two detectives out of the room.

'Yeah,' Haggard called, as the front door crashed open, broken glass tinkled, and he ran for Vine's Mondeo. 'Our photographer's snapped his last shot. If uniforms have got it right, Len Tully's topped himself.'

18

Heswall lies between West Kirby and Parkgate on the Wirral peninsula overlooking the estuary of the River Dee. Getting there from the top of Park Road in Liverpool could take anything from half an hour to double that time, but we made it in what must have been a record twenty-five minutes with me hunched over the Quattro's steering wheel clinging desperately to the tail of Vine's scruffy green Mondeo as he pushed it close to a smoke-belching ton along clear stretches.

The red Ford Escort had been found about thirty yards off a track leading from Oldfield Road down into the grassland and scrub of the Heswall Dales. It had been driven through the bushes into a· small clearing. If you listen to the news you'll know that such discoveries are always made by a man walking his dog, a lone jogger, or a hot young couple looking for soft grass and dense shrubs. This time it had been a 70-year-old bloke on a mountain bike trying out new night-vision goggles he'd bought on eBay. Either they didn't work too well, or his brain couldn't make sense of the weird green shapes he was seeing. He veered wildly off the track, crashed through the bushes and went flying over the handlebars.

When he shook the muzziness from his head, slid off the car's warm bonnet and shakily regained his feet he realized that the engine was running. All the car's windows were closed, except for one with a narrow gap at the top, and the door locks were down. He could see a man slumped in the driver's seat. Then, with a quiver of horror, he noticed the black rubber pipe connected to the exhaust and snaking into the car through that one narrow opening.

Still dazed, he didn't think of breaking into the vehicle, switching off the engine and opening the windows. Instead, he headed for home. It took him a while to get there in the dark pushing a bike with a buckled front wheel, the useless night vision goggles dangling from a neck cord and bouncing on his bony chest. By the time he reached the phone the man in the car who might once have stood the ghost of a chance had used up all his nine lives.

All this information must have been given to Haggard over the phone as he sat rigid in the passenger seat alongside a bright-eyed Willie Vine gleefully doing a Michael

Schumacher. When we hit the outskirts of Heswall and turned off Oldfield Road to bump down into The Dales the crime scene was already taped off, and floodlights blazed on the shiny red car, on tyre tracks and flattened bushes where broken branches gleamed like exposed bone, on uniformed policemen and SOCOs in strange white suits and funny bonnets.

Vine wandered away to talk to uniforms. Perhaps because I had been employed by a solicitor to look into Joe Creeney's death and was now in up to my neck, Mike Haggard brusquely told me what he knew then strode over to the car with me tagging along behind. The breeze had slackened, but was still cold. We ducked under tapes, tramped across wet grass with the damp salt scent of the river in our nostrils and mist curling like smoke under the bright lights.

Haggard moved to one side to talk to a tall, pale-faced man in plain clothes. They both glanced in my direction. I knew Haggard was explaining who I was, and my reasons for being there. Then someone called out, attracting the tall man's attention, and I had his name: DI Tracy.

I moved closer to the red Escort. The driver's door was open. Len Tully was still slumped in the seat.

Grass whispered underfoot as the two detectives joined me.

'Suicide, Dick?'

'Nothing I can see suggests otherwise.'

I struggled to suppress a smile. Dick Tracy. A cartoon character brought to life, and by his manner of speech more Vine's type than Haggard's.

'He's got identification on him, so no problem there. Len Tully.' The tall man paused for effect. 'You might like what we found in the boot.'

Haggard looked at me. 'Bright ideas?'

'A coil of rope,' I said. 'Orange nylon.'

The tall detective called Tracy looked at me with sharp blue eyes. 'Jack Scott,' he said, as if he'd suddenly discovered a bad taste in his mouth. 'I've heard about you. Superman without a badge. An amateur with pretensions. All right, Scott, so what did we find in the glove compartment?'

'Either a digital camera, or mobile phone with camera — I'd go for the phone.'

Tracy nodded. 'The phone was there, but the pics were on a Samsung digital compact. One of our younger constables played with the buttons. I've been looking with disgust at what he found.'

'We've been lookin' with dismay at where he put it,' Haggard said. 'The weird bastard

211

stuck that picture on his computer as a desktop.'

'That it, nothing else there, pornography, snuff movies?'

'Vine phoned it in from the car, a team's on its way to the house.' He shook his head. 'They won't find anything.'

'So what's going on?' Tracy said. 'The woman in the photograph is Lorraine Creeney. Last I heard, her murder was a closed case.'

Haggard nodded at Len Tully's body, then grinned savagely. 'An' it's still closed, isn't it?'

'Is it? Sunday morning an escaped prisoner was found next to his wife's still-warm body hanging by the neck in the hallway of his house. He died resisting arrest.' That last bit drew a dismissive grunt from Haggard.

Tracy said, 'That was Joe Creeney — right? Now you've got a second, Len Tully. He's got a coil of rope in his boot similar to that used in the Creeney hanging, and a photograph of the scene on his camera — and *he's* dead. So where did he fit in?'

'Accomplice,' Haggard said. 'Creeney wanted his wife dead because she'd been sleepin' away from home and he'd never got over it. He had the hanging all set up for him by this dipstick' — he jerked a thumb at the car — 'who was so proud of his handiwork he

212

took a photo before buggerin' off.'

'If the case was officially closed, Len Tully was in the clear. So why suicide?'

Haggard shrugged, patted his pockets, then remembered it was a crime scene and abandoned thoughts of a cigarette.

'It's a long story. Creeney was doing time for the manslaughter of the Tullys' younger brother, Wayne, who was the one havin' it off with his wife. When Creeney was sent down, the brothers swore they'd get him — '

'Doesn't that make nonsense of the idea Tully helped Creeney murder his wife.'

'Not necessarily,' I chipped in. 'What if the Tullys found out some time ago that Creeney had nothing to do with their brother's death?'

'Bollocks,' Haggard said. 'Joe Creeney admitted it, he pleaded guilty.'

'Yes, and because of that there was no reason for the police to hunt for an alibi. But six months ago the Tullys found out that Creeney *did* have an alibi. Wayne Tully lived in Fazakerley. On the night of the assault, Joe Creeney was miles away drinking in his brother's night-club in Brighton-le-Sands from six o'clock until he was picked up by the police — they were following up an anonymous tip off. That was some time after eleven. And Wayne Tully was definitely alive at nine: he was with his brother Frank in a local chippy.'

A photographer had arrived, and we were getting in the way. We walked away from the car, DI Tracy lifted the tape and we ducked under it and wandered out of the floodlights and into the deep shadows under a grove of silver birch. When we were clear of the crime scene, Haggard lit his cigarette, the match flame lighting the grim planes of his face. He picked up where we'd left off as Willie Vine wandered over to listen.

'Yeah, well, I can't comment because that crime's in the past, and the man who was sent down for it is dead. But this one, this suicide and what went before it . . . ' Haggard waved a vague hand. 'If Creeney didn't kill their brother, yeah, the Tullys dabbled in crime so they could've got in with him, helped him murder his wife.' He looked at me. 'But what about Frank Tully?'

'What *about* him?' Tracy said. He was leaning against a tree. The light from the nearby floods shone eerily on his pale skin.

'Frank was found hanged with the same orange nylon rope,' Haggard said. 'Which, lookin' at what we've found here, points the finger at his brother.'

Tracy nodded thoughtfully. 'And could explain his suicide. Guilt, remorse . . . '

'I got a phone call from Frank not long before he died,' I said. 'He told me he had the name of the killer. He was trying to keep his voice down because — I found this out later — his brother Len had been desperate to hear what he was saying.'

'Ah,' Tracy said softly. 'I'm not sure I like the way you're feeding this to us, but what you're suggesting is that the name Frank had was Len Tully: he'd found out his *brother* was the killer.'

Vine took that in, thought for a moment, then said, 'If Len Tully was the one knocking off Joe Creeney's wife that really *would* explain everything. Twelve months ago he killed his younger brother who was about to broadcast his guilty secret. He helped Joe murder Lorraine because he thought she was the only other person who could split on him. Then he realized Frank knew, and he killed him.'

Now Haggard was spotting the flaws. 'What the fuck's all that about? The motive's crap. Why murder two blokes and a woman over a bit of sly nooky? If his big secret came out, so what? Different if it was his brother's wife, but it wasn't, it was someone else's wife, so where's the big deal?'

'If he didn't do the murders,' I said, 'then we've got to consider another possibility,' I said. 'The rope and the camera were planted in that red car, and this wasn't suicide.'

DI Tracy shook his head. 'No. Len Tully killed himself.'

'So where does that leave the police?'

'With three closed cases,' Haggard said. 'Wayne Tully's death was manslaughter by Joe Creeney — '

'He wasn't there — '

' — then early Sunday morning Creeney killed his wife with the help of Len Tully, and today Tully killed his brother then topped himself. All right, so I said the motives are a joke, but that's one set of motives and there could be a hundred different reasons why Tully smacked his kid brother with a lead pipe then started playin' hang the man. A hundred — but who the fuck's lookin' for even one motive when all the suspects are dead?'

'And if this is not suicide, but murder?'

'It's suicide,' Dick Tracy said flatly, then he lifted a hand to Haggard and moved away to where a man with a black leather bag had climbed out of a Mercedes and was walking towards the red Escort.

Haggard glowered at me, and began walking towards Vine's Mondeo. The dirty look said it all. He'd growled a good argument, but he wasn't happy and he hadn't convinced himself, or me.

Vine was lingering, his eyes amused.

'Not good enough, is it?' He pursed his lips. 'I wonder why. Maybe Mike was right, you're holding something back.'

I was, of course. I thought of my phone call to Len that had gone unmentioned, the woman who had answered Len's mobile, the door slamming in the background and the crackle of brush. And, as if it was replaying in my head, I heard it again, unchanged, three little words crackling in my ear — only this time I knew I recognized that woman's voice.

'If I am, and depending on what comes of it,' I said softly, my eyes on the dead body in the red car as Vine turned to follow his boss, 'either Dick Tracy or a PI with pretensions is going to have to eat his words.'

19

It was after three in the morning when I got back to Grassendale. I climbed the stairs with the smell of the Mersey in my nostrils and let myself into an unlighted flat to be greeted by a black cat that curled around my ankles, and automatically found myself thinking of an old pugilist with incipient dementia out looking with bemusement for his straying black dog on a dark night when a murderer was on the prowl.

Had Rose Lane seen something important when that same dog got out earlier that night? Was it time to talk to her husband, Rocky? I really didn't know, because the truth was I didn't know if we still had a case. Two senior police officers had, with what I considered to be twisted logic and inferior deductive skills, decided that an ancient verdict must stand and two recent murders would go uninvestigated because the perp was dead. Against that decision a voice I thought I'd recognized on a mobile phone had seemed like a red-hot lead down in the scrub of the Heswall Dales, but it had dwindled to become a vague possibility during the drive back from the Wirral and was now looking ridiculous. All manner of alternatives had presented themselves as I yawned my way home, including the likelihood that sitting in front of Len's computer I'd dialled the wrong number and spoken to a woman who had no idea what I was talking about.

So I switched on some lights and wandered into the kitchen and dished up cat food and man food and we both returned to the living-room where the cat promptly fell asleep and I slumped in leather luxury and munched and drank without enthusiasm.

My cohorts were still lying low. Calum could be anywhere with Jones the Van, Sian was staying with Eleanor and I realized I should phone and had punched in Soldier Blue's mobile number and was listening to it ring when my bleary eyes looked at the clock and I was reminded of the time.

'Damn.'

I switched off. Looked towards the kitchen where a bottle of the Macallan stood in a high cupboard that suddenly, at that low point in the day, seemed way out of reach. And not that appealing. The coffee I was drinking was not doing its job. My eyelids were drooping. I looked at the cat just as it stretched and yawned languidly, thought of kicking it off the settee — and fell asleep.

I spoke to Sian on the phone at breakfast the next morning — well, later that same morning. She told me she and her ex-army colleagues were still thrashing out logistics for the forthcoming adventure training courses in Scotland, and she would be involved with them for most of that day. I brought her up to date with murders and suicides, told her the police now considered all cases closed and that I couldn't see any way to argue. Ha! Who was I kidding? I considered it my bounden duty always to disagree with Haggard and Vine, and Sian must have caught that defiance in my voice. Her chuckle was a delightful gurgle that made my neck tingle.

'You're up to something. There was a gleam in your eye when we left The Gallant Trooper, and you weren't listening to a word I said.'

'I thought I was getting close to cracking the locked room mystery. Several brilliant ideas are still simmering away on the back burner.'

'But you're not willing to share them with me so I can tear them to shreds?'

'Not yet, no, but if I'm right, then Len Tully's death was murder not suicide, there's a very clever killer out there and he's laughing up his sleeve. What I do know is that even if we can't include Len just yet, we've still had three murders. Last night Haggard rubbished the motives Vine came up with — he was right to do so — and he was unable or unwilling to offer alternatives. But I know him too well. He was saying one thing, but eyes and body language were sending a different message. I think he's torn between relief and apprehension: he's pleased those murders seem to have been solved, but I don't go along with it and he knows my record — I'm always right.'

I chuckled as she staged a loud, exaggerated yawn, then told her about the strange response when I'd called Len Tully's mobile, and my suspicion that I'd misdialled. She reminded me the number would be there on my phone, all I had to do was look, and I groaned.

'I'm a bumbling fool. How will I solve this complicated case without you?'

'You may not have to.'

'Mm. I thought you were spending today with rugged men of few words who move silently through thick jungles. Or should that be thick men and rugged jungles?'

She giggled. 'I'll mention your name when I put it to them — but, no, I'm not with them *all* day. I'll give them the slip, then set off to solve the mystery of why Joe Creeney broke out of gaol and who he believed was expecting him when you took him home.'

'Just like that?'

'A small chore, 'twill take but a minute of my time . . .'

'Tell me about it tonight and we'll crack a bottle of champagne and the case — if you see what I mean.'

'I do and I'd love to. At Calum's?'

'No, let's have it there. I haven't seen Eleanor since she came back from Gib, so, no cooking tonight, I'll arrange for a Chinese to be delivered and we'll eat and talk while the bubbles tickle your nose.'

'I'll try my best not to laugh,' she said. 'Let's make it about eight o'clock.'

★ ★ ★

I was on my way to town before ten o'clock, walking up the hill from Paradise Street car park fifteen minutes later with my sights set on the offices of Knott, Knott and Arbuthnot. I had last spoken to Stephanie Grey on Monday after Max Spackman had given me the news of Joe's death, and it was about time we both compared notes. I wanted to get her views on two deaths and a suicide, and I was looking forward to watching her reaction and listening to what she had to say when I told her Joe Creeney had walked away from a rock-solid alibi. There was also George Kingman's interesting revelation that she popped into the King of Clubs from time to time, and had been there when Frank Tully was talking furtively to me on his mobile. Not listening — but that was just George's recollection. And what did any of that tell me? Not a lot. I had met the woman just the once, trusted her without thinking about it because a job is a job and she was the go between. But in doing that job I had inevitably looked under stones, and what I'd found there was making it look as if I knew too little about a solicitor with slender fingers in several mucky pies.

Seagulls were wheeling and calling overhead and the breeze was rustling magazines and newspapers on the wooden stand when I turned the corner into Castle Street. I was walking past with my mind on what lay ahead when the *Daily Post* headlines caught my eye and the sea birds and the salt wind sweeping off the Mersey combined to whisk me into the past. Thursday morning. I was in Toad Hall listening to a Welsh detective tell me about a woman who was under arrest for the murder of Rose Lane.

MURDER SUSPECT RELEASED WITHOUT

CHARGE BY NORTH WALES POLICE.

Watched with apprehension by an elderly woman carrying a plastic bag, I wet my forefinger and made a mark in thin air. All right, so I didn't know if the suspect in the headlines was the woman taken into custody by a certain Welsh DI, but what were the odds? I was betting it was Alun Morgan's dark-haired woman in the pink blouse who was now drinking a cup of hot sweet tea at home, and if so then a link between the murders of Lorraine Creeney and Rose Lane had not yet been severed and I had begun my day with at least a half chance, a glimmer of light.

It's strange how perceptions change. On my first visit to the Castle Street premises I had the sensation of basking in old world charm where wise legal eagles pored over dusty briefs and dreamed of justice. Today I climbed the stairs through an ambience of neglect, decay and sleaze, and I wondered if what I thought I perceived now was influenced by what I had just read and what I was certain I was about to hear. Was it precognition or fancy? Had a succession of grisly murders turned a PI with his tail up into a cynic expecting the worst?

A pointless question, anyway. I *wanted* the worst, because if Stephanie came out of this squeaky clean it would mean that once again I'd got it wrong.

My feet tapped the stairs like hollow dreams. Her door was ajar and I knocked on its heavy panels and walked into her office and she greeted me with a disquieting smile that caused her black-ringed eyes to glitter. My reaction came as a shock to me. Coloured by events, it seemed that I was looking at life through dark glasses, seeing not goodness but evil — and suddenly I knew why. She rose to greet me. Her shoulder-length hair was dark, her skirt long and her blouse, hanging loose over the skirt's waistband, was a dark and dusky pink.

I looked at it, and my mouth went dry.

'What?'

'Nothing. Muzzy head. I was up late, saw something nasty on the Wirral.'

'So I believe.'

'If you know that already,' I said, 'you must talk to Haggard more often than his wife.'

'I never talk to his wife.'

She was joking and smiling, at the top of her form, and I wondered why. I took the chair she'd indicated, watched her walk around her desk and sit in the swivel chair that had been old before she was born, and wondered where I was going with what were now wild flights of fancy. How many pink blouses did Debenhams sell? Take the bottles of peroxide out of bathroom cabinets and how many women had blonde hair? But that was to ignore the voice, and in the few words she had spoken I knew I had been right first time. The last time I'd spoken to Stephanie Grey was not Monday, but Friday. Last night. She'd answered my call on a mobile phone belonging to Len Tully that had later been found in the boot of a Ford Escort abandoned, with Tully's body inside, on Heswall Dales.

Suicide? Not on your life. Doubt had gone out of the window. I'd come to listen to a voice I might have heard on the phone, and a glimpse of newspaper headlines had led me to much more than I'd expected — so much more that my head was in a whirl. But now what? Think fast, get out fast? Yes — but first throw down some ground bait and see if she nibbles.

'So, Jack, it's all over.'

'Mm. The end of a sad story that stretches back twelve months.'

'A real mess. Four men and a woman dead because two of them . . . played around, were indiscreet. Wayne and Lorraine. Then Joe lost his head. That brought in Frank and Len Tully. And so we had manslaughter, brutal murders, a bizarre accident . . .'

She spread her hands in a gesture of helplessness.

'And suicide?'

'Yes, it seems so.'

I wondered if she had got that from Haggard, and reminded myself to ask him.

'Unless something comes up at the post mortem.'

'It won't.' Her smile was sweet.

'That's it then. It was an investigation that got overtaken by events and ran out of control. Solved itself, in a very nasty way.' I climbed to my feet. 'Will you tell Caroline it's over?'

'Of course.'

She came around the desk, a woman in a pink blouse whom I now believed had stood with her long skirt whipping in the cold wind blowing off the River Dee and spoken to me tersely on the phone while in the background a man was committing cold-blooded murder.

My skin prickled as I shook her hand. My polite smile was a mask. A thought struck me, a barb that might wound took the form of words and I paused on my way out.

'Did you enjoy your trip to Conwy?'

She smiled and frowned at the same time. 'Sorry?'

'Calum thought he saw you there . . . I think it was early Sunday morning.'

'Calum?'

'Calum Wick. My colleague. He knows you from George Kingman's place. The King of Clubs.'

'I don't think so.'

'No?' I shrugged. 'He knows you by sight, so he's seen you somewhere — and he's almost certain he saw you in Conwy.' Another thought presented itself, and I snapped my fingers. 'That's right, he said you were driving a white Fiat Punto.'

'He has a vivid imagination, Jack.' The smile had become chill. 'My car's white, but it's a Mercedes, and I don't think I've ever visited North Wales.'

20

I tramped down the stairs and into Castle Street, blinking in bright autumn sunlight, and stood on the pavement with my mind working overtime.

Probing with wounding barbs was one thing, proving that my theories were more than wild flights of fancy was something else. One pink blouse does not a murder make, but add to it the certainty that Stephanie Grey had at the very least been in at Len Tully's death and a resolute PI begins flexing his muscles. In a manner of speaking.

One person who might be able to tell me if I had the right pink blouse was the eyewitness who, from afar, had watched a woman slitting Rose Lane's throat. Getting to her was easy — I'd talk to DI Alun Morgan — but I couldn't see myself dragging Stephanie along to be identified. The next best thing was a photograph — and I was standing in the right place.

During the Danny Maguire case I had found Frank Danson's missing sons. They'd disappeared twenty years ago when he and his wife were at the theatre. That case had finished just two weeks ago; Frank and I had phoned each other a couple of times since then, and Frank's photographic business, Danson Graphics, was behind expensive smoked glass windows just a few yards away.

I found him in the outer office where pink and yellow silk flowers stood in tall floor vases, carpet tiles muffled footsteps, and three desks created an island of carpeted space. He greeted me with delight, and showed intense interest when I told him what I wanted: photographs of Stephanie Grey, back and front, from several angles.

He knew her by sight — she passed his studio every day on her way to lunch — and he readily agreed to take the photographs himself. As he pointed out, a professional photographer takes photographs, and if Miss Grey happened to be in Castle Street when he was going about his business then the odds were she'd appear in several of the shots. Short odds he told me with a grin: she'd be in every shot.

The trouble was it was early November, and when Stephanie walked downstairs and into the street she would certainly have a jacket or coat covering the thin pink blouse. We mulled over that problem for a few minutes, then Frank had a brainwave. He told me he knew the snack bar where she had lunch, and had recently taken advertising shots for the owner's menus and brochure. Some of them hadn't turned out too well — he winked — and would have to be retaken. Now seemed like a good time, and as the coffee bar was as hot as Hades which forced everyone to remove their coats . . .

I agreed to wander away, and call back in a couple of hours to pick up the ten by eight colour prints he assured me he would have ready.

★   ★   ★

I wanted peace and quiet to make phone calls and I wouldn't find that sitting with Manny Yates in the American Bar. So what I did was walk up there, get him to dig his keys out of his flamboyant red waistcoat, then walk back along Lime Street and climb the stairs to the small room with its desks and banker's green-shaded lights and filing cabinets and cork boards with coloured pins where — at the ripe old age of thirty-five — I had served my private eye apprenticeship.

Manny kept his bottles of hooch in the top drawer of a heavy wooden filing cabinet of the kind that might have been nicked from Admiral Street police station in the years before the wars. Was the police station there then? I didn't know, but what I did know was that my first phone call was to DI Mike Haggard's office in that station, and for that — or the other calls — I didn't need alcohol.

I found a big white mug, filled it with tonic water from the bottle that stood alongside the gin in the filing cabinet, then sat behind Manny's desk and picked up the phone.

'Mike?'

'Christ,' he said, 'and here was me havin' one of those nice days the Yanks are always on about.'

'This will make it even nicer. I've been talking to Stephanie Grey. She's ready to tell Caroline Spackman I'm off the case.'

'She knows that anyway. Vine went to Mill Street this morning with a young female constable. He told Mrs Spackman new evidence suggests her brother killed his wife with the aid of an accomplice. And that accomplice is dead.'

'Fair enough. Of course you know I don't agree.'

'Yeah, like you don't agree Len Tully committed suicide.'

'I don't, but that reminds me,' I said. 'You're pretty thick with our Stephanie, right?'

'She's a solicitor, so we've crossed swords in court. And useful information passes back and forth. Does that make either of us thick?'

I chuckled. 'You told her Len Tully was

dead. Did you mention suicide?'

'No, because it's not official.'

'As a possibility?'

'I told her what I'd tell anyone: cause of death'll be determined by a post mortem.' The line was silent for a moment. Then he couldn't hold back. 'Why?'

'She knows, so either someone told her, she's guessing . . . or . . . '

'Jesus Christ!' Haggard said softly, 'what fuckin' wild-goose chase are you on now?'

'I'll let you know when I get back from Deganwy.'

The next call was to DI Alun Morgan. I reached him on his mobile, he prevaricated with technique refined by constant use then gave me Grace Williams's telephone number and five minutes later I was through to the eyewitness and had made an appointment to see her at three o'clock that afternoon.

The drive both ways with a chat in the middle would leave me plenty of time to order a Chinese meal for three to be delivered at eight o'clock to Eleanor's flat in Grassendale.

★ ★ ★

The marina and executive residences under construction on the Deganwy side of Conwy harbour were of interest to me because I'd recently seen the same sort of development when Sian and I were in Gibraltar. We had dined with a suspect at a night spot called Bianca's, sipping Jameson's and gin and tonics alongside placid waters where luxury yachts and cruisers rocked gently at expensive moorings. Oh, I know, every local council with a handy stretch of water's doing marinas nowadays, but when I was stationed in Gibraltar the waters of the bay practically lapped at the traffic zipping along Queensway. Now offices and flats stand on acres of reclaimed land, and two marinas — at the last count — poke their white concrete tentacles into the clear blue waters.

From those Gibraltar flats you gaze across to the Spanish port of Algeciras, from Deganwy you look across a much smaller stretch of water to Conwy Harbour, and it was when doing just that early on Monday morning that Grace Williams had witnessed murder.

I had expected to find her in one of those grand modern blocks, but instead the address I had led me up a road close to a pub called Maggie Murphy's. Grace's neat old black and white house was at the end of an unadopted gravelly lane. It stood on a grassy rise overlooking the main road, and had wonderful unrestricted views from the front garden.

I parked alongside a bird stand under a tall sycamore, climbed out of the car carrying the manila envelope I'd got from Frank Danson, and my first surprise came when a tall old gentleman of military bearing stood with a slight list as he opened the front door then, with weaving gait, led me through a house smelling of lavender and cigars. My second came when I walked into what turned out to be a bright front room and was introduced to the plump, grey-haired woman in a shiny wheelchair.

'Two dicky hips,' she said, her accent faintly Welsh, and she smiled at the look on my face. 'What did you expect, then, a toothless old crone with dirty net curtains, a brassbound telescope and a black notebook for composing poison-pen letters?'

'Alun Morgan told me absolutely nothing, so I came with an open mind.'

'Yes, well, you can tell that to the marines. What I do from my front window evokes images in people's minds — the wrong image, as it happens, in much the same way that it's wrong for those poor photographers who take pictures at school concerts and swimming galas to be branded with that awful name. I'm disabled; I do have a brass-bound telescope, but I use it for watching sea birds, fishing boats, yachts sailing in and out of the harbour — oh, I watch just about everything but I'm *not* a . . . a . . . '

'Peeping Tom?'

'Another horrible name. No, of course I'm not.'

'Unadulterated balderdash, and well you bloody know it.'

Behind me, the tall old relic had spoken in fond tones that would have been clipped if they hadn't been slurred.

'Yes, well, Roger does like his gin, and I do love my telescope and all it brings me,' Grace Williams said — and then, out of the blue, she gave me a broad wink.

So what did I make of that? Well, probably the only reason I couldn't think of her as a Peeping Tom was because of her name — I suppose you could call it her saving grace. But she certainly peeped, she had the powerful ocular equipment set up on a sturdy tripod in the bay window, and my guess was she spent more time looking into people's bedrooms than she did watching and yawning as gulls nested.

By the time I turned around, Roger had wandered off and I could hear him bumping into the furniture as he searched for the Bombay Sapphire. Grace waved me to a comfortable settee, wheeled herself silently across the thick beige carpet so that she was close to me, and watched eagerly as I opened the big envelope.

I tipped Frank Danson's ten by eight prints into my hand, held them face down.

'You saw her from a distance. These are close-ups. D'you think you can sort of close one eye and squint?'

'Give 'em here, you daft sod.'

She studied the glossy colour prints intently, placing each one in her ample lap as she turned to the next, her lips pursing and unpursing — if that's right — and a slight flush turning her powdered cheeks pink.

She looked up at me, a twinkle in her eyes.

'She's got a knife,' she said, 'but all she's doing here is slicing a Danish.'

'Mm. Did you actually see her — ?'

'Administer the *coup de grâce*?' She chuckled. 'Damn right I did.'

'This woman?'

She hesitated. Her bottom lip jutted. She glanced sideways at the big telescope; absently moved her strong hands so that the wheelchair rocked backwards and forwards.

'Probably.'

She looked through the half-dozen prints, held up one that showed Stephanie Grey on her way out of the coffee bar. Back view.

Almost full length. Long dark skirt brushing her ankles.

'The flat across the water, the one where that woman was murdered, has patio doors leading out onto a tiny veranda. Fancy iron railings. Nothing to get in the way of someone having a sly look from afar.' Her eyes were pensive. 'If you were to ask me — '

'I am.'

'Then I'm almost certain the woman in this photograph is the woman I saw commit a bloody murder.'

'How almost certain?'

'They say you can change your identity, but not your ears — I didn't see her ears then and I can't see them now, so that's not much use. But the lights in that flat across the water were bright — she wasn't worried about being seen — and it's the stance, isn't it? She didn't know she was being watched, then or today — this was taken today?'

'Lunchtime.'

'Well there you are. She was relaxed, just as she must have been on the night of the murder, acting naturally, no reason to change — '

'Sticking a knife in another human-being's neck is an *unnatural* act. She'd be tense, wound up, muscles as tight as piano wire.'

'*Unusual*, yes, and totally unacceptable,

but not an *unnatural* act in the way that I understand the term.' Again her eyes were twinkling. She took another long look at the print, said softly, 'If it *was* her it sends a shiver down the spine, looking at her.'

'And was it?'

'Oh . . . I don't know . . . ' She looked at me. 'I can't be a *hundred* per cent certain . . . '

'Eighty?'

'Better than that. Ninety.' She grinned at me, and lifted her eyebrows and a plump hand.

'Done,' I said, and leaned forward to give the delightful little curtain twitcher the awaited high five.

21

'Ladies of advanced years,' Eleanor said, 'are often a little scatterbrained.' She touched her white hair and winked at Sian. 'They're also kittenish; they like to lead gullible men up the garden path.'

'I'll point that out to Reg,' I said, 'warn him what to expect.'

'Oh, he knows, and he couldn't wait for it to happen. Why d'you think he invited me to Gibraltar?'

'If you're going to go into that,' Sian said, 'this is where I cover my ears.'

The Chinese meal had been oriental excellence in dainty edible slivers and deep-fried pouches soaked in hot grease and savoury sauces that led to frequent rinses in fingerbowls and, that finished, we were scattered around the comfortable room on settee and easy chairs, as relaxed as well fed cats. The table had been cleared (I think Sian did that), the dishes were in the dishwasher, and the table lamp with its rich red shade cast a warm glow over a room where expensive red wine glistened in crystal glasses that were held with what could only be gay abandon.

The champagne had mysteriously disappeared from my shopping list; it seems that gentlemen of advanced years are also scatterbrained, particularly those with murder in mind. And haunted by dilemma. Should I inform Haggard of my suspicions, or hold back? I seemed to have Stephanie Grey nailed on two counts, but could a solicitor be so naïve that she'd risked answering Len Tully's phone, and continued to wear the pink blouse in which she'd committed one murder while assisting in a second?

'A penny for them, Jack,' Eleanor said.

I sighed. 'Has Sian told you all about the Joe Creeney case?'

'As much as she knows, which seems to be most of it. Then you brought exciting news about a bent solicitor when you walked in, and now . . . well, what comes next? Where do you go from here? I know Miss Grey's your new suspect and you think two of the murders are linked, but there are others, and trying to pull them all together must be like trying to catch sardines in a net intended for cod.'

I smiled absently, sipped my wine and thought for a moment.

'If you know the story,' I said, 'you know some of the unanswered questions. One of them is why did Joe Creeney break out of jail and go straight to where the police were sure to find him? Another is who was already there in the house, and expecting him? Mike Haggard believes that he went there to murder his wife, and he was meeting his accomplice. But if he's wrong, and I believe he is, then the question remains unanswered.'

'Not any more,' Sian said. 'Damon Knight was very talkative. I think he was jealous of Joe.'

'I'm sure he was. Joe was getting out.'

'More than that. The plans someone had put in place for Joe included a new identity, and a new life overseas. With Lorraine.'

I shook my head in amazement, at her skill and the news.

'So all we have to do now,' I said softly, 'is find that someone.'

'If we can believe Damon.'

'Joe Creeney didn't murder his wife, so he had to have another reason for going home. The one given to you by Knight is the only one that makes sense. Once he went over the wall, Joe was on the run. Men on the run need to disappear, and the best way of doing that is to leave the country.' I tilted my head. 'Did Damon have ideas on this mysterious someone, the person who was doing the planning?'

'He simply repeated what he told Stan

Jones: the only visitors Joe had in a year were Lorraine, Declan, Caroline and — '

'Stephanie Grey.'

'Right.'

'So now we're getting somewhere. Joe got out of jail with help. When he was driven home he expected to find Lorraine with their bags packed, his mysterious benefactor holding two one-way tickets to the Cayman Islands. Instead he walked into a trap, and one of the people pulling the strings was our bent solicitor, Stephanie Grey — '

'Why?'

I blinked and looked at my mother.

'You mean what was her motive?' I shrugged. 'She's well paid, so profit's out. Hiding the truth about something that might incriminate her or someone important to her, is one possibility. Another is that she's besotted, willing to do anything for our mystery someone.'

Sian was also looking at Eleanor. 'Does it matter? If we have enough to arrest Stephanie, the police can take it from there.'

'Ah, but hold on a minute,' I said. 'Who said anything about arrest?'

'That's what they do,' Eleanor said, 'with murderers.'

'Yes, and no doubt that will happen.'

'You left out a word,' Sian said sweetly.

'He did, didn't he?' Eleanor said. 'What he meant to say was, it will happen *eventually* — but before that he's got a locked room mystery to solve. Which means there's a lot more work to do, because if Joe Creeney walked into a trap it was one devised by a fiendishly cunning mind. Stephanie's a solicitor, which suggests she's clever, possibly devious. You believe she was there when Len Tully was being . . . disposed of. And you heard a man in the background. You know a high percentage of murders are family affairs, so why aren't you looking at Declan?'

I nodded. 'Declan's always been a possible, even a probable. But Max Spackman pointed the finger at him by suggesting he was in a flagging relationship with Lorraine. That smells fishy. And I believe I saw Max in what could have been the white Fiat Punto I stopped to help. If he bopped me on the head, then he's got some explaining to do, and a possible drifts more towards a probable.'

'Max never visited Joe in prison,' Sian objected. 'If he thought up this cunning plan to murder Lorraine and implicate Joe, how did he get it to Joe?'

I thought for a moment, then gently snapped my fingers.

'Nobody,' I said, 'thought of checking on

Damon Knight's visitors.'

'Oh, that's really clever,' Eleanor said drily, 'because if you go down that road you'd need to look at every visitor to every prisoner who had the opportunity to talk to Joe Creeney.'

'Keep it simple,' Sian said. 'Damon was Joe's cell mate, he likes me, I'll talk to him again.'

'Which leaves us,' Eleanor said, 'speculating on where Frank and Len Tully come into it.'

'My instinct is to believe everything they said. Someone murdered their brother. Six months ago they learned that Joe Creeney had an alibi. Then I came into it, they discovered the name of the killer, and paid with their lives. The rope and camera were planted in Len's car.'

Sian nodded. 'And the photographs were loaded into his computer by the real killer, who broke into his house with more finesse than you showed?'

'Everyone,' I said, 'has an off night.'

Sian grinned. 'I think we should stick with that. With the Tullys resting in peace we can concentrate on the other suspects. The one clear connection to murder — two murders: Lorraine and Rose Lane — is Stephanie Grey. What do we do about her? Confront her, leave her alone and go after the man?'

'I know where you two go,' Eleanor said.

I looked at Sian. Then at my mother. 'Us?'

'Oh, come on, Jack. Sian's been spilling the beans. Telling me all about her return to that adventure training boys-own-paper stuff she loves, how the status quo's been restored, you two together but doing your own thing and sometimes those own things coincide . . . '

'So . . . where are we going?'

'Home. Bryn Aur.'

'We've been drinking.'

'Sian's had less than you. She'll take you in the Shogun.'

Sian's chuckle was lecherous.

'That's not quite what I meant,' Eleanor said, 'but if that's what floats your boat . . . '

'Time off,' I said loftily, 'is time wasted.'

'Don't try to blind me with aphorisms,' Eleanor said scornfully. 'One bloody night won't make a scrap of difference, and I'm sure you've got better things to do in the hours of darkness, in or out of the Shogun.' She winked at Sian. 'I certainly have.'

I raised my eyebrows. 'Eleanor, you don't mean . . . ?'

'But I do. Reg is arriving tonight.' Her smile was kittenish. 'When you've been led up one garden path, the prospect of another one becomes positively irresistible.'

22

Of course Eleanor was right, as she usually is. After a promise from Sian that she would return soon to spend more time with my mother, we did take Sian's Shogun to Bryn Aur, my Soldier Blue chased the halogen headlights' probing beams with speed and safety along sweeping country roads where flat lakes shone like silver, and in the stillness of my old stone house beneath the Glyders we sat on cool leather and drank laced coffee while listening to the clock chime midnight and a distant fox bark from tangled undergrowth already glistening with dew under a cold autumn moon. Some time later we walked upstairs to the bedroom, and there in silky nakedness found something to do that transformed those hours of darkness into endless moments of intense pleasure and, with our valiant efforts, earned ourselves the reward of a long lie in. The movement alongside me of a body that was at once soft and firm, warm and cool, brought me sluggishly awake at a little after nine, the window's grey rectangle told me that the light of a November day was filtering through a hanging river mist and, with Sian's arm heavy across my naked chest and her steady breathing softly warming my ear, I lay in luxurious lassitude and tried to make sense of what lay ahead.

There comes a point in every investigation when instinct warns that the end is drawing near. Usually I'm confident enough to expect a successful outcome, yet always that optimism is tempered by dread, the dread engendered by the revulsion I feel for all violence.

That probably sounds like a contradiction coming from an ex-soldier, but my military career's watershed came when, in a rapid in-and-out action in Beirut, I killed an innocent man with my bare hands and his sightless eyes and the black blood seeping from his ears — the only sign of violence — had, for the next twelve months, gone with me each night to my bed.

Sensibly I ditched a fatally stalled vocation and moved on, trying half-a-dozen jobs in Australia, various scams when back in the UK, surviving a bruising brush with the bottle and eventually arriving at toy soldiers and the investigation of, yes, violent crimes — a tale oft recounted, all of it by now old hat, but the outcome nevertheless one that in reflective moments raises an obvious question.

Why? Why go back to engage closely with what I had rejected?

Manny Yates is the obvious answer: the Lime Street dick was my saviour, my teacher; he investigates crimes and he is my mentor still. Sian Laidlaw is another — but her involvement in my cause serves only to add to the paradox for under the appearance and demeanour of a strong, immensely capable and even aggressive person there hides a nature that is both caring and gentle.

But now we begin to build paradox upon paradox for ultimately it is that lurking inner softness that impels both of us to fight the violence without. We left military careers behind, but are driven to anger and tears by reports of kidnapping and murder and so we act. You can take the soldier out of the army but you can't . . .

Well, you know the way that ends and, as a valedictory bugle note to which every ex-soldier will raise a glass, it offers the least complicated reasons for why I do what I do: restlessness; the inability to settle; in Kiplings words: *Me that 'ave followed my trade in the place where the Lightnin's are made; 'twixt the Rains and the Sun and the Moon . . . Me that 'ave watched 'arf a world 'eave up all shiny with dew . . .*

What it boils down to is my subconscious

telling me that if I worked only with toy soldiers it would be as interesting and fulfilling as rolling the lawns for the squire — which may not be accurate, nor quite how Kipling wrote that bit, but by God when he did write it he hit the nail of a soldier's yearning smack on the head!

Sian mumbled, and rolled onto her back. The duvet slipped. I grinned in the grey half light, reached out to fix it and she caught my wrist, took my hand to her mouth and breathily kissed my palm.

I said softly, 'How well did you like Lorraine Creeney?'

'Mm? It was too soon to tell. She was a new friend. But nice. And now she'll never be anything more.'

'And somewhere out there is the man who hanged her by the neck.' I could hear her breathing; the subtle change in its rhythm as my words hit home; the sudden tightening of her grip.

'I've been cogitating, trying to work out why we do what we do. I think I arrived at an answer of sorts — I've got us down as gentle people, knights errant — but that could be codswallop. You see, I know what you're capable of, Soldier Blue — and I'm scared. I'm going after your nice new friend's killer. When I find him, I want you to stay away.' I rolled towards her, placed my palm on her forehead and with finger and thumb gently lifted her eyelids. Her eyes looked at me, a smoky blue.

I said, 'Will you do that?'

'What I'll do,' she said, 'is make your breakfast.'

DAY SIX — SATURDAY 5 NOVEMBER

DI Alun Morgan rolled in when we were finishing off in the kitchen, his battered Volvo's engine rattling like dried peas in a tin can as the car bounced over the stone bridge and emerged like a rusting frigate from the morning mist. The dishes were cleared, but half a pot of coffee was still perking gently on a low light and we welcomed him with a full mug and, for a change, went through to sit in the office.

'How the hell,' I said, 'did you know I was here?'

'Prescient,' he said.

'Oh yes, more dark forces and mystic powers?'

'That's always possible, but this time something perhaps a bit more prosaic.' His grey eyes were amused. 'I called your mobile phone, got the answer I needed and here I am.'

'No you didn't.'

'Phone Eleanor. Ask her.'

'Wha . . . ?' I smacked my forehead. 'Damn. I left it there. Then you tried to phone me, and she answered.'

'Now that *is* prescient,' he said, 'but it ruins the next bit. Because if I now tell you I know all about the woman in a pink blouse, you'll realize exactly how I found out and my reputation is shot.'

'Not *all* about her,' I said. 'The one thing Eleanor wouldn't give you is the name.'

'So who is she?'

I shook my head. 'You'll know when I've got proof of what she's done.'

'More fuel to feed Haggard's anger. He won't like what *you're* doing.'

'It's not him that's here, it's you, and it's you that's interested in someone who committed murder in Wales.'

'That's as maybe, but if you can link it to more than one murder in Liverpool that brings in the Merseyside police — '

'Who at present consider the case closed.'

'Impasse,' the Welsh detective said. He sipped his coffee, thought for a moment and shook his head. 'And in my estimation more like a wild leap of the imagination or I'd be taking this much more seriously. Look at it with logic: how many women have pink blouses and dark hair, I wonder?'

'Not all that many,' I said, 'who very early yesterday morning answered my call to a man's mobile when, as far as I could gather, he was being murdered by her accomplice.'

He raised his eyebrows. 'You can prove any of this?'

'Of course not. I'm pretty sure I recognized the voice. I know I could hear a man in the background. I was at Heswall when the phone was found in the car's glove compartment. Now, brilliant sleuths that we are, we will go out into the mean streets and gather evidence.'

'Gather evidence in the mean streets?' Sian echoed, her face a picture.

'No stone unturned,' I said.

'No gutter untrod,' Alun Morgan said drily.

'It could come to that,' I said.

'Another thought does occur.'

'Go on.'

'Were you circumspect? You questioned this woman, I'm sure, and I'm sure you did it with cleverness so as to hide what you were after. But were you careless? Did you inadvertently make your suspicions obvious? Because if she *is* a killer in a pink blouse, with a male accomplice — '

'I got that wrong. She'd be the accomplice.'

'Whatever. But if you've alerted them,

they'll either disappear — '

'Or come after us,' Sian said. 'I think you're right.' She looked at me. 'Jack?'

'I told her Calum saw her in Conwy very early Sunday morning.'

She smiled ruefully. 'Not circumspect, nor careless, but reckless.'

'I have a plan.'

'So did General Custer.'

'And I've heard enough,' Alun Morgan said, 'so I want you to listen carefully. I'm investigating a brutal murder. DI Haggard has looked into two murders and a suicide, and considers all three cases closed. My advice to you is this: keep out of my way, because I don't believe one word of this pink blouse nonsense — '

'Even though Grace Williams in Deganwy is pretty sure from a photograph that I've found the right woman?'

' — and make sure you dig up proof before you talk to Haggard about mysterious women answering dead-men's phones.'

'Absolutely,' I said. 'If proof is what you're after that's what you'll get: the next time you hear from us, all cases will be solved.'

'That's not a clever man with a plan,' Alun Morgan said, swinging smoothly out of his chair, 'it's a boastful PI blowing hot air full of empty promises.'

23

Our morning lie in, followed by a late greasy breakfast, Alun's visit and heavy rain and thick spray slowing traffic on the M56, meant that it was early afternoon before Sian brushed the Shogun up against the kerb outside Calum's flat in Grassendale. Fine rain was still sweeping like mist across the flat surface of the Mersey. We ran across the road, pounded up the stairs and walked into an empty room.

Of the lanky bearded Scot there was no sign. I hadn't spoken to him since my suggestion, in The Gallant Trooper, that he should lie low, but as the American Civil War soldiers were still standing in patient ranks in my Bryn Aur workshop awaiting the arrival of their Sharps rifles, I didn't waste time trying to reach him on the phone.

Sian still had more shop talking to do with her ex-army chums, her rugged men of few words. She had arranged to meet them in a bar in Southport, but promised to talk to Damon Knight as soon as possible. I pointed out that the journey back would take her close to the prison. She rolled her eyes and thanked me politely for the information.

Me? Well, I was going to see a man about a dog.

⋆   ⋆   ⋆

I already knew that Rose Lane's house in Ash Crescent backed onto the lane where I had dropped Joe Creeney. What I didn't know was the reaction to expect from her husband, ex-boxer Rocky Lane. The man was elderly and losing his faculties. He must have leaned heavily on his wife, and now she was gone.

Two minutes waiting for a ring on the doorbell to be answered can feel like a long time. I waited twice that long, rang again and waited another long minute before I heard footsteps and saw a bulky shadow fall against the glazed door. A brisk wind was driving rain against the back of my neck and causing my pants to stick to the back of my legs. When the door was opened by a man in T-shirt and jeans who looked like a 1950's Russian weightlifter on his day off, I forced a smile, expected to wait another minute before he realized he should invite me in, but was pleasantly surprised.

'Jack Scott,' he said in a rasping voice. 'Christ, come in, you're gettin' soaked.'

He shambled off with a boxer's rolling gait, leading me into a gloomy hallway that looked and smelt like a warm, damp florist's shop when the the stock of heady blooms is going over. He must have brought all the wreaths and bouquets home from the recent funeral and stacked them on the telephone table and a fancy brocade chair, hung two from the lime-green light fitting and propped the rest around the base of the grandfather clock, along the deep skirting boards and all the way up the stairs. A stairway to heaven I thought, with the late Rose in mind, then berated myself for my tasteless thoughts and followed the old pugilist into the rear sitting room. A room, I realized, that overlooked the conifer-flanked sloping lawn that led down to the narrow lane and the back of Joe's house.

Rocky indicated a vast easy chair close to a living-flame gas fire set in a marble recess in the wall, dropped his bulk into the one opposite me as I sat down, and looked at me steadily with sharp blue eyes.

'Yeah, right, so you are . . . ?'

His accent was broad scouse. I guessed the huskiness came from strong drink and cigars, and more than one straight left-hand jab to the throat.

'Jack Scott. I rang you earlier.'

'Did you?' He frowned. 'Yeah, that's right, I

remember a call . . . ' He smiled. 'OK, and you are . . . ?'

'Jack — '

He stopped me quickly by raising a hand as big as a shovel blade.

'I've already asked that, haven' I?'

'Yes, you have. But it's OK, I do understand.'

'I wish I fuckin' did,' he said, and the tone was so ineffably sad I was relieved Sian wasn't with me.

'It's all comin' back though,' he said. 'It's about Cocky, right?'

'Cocky?'

'Cocky the cocker spaniel. My dog.'

'Mm. But not so much about the dog as what was seen when he got out on the night your wife died.' I smiled apologetically. 'By you or your wife. Whoever went out looking for him.'

'I know what I saw,' he said. 'I saw your car.'

'That's right — but how'd you know . . . ?'

'Because it's outside now. I saw you arrive, saw you gettin' out.'

'Right.' I shook my head and smiled ruefully. 'Obvious isn't it — and I'm supposed to be a private investigator.'

'Yeah, well, that's what I saw, your car — but Cocky got out a couple of times that night. He always does.'

'What I'd like to know is if you're sure he got out earlier on that *particular* night.'

'Definitely.'

'Any idea what time?'

'Nineish.'

'And who went looking for him?'

'Rose.'

'Did she tell you where she found him?'

'He'd strayed into a neighbour's garden. Across the back lane . . . '

He trailed off, his eyes distant. Death added to death. His ageing brain was fumbling as it tried to separate one from the other.

'Joe Creeney's house,' I prompted.

'Yeah. It's got a white gate. Rose shut it after her an' Cocky.'

That sounded right. The gate was shut when Joe got out of my car.

'Did she see anything while she was in Joe's garden? When she was near it, maybe when she was coming out, shutting the gate?'

'Listen,' he said, 'I haven't even offered you a cup of tea.'

'Don't worry about it, it's getting late and I've not long had coffee.'

'Yeah, well, I'll have to hurry you because I'm expectin' a visitor, see, I had a phone call . . . '

'That was me,' I said gently.

'Was it?' He frowned. 'What did you want?'

'I wanted to know if your wife saw anything when she went looking for your dog on Saturday night. No, sorry, I'm not being precise. What I mean is, did she see anyone in Joe Creeney's garden?'

'She saw Creeney.'

'What — in the garden?'

He nodded. 'Crossin' the garden. Well, walkin' down the path from the shed. Towards the house. Carryin' a ladder. I think they were decoratin' . . . '

He looked at me, puzzled.

'What did you say your name was?'

'Scott. Jack Scott.'

'Right. Jack. So, Rose didn't say nothin' to Creeney because, well, it was late, and Cocky had got in his garden. Rose didn't like tresspassin'. But she told me she saw him. Creeney.'

'And you're sure of the time? Nine o'clock?'

'It was wet, wasn' it? Rainin'. And the clock had just chimed, the big one, the grandfather clock. It's in the hall.'

'Yes, it is. I saw it.'

I saw that, but what I couldn't see was how Rose Lane had watched Joe Creeney carry a ladder out of his garden shed at around nine o'clock on Saturday night, a week ago, when at that time he was still locked up in Walton gaol.

★ ★ ★

I rang Willie Vine from the car and asked him if he could confirm the time Joe Creeney had gone over the wall of Walton prison, or whatever he had done to get out. Around ten o'clock, Vine said. Could have been later, not a chance it was as early as eight or nine because he'd been spoken to several times by prison officers.

While he was on I also asked him for the results of the DNA analysis of the blood found on Lorraine Creeney's elbow. Definitely Joe's, Vine said. A positive match. I asked how that fitted in with the idea of Len Tully as the accomplice who had set the whole thing up and then walked out. Easy, Vine said. The photograph showed Lorraine still alive. She was alive when I dropped Joe off, she was alive when Joe walked into the house. Something happened in there, and Joe got elbowed in the face.

Then Joe Creeney murdered his wife.

Case closed.

261

24

A chill dusk was darkening the eastern skies when I put away the phone and started up, and when a black car that had been parked a little way behind me switched on its headlights and pulled silently away from the kerb as I moved down Ash Crescent, I was reminded that my careless talk to Stephanie Grey had made me a target, and I was vulnerable. Uneasy, I kept my eye on the following car. It tucked in behind me along Menlove Avenue — dual carriageway, one way system so it had no choice — but at the lights it drew level and showered the Quattro with spray as it turned left into Beaconsfield. I turned right into Yew Tree Road, and breathed a sigh of relief.

I was mildly jittery all the way to Grassendale, the unease not helped by the constant rattle of Bonfire Night fireworks that sounded uncomfortably like gunshots. I kept telling myself that my fears had little justification. What was I expecting? A bullet from a high-powered rifle to come smashing through the windscreen? A car to accelerate out of a side road and turn the Quattro into mangled metal, me into a blob of strawberry jam? I suspected Stephanie Grey of complicity in murder because she was dark-haired, liked pink blouses and I'd recognized her voice, and so I was anticipating a move to silence me. But, despite Grace Williams's positive identification, time was making the pink blouse idea look silly and, if pushed, I could probably think up a dozen plausible reasons for what I had listened to on the mobile phone — top of the list being the possibility, recognized earlier, that I'd dialled the wrong number.

All right, so Stephanie's mentioning that Len Tully's death was suicide looked like a slip. But why should it? Mike Haggard couldn't be the busy solicitor's only source of information. If I'd queried her she would have come up with a logical explanation, I would have looked foolish — and as I pulled up outside Calum's flat on the banks of the Mersey, that was exactly the way I was feeling.

The big first-floor room with its familiar odours of enamel paint and cigar smoke was empty. I threw my coat on a chair, wandered aimlessly around from window to work table to the picture wall where Calum's Blu-Tacked cuttings had grown into a unique personal history of life in Liverpool. Switched on the table lamp. Looked for Post-it notes. Sniffed the air for familiar perfume. Detected nothing.

The story of my week.

It was close to five. I wandered into the kitchen and put the coffee on the stove to perk, looked in the fridge, found an open pack of smoked bacon, located tomatoes in the vegetable rack and got the lot sizzling in a frying pan filmed with lard and slid the result — crisp bacon, slightly blackened tomatoes — out of the pan onto granary toast thick with butter.

While eating I noticed that both the black moggie and its feeding bowl were missing. Had Calum been back, or had they been missing when Sian and I called in earlier? I couldn't remember. And it didn't matter. Calum and cat would be residing with Jones the Van. Sian was either chewing the fat with the army types, or already in Walton prison squeezing information from Damon Knight. When she did finish those chores I thought she might again be spending the night at Eleanor's flat.

Whatever I had to do could be done by one clever investigator.

Trouble was I wasn't feeling clever, and I hadn't a clue what I was supposed to do next. I chuckled. I hadn't a clue about *anything*.

Should I visit the original crime scene again to see if my theories on the trap to ensnare Joe held water? Call in on Max Spackman and ask him if he'd followed me to Wales and bopped me on the head? Confront Declan, find out if Max was right and he really had got tired of Lorraine? Or go back and put my suspicions to a solicitor who would be flabbergasted, then outraged enough to toss me bodily down the stairs?

The decision, as often happens, was taken out of my hands. A couple of hours later, seven or thereabouts, I was dozing fitfully on the leather settee when footsteps pattered on the stairs and Sian walked in shaking the rain from her coat.

★ ★ ★

'He had a lot of visitors, our Damon,' she said. 'Named a lot of names, too, but only one I recognized. Care to make a guess?'

'We've got Declan, Caroline and Stephanie visiting Joe Creeney. So it has to be Max.'

'Bingo.'

'Did Damon say how he knew Max, what they talked about?'

'No to the first, and when I asked him if he passed messages between Max and Joe Creeney, I got a second no.'

'Double negative.'

'Still means no.'

The small table lamp was bathing the room in a warm, intimate glow. We were sprawled on separate leather chairs knocking back coffee with a liquid additive that was working the same magic on the drinkers. Blonde hair snatched back into a pony-tail was a lustrous beacon attracting my attention, which then tended to slip without restraint in a southerly direction. Blue eyes watched me with amused affection.

'Are you thinking Max Spackman and Stephanie Grey?'

'With reluctance.'

'Why?'

'Their involvement in murder is . . . incomprehensible.'

'What, even for Max the bouncer?'

'He's nothing but a big show off. That's the way I saw him.'

'You've been wrong before.'

'That's why I'm sitting on the fence.'

'But it's all there, isn't it? Max tried to point the finger at Declan, then lured you into the Welsh woods and whacked you on the head. Stephanie's been identified by Grace Williams, and you heard her voice on Len Tully's mobile. That links her to two murders.' She paused. 'When she answered

266

the mobile, that must have been Max you heard thrashing around in the background. They were both there on Heswall Dales, murdering that poor man.'

'Mm.'

'Christ,' Sian said, 'how enthusiastic can you get. I tell you what, if we're right and it *is* them, I'm so angry at what they did to Lorraine I'll hang them myself.'

I sighed deeply. 'Trouble is, it's *not* all there, it doesn't *all* fit. Think of all the scheming involved. Joe Creeney was trapped by a cunning plan, but Max is nothing more than a stylish thug of limited intelligence.'

'Enter Stephanie,' Sian said, 'stage left.'

'Woman in pink blouse playing the master criminal? And . . . what? There's something going on between her and the leading man?'

'You said it last night: she's besotted.'

'I might go along with her brains *and* the relationship, because women like Stephanie are often attracted to men like Max, but then we have to take another gigantic leap into the unimaginable and believe she could physically plunge a knife into Rose Lane's throat. I can't see how she could do it.'

'We could go and ask her.'

'Better still, I'll go and talk to Max. The evidence that he bopped me on the head is stronger than the evidence against Stephanie.'

'When?'

'Now's a good time. If he's at work he'll be mellow, and I'll be safer in a crowd. I'll find out from Caroline where he is.'

I took my phone out of my pocket, prepared to dial — and it vibrated in my hand. I pulled a face and pressed receive.

'Jack?'

'Yes?'

I looked at Sian, put my thumb over the microphone and said, 'It's Stephanie.'

* * *

'Jack, there's something I didn't tell you.'

'It's never too late.'

'You're sweet, but in a murder case you know that can be risky.'

'We both know the murder cases we've been interested in are all wrapped up, closed.'

'They could be reopened,' she said, 'if new evidence is uncovered.'

'Then that would depend,' I said, 'on what you didn't tell me.'

'Well, it wasn't you exactly. It was Sian.'

'I didn't know you two had met.'

'Of course you do. She came to see me. Asked all sorts of questions.' She laughed. 'And I suppose she told you she sprayed perfume and I had a terrible asthma attack.'

I frowned, spread my free hand palm up on the arm of the chair and looked wide-eyed at Sian. 'I've jumped to the wrong conclusion, haven't I?' I said. 'You're Fiona — Fiona Lake.'

'Of course. Lorraine's sister.'

'You sound,' I said, 'just like Stephanie Grey,' and in the other chair Sian put her hand to her mouth.

'I know,' Fiona said. 'She was Joe's solicitor and I met her at the trial. People who know both of us often make that mistake.'

'Well, with that all cleared up, what was it you were going to tell me?'

'It's . . . it's about a possible clue. I know Caroline asked you to look into Lorraine's murder because she couldn't believe Joe had done it. This . . . clue . . . could lead you to the man who murdered Lorraine.'

'If you know that,' I said, 'you must know his name.'

'I didn't say that — and anyway, I'm terrified. Several people have been murdered; just talking to you like this is dangerous.'

'You're very brave, and you're doing the right thing. Just tell me as much as you can — as much as I need to know to take the next step.'

'This . . . bloke's been talking. He was . . . somewhere . . . and while he was there he lost something . . . '

'Really,' I said softly, my mind racing backwards as lights flashed and bells rang. 'Do you know what he lost?'

'No!'

She blurted the word. Her breathing was coming in short, irregular gasps. I could almost taste the fear, almost feel the phone tremble in her hand as she shivered.

'All right. Do you know *where* he lost it?'

'In the shed.'

'Whose shed?'

More rapid breathing. Something that might have been a strangled sob.

'Fiona,' I said, 'why didn't you go to the police?'

'Because this is going to incriminate a member of the family and' — another sob, swiftly suppressed, a gulp as she swallowed hard — 'and I don't *want* the police I want *you* to deal with it and — '

The phone went dead. She'd ended the call. Or someone had ended it for her.

Sian was watching me.

'It's a trap.'

'You don't know what she said.'

'But if she sounds like Stephanie . . . '

'Yes, I know.' I stood up, paced to the window, walked back and stood with my hands braced on the back of the chair.

'Between a rock and a hard place again,' I said. 'If I didn't dial a wrong number when I was sitting in front of Len Tully's computer then one of these women was on the Heswall Dales when she answered my call. But which one? If it was Stephanie out there in Heswall, then this call from Fiona could be genuine. If it was Fiona, then, yes — '

'It's a trap.' She smiled. 'Follow me, Super Sleuth.'

We went into the kitchen. She poured more coffee, strong, no booze. We sat at the table.

'Drink that,' she said, 'while we plan the next move.'

'The next move is a phone call.'

'To who?'

'Whom.' I winked. 'Just listen.'

I took a sip of scalding coffee, found my mobile, keyed in the number.

'Caroline? Hello, it's Jack Scott. Yes, I'm fine thanks, but I want to talk to Max. Is he there?'

I listened, shook my head slowly at Sian.

'No, it doesn't matter, because you can probably help. Remember when I called to see you? When Max had on his spare gloves because he'd lost one. He said he had it when he left Lorraine on Saturday, thought he might have dropped it when he was getting into his car . . . ' I waited, then closed my eyes, opened them and nodded at Sian. 'He hasn't found it?' I listened some more, nodded once or twice, then smiled. 'Thanks Caroline, you've been a big help.'

I ended the call.

'Max lost one of his monogrammed leather gloves. He had it Saturday night when he went to see Lorraine, had it when he left — he says — certainly didn't have it after that. And, as you heard, he still hasn't found it.'

'And presumably this is the clue Fiona was talking about?'

'We don't know. She was vague. Like, someone went somewhere and lost something. Now the someone's panicking. As they should be. Fiona heard this someone talking to another someone. The first someone thinks he lost whatever it was he lost — in Joe Creeney's garden shed.'

'Fiona actually said that?'

'She said 'the shed'. I'm a sleuth. I worked out the rest.'

'But why is it important? No, why is it a *clue*? If half of Liverpool knows Max went to see Lorraine, it's not exactly a secret. If he lost a glove there, or left it there — so what?'

'Because on Monday night I asked Max if he had gone anywhere near Joe's shed. He laughed at the idea, because the police had searched the area. But the police thought the ladder had come from the garage, and they were concentrating their search for signs of someone entering or leaving the house by the back gate.'

'And you know the shed is reached by a path on the other side of the garden because you and Calum have been to the scene,' Sian said. 'And that's where the glove is: in the shed.'

'Yes. Bearing Max's initials.'

'It's a trap. You are being lured to a terrible fate by the two killers, one of whom is Fiona.'

'That's one possibility.'

'What's the other?'

'Stephanie's the killer and Fiona has developed a conscience. Or she always had a conscience, and now she's heard these two people talking and her conscience has overcome her fear.'

'It could still be a trap. The conversation between the two unknowns could be a ploy. They deliberately had this phoney conversation when Fiona was nearby, knowing she would overhear and give the details to you.'

'I know. But Max did lose a glove, and I can't just ignore what could be a breakthrough.'

'You're too gullible.'

'How about daring, gutsy?'

'Hotheaded and irresponsible. If you're determined — '

'That too — '

' — to go, call Calum. Take backup.'

I did. He was in Manchester, they'd be starting the drive back to Liverpool within the hour, in Stan Jones's rusty white van. Far too late if I wanted to go to Joe Creeney's house now.

I told Sian. Her face was grim.

'Then I'll go with you.'

'The hell you will.'

I drawled it, like John Wayne, and I don't know whether it was that or my steely gaze, but for once I didn't get an argument.

25

Diplomatic Reg was indelicately ensconced in Eleanor's Calderstones' flat so, without a bed for the night and deciding not to spend it stretched out on Calum's leather settee, Sian phoned ahead and set off for Meg Morgan's place. I used the mobile to get back to Calum. They were hurtling down the M56. Over the rattling and roaring of Stan Jones's van I swiftly told him where I was going and what I was looking for, told him I'd hang on there as long as I could, then switched off and set about gathering together what I needed to sneak across Joe Creeney's garden and break into his shed.

Calum's spare room was mine whenever I stayed there, which was often. I went through and changed into the dark clothing I'd last worn when — different time, different thugs — we had crept warily across a greasy garage floor in Old Swan: trousers, sweat-shirt, woolly Benny and rubber — soled black shoes. Calum and I both had heavy rubber torches that doubled as weapons, but night in the city is never completely dark, crossing Joe's garden would be a damp walk in the park and for my search of the shed I took a tiny Solitaire by Mag Instrument — a Maglite.

For such an outing James Bond would have clipped a .38 Smith & Wesson Centennial Airweight revolver into a leather holster after M ordered him to get rid of his .25 Beretta in *Dr No*. I double checked to make sure I was carrying my Swiss Army knife, took a last look around the empty flat then slipped out into the night.

* * *

For the second time in seven days I drove with some stealth up the lane behind Joe Creeney's house and parked with my tyres squelching in muddy ruts and the car canted enough to the left to make it awkward to disembark. I wound my window down and sat for a moment listening. The fine rain was cold on my face, hissing gently across the Quattro's roof with each gust of wind; why did it always rain on Bonfire Night? Fireworks snapped, rockets showered sparks beneath the clouds. Traffic mumbled and growled along Menlove Avenue. A dog barked snappily, and I cast a glance right and tried to peer through the shrubs bordering Rocky Lane's sloping lawns.

Sliding in and out of dementia, Alun Morgan had said of the old boxer, and I'd witnessed it for myself — yet Rocky had spotted my car when I dropped off Joe Creeney, and remembered the number long enough to pass it on to the police. I shook my head in wonder at the fascinating mysteries of old age, then opened the door, swung a leg out and stood up in the rain to look across the car.

Joe's white picket gate was open.

Least worrying explanation: Rocky's spaniel had again gone walkabout, and forgetful Rocky had gone after it and left the gate open on his way out. Most disquieting? The trap as envisaged by Sian had been set, and the trappers had left the gate open on their way in.

There was an eerie half light in the narrow lane as city lights bounced off the low wet skies. Remarkably, when I walked around the car the deep gouge in the grass where Joe Creeney had almost lost his footing was still visible. But of more recent intruders there was no sign.

Like a cunning burglar preparing for a hasty retreat, I left the car unlocked, the gate open. A few moss-coated steps led down to a stone path. From my viewpoint it was on the left of the sloping lawn. Across the back of the unlit house there was a paved patio. The eerie light was reflecting from the wide patio-doors through which Joe had entered the big living-room. In that radiance I could see on the right of the patio — again from my viewpoint — a short path leading back up the slope to the garden shed.

No movement anywhere. No movement, no sound. I could smell wet grass, rain on stone, but no lingering cigarette smoke, no perfumed trace of human presence. The muted light reflecting from the patio doors created the illusion of lights switched on inside the living-room, of people watching television — but that's all it was, an illusion. The previous residents were dead.

I listened to the thump of my heart, the rasp of my breathing. Then I moved away from the gate. The moss-coated steps would be slippery. I avoided them, treading silently through the wet grass at the side of steps and path. Ten strides carried me to the house. I stepped up onto the patio. My back was against the wall to one side of the glass doors. I was poorly concealed in shadows weakened by the reflected city lights. Again I listened. Listened, and continued to use my eyes.

From the patio I had a different perspective. Now I could see up the sloping lawn to the open picket gate. To its left there was a high hedge bordering the lane. The shadows on the garden side of it were at the mercy of skies made luminous by the city's sodium street-lighting. No killer hiding there — but what about behind the shed?

I was still gnawing my lip at the thought when I realized that the shed door hung half open.

I had two choices. Cross the lawn and search the shed, or go home. The second wasn't an option, so I was stuck with the first. Before I took that, I had to clarify my situation. That, too, was simple. If a trap had been set, I'd already walked into it. Joe's killers were waiting to pounce. I didn't think they were hiding in the shed, so they were somewhere behind me — towards the front of the house — or *behind* the shed. Possibly both, if there were two of them. The only scrap of comfort I had was that their favourite choice of weapon seemed to be a coil of bright orange rope. Definitely no match for a Swiss Army knife.

I reached into my pocket, took out the Maglite and ran across the lawn. It seemed that around me the world held its breath. I sped across the grass cocooned in silence. When I reached the shed I steadied myself with one hand on the wet timber. With the other I pulled the door fully open. The hinges screeched like a hunting owl. The eerie light crept in like a ghostly intruder. It entered and was scattered by mechanical and chemical contents stored in disarray on floor and shelves, tools hanging from nails, the big ladder standing on its long side against the wall under a cobwebbed window glazed with plastic through which light filtered and turned two dimensions into three, but gloom was still gloom and the glove I was seeking was black.

Then I remembered my tiny torch hanging from its wrist strap. I took one step forward, turned it on, narrowed the beam. One sweep was enough. A black glove was lying on the dusty boards under a lawn mower.

I hesitated. Looked behind me. I was half in, half out. The garden was unchanged. The silence was stifling. I took that second step. Treating rusty hinges as tenderly as sick friends I pulled the door silently to behind me. Suddenly enclosed I could smell dry grass, petrol, something acrid close to my face that was probably strong weed killer on a shelf. A sneeze threatened. I put the back of my hand to my nose, pinned the glove with the torch's beam and bent down. Gold letters glinted on the wrist. I scooped up the glove, stuffed it in my pocket; switched off the torch, stood up and turned round.

As I did so someone celebrating Bonfire Night let off an enormous banger in the next garden and I jumped out of my skin. Sweating, I closed my eyes, tried to forage calm out of galloping panic.

Then my eyes snapped open as someone kicked in the shed door. Hinges screamed. A black shape loomed, wide shoulders blocking the light. I saw one of those shoulders dip. A fist shot out of the blackness and slammed into my face. My nose cracked. I reeled backwards. On the way down my flailing arm caught one of the hanging tools. It leaped off its hook, hit the boards with a musical clang.

My eyes were streaming. I could taste blood, feel it warm and wet on my chin. My breath bubbled. I snuffled, struggled to roll, get to my feet. A swinging foot drove into my ribs and I gasped. Again I thudded to the boards. Metal clattered as my head and one arm got tangled in the handles of a lawn mower. I fought free, kicked out. My foot scraped across a shin. The man let loose a string of curses. I planted my shoulders, forearms and flat hands, launched a double-legged piston kick and drove both feet into a fork of soft flesh covering vital organs. The curses turned into a drawn-out groan of agony.

I swept a hand across my streaming eyes,

struggling to see, my vision blurred. My attacker had staggered back. He was crouching, hands pressed to his groin. I rolled onto my knees, staggered to my feet. He lifted his head, saw me. Straightening, he lashed out with his foot. I twisted, took the kick on my thigh. Then he sprang forward. His right hand grabbed my shirt front. He brought his other forearm round in a sweeping blow to the side of my jaw. It was like being hit by a log. I felt myself wobble. Lights flashed behind my eyes. There was a singing in my head. I grabbed for the hand holding my shirt, felt the hard fist inside the tight leather glove. Then we were locked together and struggling. We swayed one way then the other. The walls were thin. They creaked and groaned as heavy bodies crashed into them and rebounded. More tools were dislodged from nails and fell, ringing. Once, my attacker went to his knees as an ankle rolled. He hung on, his weight buckling my knees, then pulled himself up by clawing at my neck and together we fell against the wall. We were too close, the embrace too intimate. My blood was spattering his face as I snorted; it was a gory film, slick and slippery as we rubbed heads like warring bulls. I couldn't see him through streaming eyes, couldn't tell who I was fighting — and neither of us could land a telling blow. We were gasping like lovers, sweating like pigs — and weakening.

And then over it all a voice said, laconically, 'If you don't mind me sayin' so, I've seen more genuine action from a gaggle of wee five-year olds having a punch up in a bouncy castle.'

★ ★ ★

'Gaggle?'

'Aye, well, you weren't seeing it from my angle. Actually, it was like something out of Buster Keaton, you know? All this rattling and clanging and thumping and sonorous groans and the sides of the shed bulging every now and then and dust puffing out of every crack . . . '

'Buster Keaton or Tom and Jerry?'

'Your choice, pal,' Calum said, grinning, and he continued wiping my face with an old rag he'd found in the shed and dampened by rubbing in the rain-soaked grass. Neither nose nor ribs were broken but I was seriously considering giving up breathing because of the pain from both, and I recalled with sadistic pleasure the kick that had connected with my dancing partner's goolies and threatened to send them back from whence they came.

The shock of Calum's arrival on the scene had galvanized my attacker. With sudden brute strength he'd sent me crashing like a discarded scarecrow across the lawn mower. Then, with amazing speed, he had leaped from the shed, caught Calum a glancing blow with his forearm and bolted around the side of the house.

'Leave him!' I'd yelled — then rolled off the lawn mower and sank with a groan onto the boards as Calum poked his head through the door to admire the carnage.

That had been five minutes ago. The killer had that much start on us, but I was unconcerned because what I had learnt in the bruising close-contact scuffle meant that he could have five days, or five weeks — and it would still not be enough.

'So why did you tell me to leave him?' Calum said now, tossing the blood-soaked rag aside.

'I need to catch my breath, marshal my thoughts — '

'Fix your make-up and adjust your attire — what the fuck are you talking about, Jack, we had a killer at our mercy?'

'He's still at our mercy,' I said, 'if in the past few hectic minutes I have discovered his identity.'

We were outside the shed, our backs to the

door. Rain from the overhanging trees was pattering on the tar-paper roof. Fireworks crackled. The smell of smoke from a thousand bonfires was strong on the damp air.

'Care to explain?'

'In the struggle, I grabbed my assailant's hand.'

'Aye, well, silly of me to miss that significant and may I say poignant moment — '

'And what happens now,' I said patiently, 'is we phone Caroline Spackman and get her to come here with the house key. Then we go over the killing area — hall, stairs, living-room — but stand well back while she does some sharp-eyed nosing around.'

Calum stroked the fine droplets of rain from his beard and nodded thoughtfully.

'Bringing Caroline Spackman in — does that mean you suspect Max?'

I shook my head. 'I found his glove, as I was supposed to, but I'm pretty certain he didn't attack me — tonight, or in Wales on Tuesday.'

'All right, then you're asking Caroline to open up the house because there's something in there that will confirm your suspicions about the person who is now your number one suspect?'

'Not directly. I'm hoping what Caroline

sees — what she notices — will tell me my *other* theory is good; that I know how *the trap* was set. If that happens, then, yes, something at the crime scene — something I noticed when you and I were there — could nail the killer. Before that, as a small step in that direction, I'm going to pay Rocky Lane another visit because when I was there this afternoon I missed the significance of what he was telling me.'

'And I wait here for Caroline?'

'Please.'

'But you're not willing to share any of your brilliant theories?'

'If they're wrong, I'll look foolish.'

'If they're right, and you've kept mum to the bitter end, you'll take all the credit.'

'Would I do that.'

'What, and you a modest Sassenach? Now what on earth gave me that preposterous idea . . .'

★ ★ ★

My nose was still seeping blood when I walked up Rocky Lane's path and knocked on his front door. This time he answered almost immediately, and I wondered if the explosions that were like the rattle of distant rifle fire or the rockets trailing fire across the night skies like battlefield tracer bullets would disturb a man in his condition.

I had seriously underestimated the old bruiser.

'D'you find anything?' he said, as he led the way through the unlit hall smelling of decaying vegetation where my feet rustled against wilting leaves and fading petals trailed in my wake.

'You were out there watching, weren't you?' I said, as we entered his living-room.

'Yeah, Cocky got out again.' He grinned. 'Only as far as the bottom of the garden, but from there I could see you moving around by Creeney's shed.'

'Like Creeney was doing.'

He frowned. 'What, tonight?'

'No. The night you saw my car.'

The frown remained, but it was joined by a relieved smile.

'Of course,' he said. 'The night of the murder. They were decoratin', weren't they, and he was carryin' a ladder.'

'From the shed, to the house,' I said, carefully jogging. 'Joe Creeney.'

Again the frown. I thought I'd lost him. I had, but in another way.

'Sorry,' he said, 'but what was your name again?'

'Jack Scott. I came to see you this afternoon.'

'So you did . . . ' His eyes were puzzled. He glanced at the clock over the gas fire and said, 'Christ, it's getting late, did I give you somethin' to eat an' drink or . . . ?'

'I didn't stay,' I said gently. 'I drove away, and came back a couple of minutes ago — '

'Yeah, but Joe Creeney's in prison.'

His mind had jumped again.

I nodded. 'He *was* in prison, yes.'

'So what makes you say he was carryin' the ladder from the shed? He couldn't have, could he?'

'I didn't say . . . ' I paused to give his thoughts time to settle, then said, 'He couldn't, no. But if it wasn't Joe — who was it?'

'I told you. It was Creeney.'

'Yes, but which one?'

'The lad I used to train, years ago.'

'The boxer?'

'Joe's brother, yeah. Declan.' He nodded at my face, his eyes amused. 'By the look of your nose,' he said, 'you could do with a few tips yourself.'

★　★　★

'He meant tips on how to deliver a right hook,' I said to Calum, 'but what I really need is a refresher course with Manny Yates. In

288

today's parlance, my investigative technique sucks.'

I was talking quietly as Caroline Spackman unlocked Joe's front door. We followed her inside out of the rain. Rocky Lane had let me out the back way, and I'd crossed the lane and come through Joe's garden and around the house. Calum had been waiting with Caroline. I'd thanked her for coming, and now she turned to me with a questioning look.

I closed the front door behind me.

'Right. Calum and I have been here before, as you know. But we're strangers, and in your sister-in-law's house you'll see things we'd miss. What I want you to look for is anything that's out of place. Look — but don't touch.'

'What's this about? Stephanie told me you were out of it, the investigation was over.'

'It is — and yet it isn't.' I smiled reassuringly. 'Can you just bear with me, for the next few minutes?'

'OK, well, that for starters,' she said. She was pointing at the can of beeswax furniture polish standing on the telephone table.

'Is that because Lorraine was asthmatic?'

'She couldn't stand sprays of any kind. For furniture she used a chamois leather, and water with a drop of vinegar.'

'So does my mother,' I said, 'when she's feeling energetic.'

Caroline pulled a face. 'I'm always too bloody lazy. So's Fiona. She uses spray polish, but she buys those disposable masks and they seem to work.'

'Fiona, Lorraine's sister.' I shook my head sympathetically. 'Asthma's a terrible thing, and it runs in families. Were they alike in other ways?'

'In *every* way,' Caroline said. 'Tall, fair hair, wore similar clothes . . . '

'*Fair* hair?'

She nodded, but her eyes were again busy. She walked across the hall, looking up the stairs. I thought I saw her shiver. Then she turned towards the living-room. The door was still open. It had been like that when Calum and I left with Declan Creeney on Wednesday.

Caroline had gone straight to the tray I'd leaned against the wall.

'What's this doing here?'

She was looking at Calum. He spread his hands. She shook her head.

'Sorry. That was automatic. Of course you wouldn't know, but this belongs in the kitchen. And the cloth. Lorraine wouldn't't've stood the tray here.'

I said, 'That was me.'

'What — you brought the tray and the cloth in from the kitchen?'

'No. I stood it there. The cloth and tray were on the floor when we walked in.'

'Why?' And again she shook her head. 'Sorry, stupid question, I'm acting daft. It's just, being here, you know, where Lorraine was . . .'

I let her wander around, but the only areas of interest to me were the living-room and large hall and she found nothing else that jarred, nothing out of place. I had all I needed, anyway, and after a few more minutes I called a halt and we walked out to find that the rain had finally died away.

We stood by Caroline's car. Rocky Lane had given me a name, Caroline had confirmed my more outlandish theories, but there were still unanswered questions, suspects to be cleared.

I said, 'I thought I saw Max in Wales the other day. Tuesday. Would that be right?'

She smiled and shook her head.

'Wrong feller, Jack. We were down town shopping.'

I thought for a moment. If not Max and his daughter, then who? *Somebody* had attacked me. Then on Friday I'd recognized a voice on a mobile phone, which might put Fiona on Heswall Downs where Len Tully had died, but fair hair seemed to rule her out for the Rose Lane killing unless she'd worn a wig.

291

However, the woman who had flagged me down on the Llanrwst Road *certainly* had fair hair.

'What car does Fiona drive?'

'A white Fiat. A little one. But most of them are, aren't they?'

I grinned and asked her what that said about Italians, when in reality I was wondering what it told me about Fiona Lake and . . . who? Not Max, certainly. Clearly he had *not* attacked me on the Llanrwst road, and one simple test would tell me if he was the man who had attacked me in Joe Creeney's shed. Simple and necessary — but a waste of time: I already knew the answer.

Caroline was smiling absently as she opened her car door, her thoughts elsewhere. As she slipped inside I rested a hand on the roof and held the door open.

'Caroline, do you know where Max is now?'

'Yes, he's at the Sleepy Pussy.'

'Mm. Look, would you mind doing me a favour? Give him a quick call on your mobile, now, see if Declan's there tonight.'

She did. He wasn't. I could almost feel my eyes gleam.

'Ask him if he's expected.'

He was, Caroline confirmed. Quite soon. He'd phoned in, mentioned a puncture. And now Caroline was looking hard at me. There was something in her eyes I suspected was hope, tinged with understandable apprehension.

'Stephanie was wrong, wasn't she? It's not over. You're still working on all these killings?'

'It's *almost* over.'

'What does that mean?'

'I'm pretty sure I know who murdered Lorraine. And I *do* know how it was done.'

'Jesus!' she said softly. 'D'you mean it really wasn't Joe?'

'Joe was set up. That's what I'm saying: I know how he was trapped.'

'So — who was it?' Her eyes were moist. 'You've mentioned two names, Declan and Max, and I'm not exactly stupid so I do know where you're going so — '

I stopped her by resting a hand on her shoulder.

'Joe didn't murder Lorraine, and I'm sure Max has done nothing wrong. That's all you need to know — isn't it?'

'I suppose.'

She was breathing hard. Her hands were tight on the steering wheel. She was looking straight ahead. Then, abruptly, she started the car. I stepped back and slammed the door, and she gave me a quick smile and drove away.

'The man who knows everything,' Calum said softly. 'So what now? Is it time to let me in on the secret?'

The Quattro was in the lane. We walked around the house and up the moss-coated path and through the little white gate. I looked across at Calum.

'One secret's out already: Declan Creeney's our killer. What we need to do is toss around the whys and the wherefores so that I've got plenty of ammunition when I tackle him. I'd like to pounce on him with motives and opportunity and tricky little details, and watch the shock and fear in his eyes, so we'll do some talking in the car.'

'And you got Declan's name from a geriatric boxer who slips in and out of reality?'

'Yes. His wife saw Declan carrying the ladder from the shed. Which is why she was murdered.'

'Right. She's no longer with us and can't back up his story; corroborate, if you'd prefer the big word.' He grinned, his bearded face wolfish in the strange half-light. 'So isn't that a slender wee thread you're using to link Declan Creeney to violent death?'

'Works well for the Bolas spider,' I said, as we climbed into the car. 'Come on, let's go to the Sleepy Pussy and polish this off.'

26

It was pushing 11.30 when we left Joe's house in Calderstones, almost three-quarters of an hour later when I drove into the Sleepy Pussy's car-park in Brighton-le-Sands and pulled up under the yellow light of an ornate cast-iron street lamp. Several were dotted round about. Reproduction. Probably plastic. Pools of light fell on perhaps a dozen cars, several of which were metallic silver.

From where we sat we could see across the car-park to the club's main entrance. The doors were open. Red walls and dark wood panelling glowed in the warm lighting. A tall man was standing talking to a young woman in some sort of night-clubby uniform. He was wearing tailored jacket and jeans, driving one fist into the palm of his other hand as he talked. A poser in black leather gloves and designer shades.

'Max Spackman,' I said.

Calum and I looked at each other. Our eyes met, and all I could see in his was a reflection of my own elation. Then, as one, we climbed out of the Quattro and slammed the doors.

Calum had been right to point out that there was but a slender thread connecting Declan Creeney to murder, but in my opinion that thread was strong, and firmly anchored. As we drove away from Calderstones, I told him that Max had planted the seed in my mind as early as Monday.

'He told me then that Declan had something going with Lorraine. I did nothing, because it could have been Max shifting suspicion. Now I'm sure he had it right.'

'So what about Wayne Tully's murder?'

'That was Declan.'

'Why?'

'The prosecution's case was that Joe killed Wayne Tully because he believed the lad was having it off with Lorraine. But I think Declan was already playing around with his brother's wife. Wayne found out, and threatened to tell Joe.'

'So if Declan murdered Wayne, why did Joe plead guilty?'

'Because he *felt* guilty. As far as Joe knew, Declan had got rid of the lad who was playing around with his wife. The elder brother he looked up to had saved him from being branded a cuckold, so he took the rap.'

'Accepting all that, because it does indeed

have the ring of truth, then when did Declan decide that Lorraine had to be got rid of?'

We'd reached that point in our talk just as I was driving up the slope of Queen's Drive and passing Declan Creeney's house. I could feel Calum's eyes on me as I looked across at the unlighted windows. Me? Well, I was remembering Creeney standing outside his garage, spitting on his own expensive stone steps, and only now realizing the contempt he must have been feeling. Looking at me, laughing at me as he protested his innocence.

'I think Declan was already planning Lorraine's death when he framed Joe for Wayne Tully's murder. And if we weigh all the evidence, examine what we know, then I think the reason Lorraine had to go sooner or later was because Declan had taken a fancy to her sister: to the pretty widow, Fiona Lake.'

'OK. So that fancy turned to thoughts of, well, doing something about it. Declan ended up sleeping with Fiona *and* Lorraine at the same time, Lorraine learned the truth and went bloody hairless — as one would.'

'Right.'

'Aha,' Calum said. 'And at that point Declan concocted his fiendish plan and arranged for Joe to get out of jail free.'

'In my opinion the promise of an early release had always been there, or Joe might not have taken the rap. But, yes, you're right. The cruel twist, of course, is that in the end Fiona was helping Declan to kill Len Tully — probably because she was in over her head and being threatened.'

'But what about Lorraine? Surely you're not suggesting Fiona would help to kill her own sister?'

I shook my head. 'I don't think she found out about the killings until later. After Frank had died.'

'So what about Rose Lane? She was silenced that very same night.'

I glanced at him. 'That wasn't Fiona. Not if we can believe the eyewitness. A dark-haired woman, she said, wearing a pink blouse. And you heard Caroline: Fiona has fair hair. All right, she could have worn a wig, but I really don't believe it. No, that's my one blind spot, the one killing about which I may have to ask Declan Creeney a blunt question.'

As it happened, of course, it wasn't necessary.

DAY SEVEN — SUNDAY 6 NOVEMBER

'Evening, Max.'

The rain had started again as we crossed the car-park and, as the wind whipped it across the lights like swirling mist, we broke into a trot. The lean bouncer had crossed the tiled floor to meet us as we ran into the foyer. The young lady had slipped back into the cloakroom and was watching from the counter.

I stuck my hand out as I greeted him. He took it, his eyes amused, shaking my hand with the gloved fist that usually decked belligerent drunks and he couldn't see why, couldn't see what I was playing at.

'Something's missing,' I said. 'When I shook hands with you on Monday I felt a lump where a broken bone had been badly set.'

'We didn't shake hands,' he said.

'Then if it wasn't you,' I said, 'it must have been Declan.' I waited, met his blank gaze and shrugged it off as if of no importance. 'Is the boss around?'

'Came in fifteen minutes ago.' He grinned. 'Something must've got up his nose. He sat down, hung on with a small pair — threes, I think it was — an' lost the first big pot.'

'That's not all he's going to lose tonight.'

There was a tense silence behind us as we stopped inside the doorway of the main room where smoke from cigarettes and cigars hung like a blanket of smog under the lights and background conversation was the muted roar of a waterfall, the movement of poker chips across green baize the wet clicking of pebbles.

Calum said softly, 'I take it the handshake has told you Max was not the man in the shed?'

'Mm. It was that man over there,' I said, pointing to the flashy character in a grey charcoal suit sitting on the far side of the poker table, his face filmed with sweat, gold glittering at his wrists as he dealt the cards. 'That's Declan Creeney. I shook hands with him on Monday. He's an ex-middleweight with fragile bones.'

And then it happened.

We made for the bar. Calum ordered Jameson's on ice, a Holsten Pils for me. We turned, leaned back against the oak top to wait, and watched Declan Creeney push his chair back and stand up awkwardly. I'd already noticed the sweat. The man was on fire, probably in pain, and, as we watched, he slipped out of his jacket and hung it over the back of his chair. When he sat down gingerly, like a man suffering with piles, there were two dark patches under the arms of his shirt. His *pink* shirt.

'Jesus Christ!' I said softly, as he reached behind his neck with both hands, slipped the loop off his pony-tail and with a toss of his head shook free his thick dark hair.

Behind us glasses clinked and the barman said, 'He looks like a bloody woman when he does that.'

'A lady killer,' Calum said.

I picked up my drink, tasted the ice-cold lager and looked at the barman.

'A thought has occurred.'

The barman shook his head. 'Painful, that.'

'What?'

'Thoughts occurrin'. Can ruin your night.'

'I'm about to ruin someone's.' I presented my face to him. 'Remember me?'

'Go on,' he said, 'give us a jog.'

'A week ago, Saturday night, Sunday morning, you got a telephone call, and asked me to pick someone up.'

'Yeah, right. Feller called Joe.'

'So, when you answered the phone, was I asked for personally, by name?'

He shook his head. 'He asked for Robbie. It had all been arranged. Only Robbie didn't turn up, for some reason. I think he was sick.'

'So a plan was falling apart. All right, what then? I was at the bar, looked as if I was about to leave — and you asked me?'

'Yeah, that's about it.'

'Pure coincidence?'

'Absolutely.'

'OK. Now think carefully. The bloke over there at the poker table, he limped in a while ago and you just watched him let his hair down. On that Saturday night, was he the one on the the other end of the phone asking for this Robbie, the one desperate to get someone to pick up the mysterious Joe?'

'Not so mysterious. Yeah, it was Declan who phoned, and who else could it have been he wanted pickin' up but his brother?'

'But his brother was in Walton,' Calum said.

The barman tapped the side of his nose, shook his head.

'I serve drinks, take messages, mind my own business.'

'And keep the playing cards behind the bar?'

He frowned. 'Yeah, why?'

'Last time I was in I saw a woman reading the tarot. Have you got that pack?'

'Got 'em all. How about Happy Families?'

I smiled. 'I'd like to borrow the hanging man out of the tarot deck.'

He found the deck, riffled through it and handed me the card I wanted, then wandered away to serve another customer. When he was out of earshot I turned to Calum.

'I'm going to drop this on the table in front of Creeney, frighten him to death. At the same time I'll threaten him with the police if he doesn't get up and follow me outside to my car.'

'And then?'

'I'll tell him what I know — '

'All circumstantial.'

'So far.'

'And you want me to lurk in the shadows, ready to pounce if he gets tough?'

I grinned. 'Stay here, enjoy your drink. I'm expecting him to leave in a hurry when we finish talking. When he does, I'll come in for you and we'll follow him.'

'Let me guess,' Calum said. 'You're giving him the rope to hang himself?'

'Metaphorically speaking.'

'Of course.'

★   ★   ★

Declan Creeney was slumped in the Quattro's passenger seat. I could smell sweat and deodorant, the same cheap perfume that had pervaded his living-room. He had the window down. He'd put on his jacket but his dark hair was still loose and lifting in the cool breeze. As he stared at me he was flicking the tarot card with a fingernail.

'What's this supposed to mean?' He flicked the card again, grinned to show his contempt. 'A hanging man. Even the sex is wrong. And I told you it wasn't me murdered Lorraine.'

'Somebody did. It wasn't Joe. I believe it

303

was you. Unfortunately, I can't prove anything.'

'Damn right you can't.' He shrugged his shoulders and rocked his head from side to side, a boxer sitting on the stool in his corner, still oozing confidence, still seeing nothing to fear.

'So what do you think? Are you telling me Joe got out of prison to murder his wife?'

He shrugged. 'It's finished, the case is closed so it's all in the past.'

'That's right. It is. Because it began twelve months ago when you murdered Wayne Tully — '

'Hang on, what the fuck — ?'

'Just listen.' I clamped a hand on his wrist. The tarot card fell to the floor. 'I told you I can't prove anything, so you've got nothing to lose by listening — right?'

He was tense and breathing hard. He shifted in his seat, glanced through the drifting rain towards the yellow lights of the club. I saw a dark shape silhouetted in the doorway, knew it was Calum, and I knew Creeney had seen him. He took a deep breath; angrily shrugged off my hand and settled back.

'You murdered Wayne Tully,' I said, 'because he found out you were knocking off your brother's wife. You murdered Lorraine

Creeney because you were fed up with her, and wanted her sister, Fiona. Then you murdered Frank and Len Tully because, after a lot of digging, they found out what you'd done to their brother.'

'Joe admitted he went after Wayne,' Creeney said. 'He pleaded guilty, and he was convicted of manslaughter. All the others're fuckin' nonsense. Especially Lorraine. Christ, I was miles away in the Copacobana.'

'But you were in Joe's house earlier that night. You were seen carrying the ladder into his house, by Rose Lane. And you saw her watching you. You knew you couldn't let her live, so you went after her that night. You murdered her with a knife, to save your skin.'

'Bollocks.'

'No. And for that one there is proof. You have a nasty habit. You spit. You spat on the carpet in Rose Lane's Conwy flat.' I smiled. 'Ever heard of DNA?'

He'd started to sweat again. He dug out a handkerchief and wiped his brow, then shook his head in frustration.

'Bein' in Joe's place earlier still doesn't explain how I murdered Lorraine a couple of hours later when I was in West Derby, in my own fuckin' club.'

'You slipped up.' I shook my head. 'Killers always do.'

'Slipped?'

'Mm. A good word, in the circumstances. Because that's how it was worked, wasn't it? Slipping. Sliding.'

'You tell me.'

'The ladder you were carrying into the house when Rose Lane saw you had the safety rope missing. The legs couldn't be secured; unless the feet were up against something, they'd slide apart and the ladder would end up flat on the floor. So you stood that ladder in Joe's hall — crosswise: one set of legs against the panelling on the side of the stairs, the other set against the living-room door. You polished the parquet flooring with Pledge. And under the legs up against the living-room door, you placed a white tray cloth.'

I looked at him. 'Care to finish it for me?'

He grunted. 'It's your fairy-story.'

'All right. So then you forced Lorraine up the ladder, and put a noose around her neck. We know how she was bound. We don't know if she was standing, sitting . . . it really doesn't matter. Because then you left her. Joe had got out of gaol and you picked him up in your silver car. You took him to the wrong side of town, because you couldn't risk being seen anywhere near his house. Then it almost went wrong. The man called Robbie' — I saw him glance at me sharply — 'who was supposed to be in the Sleepy Pussy, was sick. Luckily, I was there and doing nothing, your barman spoke to me, and I agreed to pick up Joe and drive him home.

'I dropped Joe *behind* his house. He told me he was expected. We've spoken to his cell mate, so we know he thought you would be there with two plane tickets and new identity documents. But the only person there was Lorraine. Bound and gagged. Waiting at the top of the ladder. And Joe went in through the unlocked patio doors, as you had told him to do. Perhaps he shouted out. You know, 'Darling, I'm home'. And then, in a rush to see her, he crossed the living-room — and opened the door.'

'Guesswork,' Declan Creeney said hoarsely.

'Deduction,' I said. 'I saw a bloodstain on the inside edge of the living-room door. When Joe opened that door, the wooden legs slid on the tray cloth as Lorraine's weight drove the ladder downwards. The ladder fell flat, she dropped like a stone and her neck was broken. The living-room door was flung open, so hard and fast it hit Joe in the face. There was blood on the inside edge of that door, blood on Lorraine's elbow that was smeared there as he tried to get her down, save her life.'

'The blood puts Joe there,' Creeney said. 'The police *know* he was there, because they kicked the door in and he was standin' there with the ladder. But there's not one bloody thing to prove I was near the place that night.'

I gave an exaggerated sigh. 'No. You're right. Rose Lane saw you, but she's dead. And who's going to take the word of Rocky, a confused old man?'

He was watching me, waiting. I said nothing. He licked his lips, then sighed, feigning boredom.

'You said the killer slipped up . . . '

I hesitated, deliberately, as if I was thinking. Then I shook my head.

'I'm not sure, now. I thought at first,' I said, 'that the can of Pledge was a possibility — '

'The *what*?'

'You left the polish there, Declan. It had to be the polish *you* used, because Lorraine was allergic to aerosol sprays. So it was your polish and I hoped there might have been finger-prints on that shiny container, and then I realized you would have worn gloves . . . '

'You're right,' he said, and his grin was relieved. 'Any self-respectin' killer'd wear gloves, wouldn't he?'

'But not in the supermarket. Not when you were in Tesco's, or Sainsbury's, *buying* the polish. Your fingerprints would have been on the can then, had to be — but of course, I told myself, you would know that. You wiped the can before you put the gloves on in Joe's house — didn't you?'

But he'd lost interest.

'Is that it?'

'It's what I've got. And I think I'm pretty close.'

'But not close enough to go to the police. Nothing to put me near any of them: Wayne, Frank, Len . . . Lorraine.'

'No . . . There's always Fiona, the police could talk to her. She answered Len's mobile on Heswall Downs; you were there so you must remember . . . ?'

He clicked his door open, stepped out, held it open.

'Forget it. It's goin' nowhere, so go an' have a drink to clear your head. Tell 'em from me it's on the house, you and your mate.'

'What about you?'

'Past my bedtime, I'm headin' home . . . '

But he was already running for his car, shouting to me over his shoulder. I watched him climb in the big silver machine, start up, burn rubber out of the car-park, rain sweeping through the halogen beams.

He was off, he was in a hurry, and he wasn't going home.

I sat still, did exactly as he had suggested and cleared my mind. Then, without haste, I went to get Calum.

27

He was in the foyer, pacing, watching me.

I said, 'I've got a couple of phone calls to make. Creeney's on his way to Joe's house to destroy evidence: a can of Pledge.'

'As in polish?'

'That's the start. He'll be scrubbing hell out of that can of polish, hoping to remove fingerprints that might or might not be there. Even he can't be sure. But I think he'll also go looking for bloodstains on doors and generally make a fool of himself. It's all over for him. DNA will link him to the murder in Wales, and after that he'll fall apart.'

'Are you inviting Haggard to the party?'

'Indirectly.'

I moved away, found my mobile and keyed in Haggard's number. As I did so I looked at my watch. One o'clock. At the other end the phone was picked up and I heard a smoker's cough.

'This better be good,' the DI growled.

'A PI never sleeps.' I listened to his snort and said, 'What did forensic say about Len Tully?'

Haggard grunted. 'Murder. Dick Tracy was

wrong. Tully was knocked out, then stuffed in the car.'

'Go and talk to Fiona Lake.'

'What, Lorraine Creeney's sister?'

'Ask her what she was doing on Thursday night, Friday morning.'

There was a weary sigh. 'All right, go on, what *was* she doin'?'

'She was on Heswall Dales with Declan Creeney, doing nasty things with a red Ford Escort. She picked up Tully's phone when I rang. Big mistake.'

Silence. Then, 'Are you sayin' Creeney murdered Tully?'

'Frank and Len. And the others: Wayne Tully, Lorraine Creeney.' I paused, thought back to that first day, and said, 'When I spoke to Declan Creeney on the morning after the murder, he mentioned a ladder being used in Lorraine Creeney's hanging. I asked him how he knew. He told me the police had visited him at around four that morning — the morning Lorraine was murdered.'

'Wrong. We got to him later that day. Me and Willie Vine — and no ladder was ever mentioned.'

'Stephanie Grey knew. I spoke to her in her office at three o'clock. She could have told him.'

'Could've, but didn't. An' anyway, why

would Creeney lie and say he heard about it from us at four in the morning?'

'I don't suppose the time you got to him matters, does it? The point is he knew all about the ladder, Mike.'

I could sense the tension on the line, the sudden excitement.

'So if Creeney's the man, why'm I talkin' to Lake?'

I chuckled. 'It all began with her, twelve months ago. She's his accomplice, and the weakest link. I think she'll snap. But if you want to go straight for Creeney, he's just left the Sleepy Pussy, heading for home.'

'An' here was me thinkin' I was in bed . . . '

The phone clicked, and I was listening to silence.

I punched in another set of numbers, spoke to a drowsy DI Alum Morgan in his home beneath the towering peaks of Carnedd Dafydd and gave him the good news about the dark-haired woman in the pink blouse. He asked where he could find Declan Creeney. I told him Haggard was on his way to arrest him at his home. The phone went dead again, this time cutting off a stream of Welsh curses — lots of double Fs and double Ls either side of much throat clearing.

When I turned, Calum was watching me with amusement.

'Did I just catch you lying to the police?'

'Definitely not. Creeney did tell me he was going home. When Haggard gets to the house on Queen's Drive he'll find it empty, wait to see if Creeney arrives, then work out where he's probably gone and race around to Joe Creeney's house.'

'But we'll be there first?'

'Of course.'

'Except for Sian, who's closer than we are.'

I stared. 'What the *hell* are you talking about?'

'While you were busy I phoned her and told her what was happening — '

'Jesus Christ!'

'Is there a problem with that?'

'Only that one of the more direct comments made by her in the past few days was that she would willingly hang the killers for what they did to Lorraine.'

'That being so,' Calum said, his face suddenly bleak, 'why the hell are we hanging around?'

28

For the second time in a week I pulled out of the Sleepy Pussy's car-park in the wind and rain to drive across Liverpool to Joe Creeney's house, but this time I was not annoyed, but frightened. In those seven days four people had died violently, and I was pushing the Quattro way beyond the speed limit in a desperate race to prevent another death.

But whose? Who would die tonight? Declan Creeney — or my Soldier Blue?

It was that sickening uncertainty that drove me around the sweeping bends of Breeze Hill and into Queen's Drive hard enough to set the tyres howling, flung Calum about in his seat like a rag doll as he pressed his mobile phone to his ear and tried to undo the damage.

'No answer,' he said. 'Her mobile's switched off.'

'Try Meg Morgan's land line.'

He did. Same result — with a slight variation which told another story.

'Engaged. I've tried three times.'

'Meg's in bed. Sian's walked out and taken

the receiver off the hook.'

'What about Meg's mobile?'

'Don't know the number. Forget it. We're way too late. It's less than five minutes from Meg's to Beech Crescent. Sian will be waiting for Creeney when he arrives.'

One thirty. Traffic sparse. No police cars — yet. I gnawed my lip, tried to put myself inside Sian's mind. Could she kill? Was she strong enough to overpower Declan Creeney? Ex-army, trained in unarmed combat, in her forties and fit. The answer was yes, she knew all the tricks so she had the capability. But was the suffering inflicted on a casual friend sufficient motivation?

'What was your thinking,' Calum said above the roar of engine and tyres, 'when you sent Creeney after that can of lavender-scented Pledge?'

'If he was guilty, he'd do everything to get rid of his prints. If he was innocent, he'd do nothing.' I flicked a glance sideways. 'I suppose I was looking for some kind of proof.'

'But if he's not there, that still proves nothing. Because even if he's guilty, he could still be confident enough to call your bluff. Because that's what it is — right? A bluff.'

I smiled thinly. 'Yes. But he'll be there, and so will Sian.'

I left the terrifying possibilities of what we might find unuttered, gritting my teeth as I thought ahead for the quickest route and opted for main roads and straight driving rather than short cuts where the speed would be reduced by too many junctions and too narrow roads.

That decision was thrown out of the window when I powered up the hill from Childwall Five Ways and hit the lights on red at the junction of Queens Drive and Woolton Road and saw, 200 yards down the hill from the brow, Willie Vine's green Mondeo pulling into Declan Creeney's drive.

'Change of plan,' I said tightly, 'to avoid being seen,' and when the lights turned green I swung hard left into Woolton Road.

'Take Hornby Lane,' Calum said. 'Half a mile on the right.'

I grunted. How long would Haggard and Vine wait for Creeney? I'd spoken to Haggard just two minutes before leaving the Sleepy Pussy and driven most of the way at seventy. The DI would be expecting mildly intoxicated nightclub owner Creeney to drive carefully within the speed limit; with stops, twenty minutes for the distance compared with my eight.

That meant we had some ten minutes before they gave up on him, fourteen at the outside before they pulled up in front of Joe Creeney's house.

Druids' Cross Road was the crosspiece of the T junction at the end of Hornby Lane, Beech Crescent a short way up the hill after the left turn into Druids' Cross. But before that there was the smaller opening into the narrow lane that ran behind the crescent, and I saw there what I had been dreading.

Halfway up the slope, probably with its four cross-country tyres planted in the muddy ruts left by my own car, Sian's metallic Shogun glistened in the rain.

'Aye,' Calum said, as I tossed him a grim look. 'She's made it — and I doubt if she's sitting there twiddling her thumbs.'

'Creeney's car's there, in front of the house, no sign of him.' I said, pulling up. 'Jump out. If she's just got here, you might catch her before it's too late.'

'And if it is too late — break in?'

'Do what's necessary.'

He jumped out. The car door slammed. I watched him jog up the lane, Timberland boots splashing water. Then I drove the remaining thirty yards and parked behind Creeney's silver car.

Drizzle dashed my face icily as I climbed out. The cold breeze plucked at my hair. As I walked quickly up the path I could see a light on the other side of the small glazed panel in the front door. Did I see shadows moving on the other side of the glass? No. The wind was tossing the shrubs at my side. I was looking at reflections but seeing hope.

I rang the bell. Hammered on the door with the side of my fist.

Nothing. No sound.

I pressed my face to the square of coloured glass. The main light was on, rays from the three bulbs like shards of splintered rainbows through the frosted glass. But the light was too close to the door. No shadows fell across the square window, and what lay further down the hall was brightly illuminated but impossible to distinguish.

'Sian! Creeney!'

My yells bounced back like flat, lonely echoes.

'Creeney, I know you're in there, I know there's a woman in there with you. Leave her alone; don't touch her; don't harm her — you hear me?'

I was talking to myself. Annoying the neighbours. Amusing Creeney. But what of Sian?

I slammed my palm flat against the door, my head spinning as panic began ripping me apart. Turned away, squinted against the rain and looked desperately down the road, almost praying for the sight of Willie Vine's Mondeo. Saw a light flick on, heard a front door open. Spun back to face the house.

'Creeney, open the bloody door before I — '

And then I heard a musical sound that froze the blood in my veins.

Somewhere at the rear of the house, a big pane of glass shattered, the fragments tinkling on a stone patio.

'Jesus Christ!' I whispered. Because, suddenly, what I had done came roaring at me out of the dark like a wild beast to rip my soul from my breast, turn my bowels to liquid, my knees to rubber.

'*And if it's too late — break in?*' Calum had said.

'*Do what's necessary,*' I'd told him.

But what I had not done was give him details of the trap set by Declan Creeney that one week ago had been triggered by his brother Joe, set in motion a makeshift gallows and broken Lorraine Creeney's neck.

'Calum!' I roared, 'stay where you are, don't come through into the hall, for God's sake stay there, stay, don't open that fucking door, *don't open it* — '

And then I kicked in the front door.

White wood flew as the jamb splintered. The door exploded inwards, hit the rubber stop and bounced. It banged back against my foot and again swung open as I stepped into the hall.

And stood, paralysed.

It was as if, the moment I kicked in the door, the ghastly scene had been illuminated by dazzling electronic flash that fired in a blaze of brilliant white and turned everything within its compass to stone.

Sian was sitting halfway up the carpeted stairs. She had on jeans, a sweater, black Doc Marten's smeared with wet mud. Her blonde hair was wet, tied back. She was looking down as she idly and repeatedly turned a can of Pledge in her hands.

In the narrowest part of the hall, Declan Creeney was standing at the top of a ladder. He was so high in the stair well I had to tilt my head to look up at him. The upper floor was in pitch darkness. He was illuminated by the light from below, that weird light coming from an unnatural direction that transforms the ordinary into the macabre. About his neck there was a noose. From it the length of orange nylon rope hung slack. I knew without thinking that it had been measured and, if he fell, it would snap tight before his feet hit the floor.

His ankles were bound. His wrists were

tied in front of him. A gag prevented him from speaking.

The ladder on which he stood had been placed across that narrow section of the hall. The legs on one side were lodged in the angle between the floor and the panelling at the side of the stairs. Those on the other side were against the bottom of the closed living-room door. Under the legs hard up against the living-room door a white cloth had been placed flat on the shiny parquet flooring.

The ladder's legs were not restrained by a safety rope.

Declan Creeney was looking at me. There was a strange, excited gleam in his eyes. Despite the cloth gag that was tight enough to wrench his mouth out of shape, I could see he was trying to smile. Then he nodded, slowly, and his eyes closed and I thought I saw his chest heave in an immense sigh of relief.

Every detail of the hellish scene was branded indelibly in my brain in that single, frozen moment when I stepped through the front door and time stood still.

Then Calum opened the living-room door.

EPILOGUE

It was as if the hangman had pulled the lever that dropped the heavy trap from under Declan Creeney's feet.

The living-room door was driven inwards as Creeney's weight bore down on the ladder and its legs shot apart on the polished floor. There was a crack and a grunt in the living-room as the door hit Calum. Simultaneously there was the sickening crack as of a wet branch snapping, and Declan Creeney's slack body hung spinning at the end of the orange rope. The toes of his slip-on casuals were inches from the floor. His head lolled to one side, driven to a terrible angle by the big hangman's knot that had broken his neck.

Sian hadn't moved.

Calum stepped out of the living-room. There was a red bruise high on his cheekbone above the grey of his beard. He reached out a hand, steadied Creeney's slowly rotating body. Looked at me, then up at Sian.

I nodded my understanding.

Behind me I heard running footsteps, then someone gagged, choked as they tried to say something, and I remembered the light coming on down the road, the front door opening.

I turned. A man was standing in the path in slippers and a white towelling dressing-gown, his hand over his mouth, his eyes huge.

I said, 'Cal, would you go with that gentleman and call the police. I'll stay here, see what I can do . . . '

Calum brushed past me and I heard his soft voice reassuring the man as they made their way to his house and a phone. But I knew that the stranger had read a different meaning in my words. He had seen the body swinging slowly at the end of a rope and assumed I would cut him down, search for signs of life, but the only person I could do anything for in that house was Sian and I eased the front door shut then trod softly across the parquet floor to sit close to her on the stairs, on the outside, placing myself between her and Declan Creeney.

I took the can of polish from her hand and stood it on the stairs and took her cold fingers in mine.

'What was all that about, Soldier Blue?'

'Fifty-fifty,' she said, her voice odd.

'As in . . . ?'

'One of two things could happen, so that's fifty-fifty, isn't it?' she said. 'Like Russian roulette, but with the odds even.' She chuckled at the sound of that, but the chuckle was cold and I could feel the tremor within her that was unceasing.

'Mm. One thing or the other. And he thought he'd made it. There was something in his eyes when I kicked open the front door. A flood of relief. He tried to smile. Because he'd watched me, and it was his plan so he knew from experience if someone came in through the front door he'd live, but if they came through from the living-room . . . '

'But it wasn't fifty-fifty, was it?' she said. 'I should have known the way you and Calum would work it. One front, one back, exploding in on a given signal. He didn't stand a chance.'

'There was no signal,' I said, 'because Calum didn't know what was going on, didn't know how the trap worked.' I squeezed her hand gently, reached out a finger and tilted her chin so that her empty blue eyes were looking at me.

'How did Creeney get up the ladder, Soldier Blue?'

'How would you get up a ladder?'

'Well, I'd put one foot in front of the other and climb.'

'There you are then.'

She was right, of course. Left foot, then right foot, one after the other all the way to the top. And what did it matter anyway. A killer had stood at the top of the ladder with a noose around his neck and, just as a young woman had done seven days ago, he had waited in deathly suspense, and then he'd died.

But the answer wasn't quite what I was pressing for.

I knew that Sian the survival expert could have forced Creeney up there, first breaking his will by the use of exquisitely sensitive pressure points to leave him writhing in agony, then lashing his hands and driving him upwards to the waiting noose with the threat of more pain. But it was also possible that she had deliberately placed herself in the position of disinterested bystander, walking in through the patio doors and across the hall when Creeney was setting up his bizarre suicide then sitting on the stairs and dispassionately awaiting developments.

Yet no matter how it began, the end could have been so different. Pricked by conscience, suddenly appalled by what was happening, Sian could have leaped to open the front door when I hammered on it, or screamed out a warning to Calum as the glass shattered and he walked towards the living-room door.

She had done neither. A man's life had

been in her hands, and she had let it slip away.

But could I be certain of that? Could I be certain of *anything*? Well, I thought I could, on one point at least: Calum Wick, who had come bursting into the unknown, could no more take the blame for Creeney's death than could Joe Creeney for the death of his wife.

Impossible hangings. A woman and a man had died — but by whose hand?

'You did well,' Sian said, watching me.

'We always do.'

'We?' Her chuckle was dismissive.

'Together,' I said huskily. 'Always and forever.'

She clutched my hand, squeezed hard.

'I know. Really I do. And I also know that, with another tricky one solved, quite soon there'll be one of those mysterious phone calls requesting your help because word's getting around about this brilliant private investigator . . . '

I shushed her with a finger placed gently on her lips.

'Bumbling private investigator,' I said, 'and his brilliant team.'

And again I turned her head towards me and this time, as she looked at me with blue eyes that had softened, had regained some warmth and life and now shimmered wetly, I leaned forward and kissed her softly on her damp forehead.

We were like that, fingers tightly interlocked, our faces pressed together and the salt of her tears on my lips, when I heard the wail of a siren and I knew that the uniforms were going to arrive before Haggard and Vine and that although there was still a myriad questions to be asked by a burly detective inspector who smoked king-sized cigarettes and a dapper sergeant who was a closet novelist obsessed with words, one way or another, it was over.

But of course, Sian was right about the phone call.

Other titles published by
The House of Ulverscroft:

THE CLUTCHES OF DEATH

John Paxton Sheriff

When photographer Frank Danson took his wife Jenny to the theatre, they had two beautiful baby boys at home. But when they returned the boys had gone — presumably kidnapped. The loss was too great for Jenny to bear and Frank was left alone to grieve for his family. Then, twenty years later, the memories come screaming back. Who is sending him photographs hinting at unimaginable horrors, and taunting notes in blood? As the killings begin, amateur private eye Jack Scott must solve a mystery once buried in the past but now disinterred to make Frank's life a waking nightmare.